The Whispers

ALSO BY ASHLEY AUDRAIN

The Push

The
Whispers

Ashley Audrain

PAMELA DORMAN BOOKS
VIKING

VIKING
An imprint of Penguin Random House LLC
penguinrandomhouse.com

Simultaneously published in hardcover in Great Britain by Michael Joseph,
an imprint of Penguin Random House Ltd., London

First United States edition published by Pamela Dorman Books/Viking

A Pamela Dorman Book/Viking

LIBRARY OF CONGRESS CATALOGING-IN-PUBLICATION DATA

Names: Audrain, Ashley, 1982– author.
Title: The whispers: a novel / Ashley Audrain.
Description: First. | [New York]: Pamela Dorman Books/Viking [2023]
Identifiers: LCCN 2022051777 (print) | LCCN 2022051778 (ebook) |
ISBN 9781984881694 (hardcover) | ISBN 9781984881700 (ebook) |
ISBN 9780593655733 (international edition)
Classification: LCC PR9199.4.A9244 W55 2023 (print) |
LCC PR9199.4.A9244 (ebook) | DDC 813/.6—dc23
LC record available at https://lccn.loc.gov/2022051777
LC ebook record available at https://lccn.loc.gov/2022051778

Printed in the United States of America
1st Printing

DESIGNED BY MEIGHAN CAVANAUGH

For every mom hanging on by a thread.

And for those trying desperately to be one.

What I increasingly felt, in marriage and in motherhood, was that to live as a woman and to live as a feminist were two different and possibly irreconcilable things.

—Rachel Cusk, in an interview with
The Globe and Mail, 2012

He lifts two fingers to his nose and smells the child's mother as his eyes grow wide in the dark of his kitchen. The clock on the oven reads 11:56 p.m. His chest. Everything feels tight. Is he having a heart attack? Is this how a heart attack feels? He must move. He paces the white-oak hardwood and touches things, the lever on the toaster; the stainless-steel handle of the fridge; the softening, fragrant bananas in the fruit bowl. He is looking for familiarity to ground him. To bring him back.

A shower. He should shower. He scales the stairs like a toddler.

He refuses to look at himself in the bathroom mirror.

His skin stings. He scrubs.

He thinks he hears sirens. Are those sirens?

He wrenches the shower handle and listens. Nothing.

Bed, he should be in bed. That's where he would be if nothing had happened. If this was just another Wednesday night in June. He dries himself and places the towel on the door's hook where it always hangs. He fiddles with the way the white terry cloth falls, perfecting the ripple in the fabric like he's staging a department store display, his hands twitching with an unfamiliar fear.

His phone. He creeps through the dark house looking for where he's put it—the hallway bench, the kitchen counter, the table near the foot of the stairs. His coat pocket, that's where it is, on the floor at the back door, where he'd dropped it when he came into the house. He brings the phone upstairs, his legs still feeble, and stops outside their bedroom door.

He can't be in there.

He'll sleep in the spare room. He lies down slowly on the double bed, noting the care with which the linens have been smoothed and tucked, and places the phone beside him. He has an aching urge to call her.

What would he say? That he misses her? That he needs her?

It's too late.

But he stares at the phone anyway, imagining himself hearing the steady march of the ringtone while he waits for her to pick up. And then he closes his eyes and sees the child again.

Sometime later he feels the mattress tremble. Someone has joined him. He waits to be touched. But no, it's a vibration. And then again. And then again. There's a streak of tangerine light piercing through the room. He swipes his thumb across the reflection of his bleary face on the phone's screen to answer.

The pained pitch of her voice. He has heard it before.

"Something terrible happened," she says.

SEPTEMBER

The Loverlys' Backyard

There is something animalistic about the way the middle-aged adults size each other up while feigning friendliness in the backyard of the most expensive house on the street. The crowd drifts toward the most attractive ones. They are there for a neighborly family afternoon, for the children, who play a parallel kind of game, but the men have chosen nice shoes, and the women wear accessories that don't make it to the playground, and the tone of everyone's voice is polished.

The party is catered. There are large steel tubs with icy craft beer and bite-size burgers on long wooden platters and paper cones overflowing with shoestring fries. There are loot bags with cookies iced in each child's name, the cellophane tied with thick satin ribbon.

The back fence is lined with a strip of mature trees, newly planted, lifted and placed by a crane. There's no sign of the unpleasant back alley they abut, the dwellers from the rehab housing units four blocks away, the sewers that overflow in the rain. The grass is an admirable shade of green. There's an irrigation system. The polished concrete patio off the kitchen is anchored with carefully arranged planters of boxwood. There is a shed that isn't really a shed—its door pivots, there's a proper light fixture.

Three children belong to this backyard, to the towering three-story home that has been built on the double lot, unheard-of in an urban neighborhood like this. The three-year-old twins, a boy and a girl, are in matching seersucker, and they've let the mother of this audacious house style their hair nicely, swept, patted. The older boy, ten, insists on wearing last year's phys ed uniform with a stain on the T-shirt. Hot chocolate or blood, the guests will wonder. But Whitney's husband had convinced her to pick her battles wisely in the fifteen minutes before the party begins.

By three thirty in the afternoon, she has let go of the urge to rip the gym shirt off him, to wrestle him into the powder-blue polo she bought for the occasion. She has let go of the hosting stress and feels the satisfying high of everyone enjoying themselves. She has impressed them all enough. She can tell from the glances, the subtle pointing between friends who notice the details she hopes they will. She thinks of the photos that will smatter social media tonight. The hum is loud and peppered with laughter, and this air of conviviality satiates her.

This noise is the reason Mara, next door, doesn't come. She got the heavy-cardstock invitation in her mailbox the month prior, like everyone else, and slipped it straight into the recycling bin. She knows these neighbors don't really want people like her and Albert there. They think she's got nothing to offer anymore. Her decades of wisdom don't matter in the least to those women, who march around like they've got it all figured out. But that's fine. She can see and hear everything she needs to through the slats in the fence, while she tidies her own garden, plucks at the tips of new weeds until her lower back is too sore, then she'll move to the mildewed patio chair. She notices something in the crispy-petaled branches of her hydrangea bush. She gives it a shake. A paper airplane falls nose first into the dirt. Another one she's missed. She found several in her yard Thursday morning. She bends to collect it as she hears Whitney's voice crest above the guests, greeting the couple from across the street.

That couple, Rebecca and Ben, make a point of finding the host as soon as they arrive. They've got twenty minutes and a potted orchid to give her. Rebecca has to get to work. Ben has Rebecca to appease, or he'd have stayed home. He is quiet while Rebecca and Whitney exchange pleasantries. Whitney compliments and inquires, she paws Rebecca's hand and then her shoulder, and Rebecca concedes. She is charmed in a way she isn't usually. She hopes nobody interrupts.

Ben's hair is still damp from the shower, and he smells like the morning. He feels Whitney glance at him while she speaks to his wife. His hand is in the back pocket of Rebecca's white jeans. He pulls her closer. Rebecca can sense that he isn't listening to her conversation with Whitney, not really, and she is right. He is watching the magician twirl a colorful scarf around one of Whitney's giggling twins, the girl, she has found Ben's friendly eyes. He's not overly social with other adults, but the children are always drawn to him. He is the favorite teacher. He is the playful uncle. He is the baseball coach.

From across the yard, Blair watches as Ben and Rebecca find subtle ways to touch while they listen to Whitney orate, like they still find in each other every last thing they need. They are childless, child-free, and so they have not yet been irrevocably changed, not like the rest of them. They speak to each other in fully composed sentences with civilized inflection. They probably still fuck once a day and enjoy it. Fall asleep in the same bed with their limbs tucked into each other's crevices. Without a pillow wedged between them to separate her side of the bed from his, to imagine the other isn't there.

Blair watches her best friend, Whitney, begin to drift as she wraps with Rebecca, in subtle search of her next conversation. Aiden, the loud man who sleeps on the other side of Blair's barrier pillow, booms from the corner of the backyard. He has an audience, always an audience. He is building to a punch line she has heard before, he has caught Whitney's attention as she passes, and Blair is painfully aware she is standing by herself. She looks for Jacob, Whitney's husband, whom she spots with a couple she hasn't met. A toddler with tight braids wedges herself between the mother's legs. Jacob is gesturing to his house, drawing the shape of the roof with his finger, explaining a part of the design. He's wearing his signature black T-shirt and black chinos rolled at the cuff, he is sockless in crisp white designer sneakers, his hair, his brows, the rims of his Scandinavian eyewear, it's all intense and cool, but he's so gentle. He lifts a hand in Blair's direction, hello. She blushes, she has been staring. He is easy to stare at. Her eyes search again for his wife.

Whitney is speaking now to a group of mothers from her older son, Xavier's grade. They have a group chat that Whitney rarely responds to, because she doesn't know the answers to the questions they ask about the first-term project and the hot lunch menu and the deadline for ordering class photos. But she likes being in the group chat anyway. Sometimes she chimes in with an emoji, as she arrives at the office early in the morning to her third cup of hot coffee and the pleasure of silence and thought. Thumbs up. Red heart. Thanks for the updates! Nothing helpful, slightly mocking. Whitney can feel the women's attention follow her now as she makes her way to say hello to their husbands, who stop their conversation, straighten their backs as they greet her.

B lair catches Rebecca's attention instead, and it's their turn for the pleasantries now. Blair can think only of the weather, always the goddamn weather, how early the evenings grow cool now, and then Rebecca's grueling hours at the hospital, where she's due in forty-five minutes. But Rebecca loves those grueling hours. The two women have nothing in common but their proximity. Rebecca offers herself to Blair as an on-demand medical encyclopedia, answering every text she sends about her daughter's new rash or barking cough or itchy eardrum or grayish-colored poop. The kinds of things that can occupy Blair for days. Blair wonders how it feels to be so purposeful. To wear white denim to a family barbecue.

R ebecca's eyes fall every few seconds to Blair's seven-year-old daughter. She can't stop looking at her. Wondering what it would be like to be here with her own. She lets herself run with this version of her future and it gets longer and longer and longer, like the scarf from the magician's hat. The girl is drawing in chalk on the patio concrete with the twins, who are waiting for their turn with the rabbit. The two women watch Blair's daughter together now, each pretending to be more amused by the children than they are.

W hitney joins them, her drink refreshed, and Blair and Rebecca come alive. She drapes her hand on Blair's shoulder and pretends not to be annoyed by the chalky colors covering the twins' palms. How sweet they are together, Whitney drawls, how good Chloe is with the littlest ones. She takes an inconspicuous step back, in fear of powdered handprints on her dress.

Rebecca tries to imagine what it's like to be interested in doing this kind of thing, the hosting, the display. She has three minutes left and her brain will tick through all one hundred and eighty seconds because that is what it does. She, too, comments on Chloe's good nature while the seconds tally.

"Delightful" is the word Rebecca uses. Blair smiles, downplays her only child's perfection, but she is buoyed in the way only this kind of comment can achieve. As perfunctory as it might be.

The word "delightful" makes Whitney wonder where her undelightful son is. She can't see him in the backyard. Blair said she last saw him a half hour ago, standing at Mara's fence with his face between the slats. He is never where he is supposed to be. Whitney has warned him to be on his best behavior, to entertain the smaller children, to be friendly. Just this once. Just for her. He should be out here. The magician is nearly done.

Maybe he just needs a moment alone. Blair says this slowly, quietly, wondering if she shouldn't.

But no. Whitney will find him.

Can't he just do what she asked him to? Can't he be more like Blair's daughter? She thinks of his perpetual pouting, of how it borders on a scowl, people asking why he's in a grumpy mood when it's just the way he looks. Long faced. Morose. In need of a haircut he won't agree to. She moves quickly through the house calling his name. The pantry. The living room. The basement playroom. She shouldn't have to do this in the middle of a party with fifty-odd guests in the backyard. Is he hiding? Has he sneaked the iPad again? *Xavier!* Must he always push her buttons like this? She hurries to the third floor and opens the door to his room, and he is there, on his bed, with the stolen loot bags for the children emptied around him. Every last one. There is chocolate on his face and on the sheets. He is licking the icing from a cookie wrapper stickered with another child's name.

"XAVIER! WHAT THE FUCK ARE YOU DOING?" She swoops to rip the licked cellophane from his hands as he shrieks and recoils from her. "WHAT THE HELL IS WRONG WITH YOU?"

Xavier's face crumples and his bottom lip curls down like that of a child half his age, and she will not allow the irritating whine that will crescendo next, the whine that makes her want to smack him. "NO!" she shouts, grabbing him by the arm as he whimpers and goes limp. She cannot stand him like this. "GET UP, YOU LITTLE SHIT!"

But then she lets go. Because she realizes the jovial purr below has deadened.

The party has gone silent. There is only the thump of her furious heart in her ears. And the ringing of her own venomous, murderous yelling. The familiar echo of her rage. The fear of possibilities registers. And then she notices. The wide-open window. Everyone has heard.

The shame pulls her to the ground. To the nest of discarded satin ribbons from the cookies, the ends cut like the tip of a snake's tongue.

She knows then what she has lost.

NINE MONTHS LATER

1

Blair

It's five thirty in the morning on a Thursday in June. Blair Parks sips her coffee and thinks about her husband spreading the thighs of another woman as wide as butterfly wings.

She imagines him smelling her. And then tasting her, his tongue circling, flicking.

Blair's hand covers her mouth. She puts her cup down.

She can't sleep. But she's been doing this in the morning now, indulging these obscene thoughts. Nothing feels good about starting her day like this, but it helps to satisfy her obsessive worrying so she can move on. Otherwise, she'll find herself consumed when she doesn't want to be. Staring at the shelf of stain removers at the store, the ones in commercials that desexualize middle-aged stay-at-home mothers like her, while she imagines a younger woman's mouth filled with her husband's semen.

She pours a second cup that won't taste as good as the first and thinks about how hungry she is for something more. Although what, she can't name. The problem isn't just boredom. Or a wistful longing. Not her sedate, ten-year marriage and the ticking clock to complete irrelevance. Is this normal? Is this how other women her age feel?

The idea of saying any of this aloud, to anybody, makes her diaphragm tighten. More than usual. It's better to lift her chin and quietly face whatever hour is ahead of her. And the next hour after that, lest anyone suspect she's this miserable. It's beneficial for everyone, she knows, if the indifference takes over. If she soldiers on, without the energy to care about what it is she really wants. Or how she really feels when her alarm goes off in the morning.

Vulnerability, she knows, is something she should work on, something women are now supposed to exercise like a muscle. The books and podcasts and motivational speakers have told them so. She tries to admire the ones who admit they've made choices they regret and resolve, loudly, to change. But that kind of upheaval is not for her. She cannot see any other life for herself. And she cannot separate the shame of having gotten it all so wrong.

Another cup later, her daughter's bedroom door squeaks on its hinges upstairs. Her footsteps tap down the hardwood in the hallway. The toilet flushes in their only bathroom, and the plumbing hisses through the house. Blair wipes her hand across her tired face.

Somewhere along the line, blaming Aiden for the way she felt about her life became convenient. He's been a reliable depository for her anger. She dumps and dumps and dumps, and he never seems to overflow. In her mind, there was little consequence to this—they are married, and separation isn't an option for Blair. The dismantling, the shape of everything changing. The perception. The impact on the daughter upstairs. She can't fathom it.

The water runs from the bathroom tap. She hears Chloe pop open the mirrored cabinet where their three toothbrushes share a cup. She puts a bagel in the toaster for her daughter's breakfast. She's already taken the cream cheese out of the fridge so it's room temperature, the way Chloe likes it.

Attributing her misery to an underperforming marriage had helped her cope well enough, until a week and a half ago, when she found a tiny piece of foil wrapper in the pocket of Aiden's jeans. Less than a square inch. Garbage, to any other person who was to pick it up from the laundry room floor after turning the pants inside out for the wash. But she recognized the texture of the ribs in the packaging. And the emerald jewel tone. It looked exactly like the condoms they used years ago. Every morning since she found it, she's opened the drawer where she keeps it and places it on her palm to wonder.

There are countless other things it could be from. A granola bar. A mint from a business lunch.

But more than any proof she has, is a feeling.

She'd once heard them described as the whispers—the moments that are trying to tell you *something isn't right here.* The problem is that some women aren't listening to what their lives are trying to tell them. They don't hear the whispers until they're looking back with hindsight. Feeling blindsided. Desperate to see the truth for what it is.

But maybe she's just paranoid. Too much time on her hands to think.

She hears Chloe's feet hit the stairs and spreads the cream cheese carefully. The wide-open thighs come back to her. Aiden's fingers opening the woman's tight, waxed lips. How nice he'd be to her afterward. Maybe she makes him laugh. The hair rises on Blair's arms. She thinks again of how Aiden didn't ejaculate during the only night they had sex last month. Of how he's been checking his phone more than usual.

Chloe is nearly at the bottom of the staircase. She closes the imaginary thighs and puts the halves of the bagel together. And then she turns around and forces herself to smile, so that like every other morning of her daughter's life, Blair's beaming face is the first thing Chloe sees.

2

Rebecca

HOURS EARLIER

The resident briefs her as they hustle through the double doors to the resuscitation bay, their sneakers squeaking on the resin floor. She feels the humid air from outside before she sees the paramedics push the gurney into the hands of her team. A ten-year-old male found unconscious at 11:50 p.m., suspected primary brain injury from a fall, no obvious signs of trauma. The nurse steps back as Rebecca snaps on the blue gloves and turns to lift the patient's eyelids.

Her hands pull back. The child's face. She looks up at the nurse on his other side.

"I know him. His name is Xavier. He lives across the street from me."

"Do you want to—"

"No." She shakes her legs to get the feeling back. The curtain is about to lift. "I'm okay, I'm fine. Vitals? Let's go, come on."

Her hands are firm on his small body as she calls the orders, and in seconds the choreography she's performed for years takes over. Tracheal intubation. Veins punctured. CT scan ordered stat. She is never with a child on the trauma table for long, but each minute is crucial and methodical, each second squeezed of its potential, and yet at the end, when everything that can be done is done, she only looks back on those minutes as a mass of time with either one outcome or the other.

"The parents, are they here? Where are they?" She peels off her gloves and pitches them in the garbage bin. She looks back to Xavier's gray face, his mouth gagged open with the tube she'd guided into him. She brushes back a strand of his damp hair. The ground where he landed would still be wet from yesterday's rain. She touches his cheek.

Hundreds of parents have sat waiting for her in the vinyl-covered hospital chairs. The ease with which she can form the words sometimes concerns her. But she has never known her patient before. She has never watched them wash the neighbors' cars in a mound of suds, or known that their bike is cobalt blue with neon-green handlebar grips. She's never had to tell a friend that her child may never recover.

Her adrenaline settles as she leaves the trauma room. She sees the reflection of fluorescent light on the hallway floor, and her senses start to return: the respiratory fellow being paged, the whine of a child in the waiting room, the antiseptic in the air. She takes her phone from her pocket. She wants to call Ben, to feel the calm of his voice, but he'll be asleep already. And Whitney is waiting for her.

Rebecca knocks on the open door of the small room where they've put her. She's sitting at a round table, staring at the box of rough tissues she's been given. She doesn't look up.

"Whitney, I'm so sorry."

Whitney moves her head slowly like a robot with a battery running down. She says nothing. Rebecca takes the seat beside her and puts her hand on Whitney. She does this, touches the parent on the arm or the shoulder, to make the words she says next feel more personal, less routine. This had been, years ago, a part of the emotional order set she created for herself. Empathy hadn't always come as easily to her as it does now. When she was younger, she'd been better at other parts of her job, things that were definitively measured, assessments of her competency. Things she could prove.

Whitney's eyes close as her mouth opens, but her voice is strained. The beginnings of words she has forgotten how to form.

"Can you tell me what happened?"

Rebecca waits for her to repeat what the first responders reported: that she checked on him before she went to sleep, and he was gone from his bed and the window was open. She looked down to see him on the grass below. That she has no idea what happened. *Come on, Whitney, tell me exactly that.*

She thinks of the backyard, the rectangle of manicured grass the paramedics would have lifted him from. Rebecca had last been there in September for the neighborhood party.

She doesn't want to think of Whitney's anger that afternoon. Of the child's cries from his room as she screamed at him.

"I want to talk to you about Xavier's condition."

Whitney covers her face with one hand. "Just tell me if he's going to die." Her voice squeaks in an octave barely audible.

Rebecca reaches for Whitney's other hand. Her fingers are cold and curled into a fist. Whitney pulls back, but Rebecca squeezes her firmly until she gives in. Rebecca isn't intimidated by much, but there was something about Whitney when they first met. Her verve, her polish, the astuteness of her words when she spoke.

But over time, as their lives quietly orbited each other's, that effect wore off. There is a strong sense of familiarity about someone whose life shares such close physical proximity, given all the possible coordinates on the planet. She and Whitney breathe from the same tiny pocket of air. She sees her garbage cans on Wednesdays and knows they don't recycle everything they could. She knows she has a shopping habit, sees the stacks of packages teetering at the front door, nice department stores, courier bags left for the nanny to collect. She knows one of them— either Whitney or Jacob—doesn't sleep well. Rebecca sees the kitchen lights flick on when she comes home in the middle of the night. She sees the empty wine bottles in the transparent blue recycling bags.

The backyard party isn't the only time she's heard Whitney yell. Right through those towering panes of glass at the front of her home, the unmistakable pitch of a mother who has had enough. She'd felt unsettled every time, like she had at the barbecue, embarrassed to have heard her. What else happens in that house, she isn't sure, but that kind of speculation makes her uncomfortable. She is a doctor, and what she cares about are facts. She finds comfort in facts.

"Xavier has significant injury—we're worried about his head. He's in the ICU, in a medically induced coma to rest his brain. They're going to talk to you there about what to expect for the next little bit, okay? In situations like this, we learn a lot in the first seventy-two hours. I know this is hard to hear, Whitney, but I need you to understand there's a possibility he might not regain consciousness."

Whitney is unmoved.

Rebecca pauses to soften her voice. "Do you understand?"

She feels Whitney's hand begin to quiver and she looks closely at her striking face. The tight sheen of her forehead. Her microbladed eyebrows. Of the outward perfection.

"Is Jacob with the twins?"

Whitney closes her eyes and shakes her head. "London. For work. Our nanny came over right away, but I had to wait for her." Her voice curls. "I couldn't go with him in the ambulance."

Rebecca tells Whitney she'll take her to see him now, that he's intubated, and there is swelling. That this might frighten her, but he's not in any pain. Another doctor will have to take over from there. The door slides open behind them and Rebecca turns to see a nurse with two police officers.

They'll want to speak with Whitney; it's routine. Rebecca registers the discomfort of this, although the questions they'll need to ask don't concern her, not technically. Rebecca shakes her head in their direction—*Please, not now, not yet*—and the nurse guides the officers down the hallway instead.

"There are studies that show patients in this condition know when family members are with them. You can hold his hand and talk to him, like you would if he was awake. Okay?"

Whitney stands and gathers the hem of her sweatshirt in her hands. She lets Rebecca slip her strong, steadying arm under her as they walk down the hall. Until Whitney becomes rigid. She turns her face toward Rebecca and their eyes meet for the first time.

"Is this why you don't have children?"

Rebecca pauses. She doesn't know what to say. This job? This hospital? This constant fear of something going wrong, the unbearable pain if it does?

She thinks of the hours she has spent on the floor of her bathroom. The bloody orbs sinking to the bottom of toilet bowls, the dancing strings of mucus. The weight of the hand towel on her lap on the way to the hospital.

Why doesn't she have children? Because she cannot keep her own alive.

3

Blair

G ood morning, darling girl. How'd you sleep?"

Chloe slips her arms around Blair's soft middle and squeezes. She's a slate wiped clean each morning. Blair rips a banana from the fruit bowl and puts it on her plate, along with one of the muffins she made yesterday while it rained in the afternoon. Because it had been Wednesday, and that is what she does on Wednesdays. The muffins, the bedsheets, the rinsing of the washing machine drum with white vinegar and baking soda. Sometimes she feels embarrassingly unevolved.

Chloe licks the excess cream cheese from the side of the bagel and makes noises of approval.

She wonders if Aiden ever notices the list she works her way through every day. Or the schedule she writes in the squares of the kitchen calendar. She wonders if he knows an eleven-year-old washing-machine drum needs to be cleaned at all. Maybe she'll leave the soiled rags on his side of the bed tonight, so that at least he'll know what an eleven-year-old washing machine smells like.

But now, it is Thursday. The bathroom. Chloe's library books are due. Blair packed them in her knapsack last night, along with the bento box and clean gym clothes and a note to say she loved her, after she'd emptied the bits of crumb and playground sand into the sink. And then she'd taken two Advil for a headache and gone to bed early. Aiden said he had to work late on a presentation.

He'd already left for the gym when she got up; he must have had an early start today. She doesn't remember feeling him in the bed beside her last night. But sometimes he sleeps in the spare bedroom so he doesn't wake her up when he comes home.

She is peeling the paper from the base of her bran muffin when she lets herself wonder: *had* he come home?

She puts a chunk between her teeth. She imagines Aiden slipping in quietly to kiss their daughter as she sleeps, with a mouth covered in the filth of another woman. She can't swallow the muffin. She spits it into the garbage.

"Coat and shoes, Chloe, time to go!"

She is a good girl, a smart girl, an only child who likes routine and clean hair and always says please, and yet her needs consume Blair. Or Blair finds herself needing to be consumed. She'd once felt she was the only person who could do what she does for her daughter in the way that she does. It's why she never went back to work eight years ago after Chloe was born. And why she's ended up where she is now. Feeling unremarkable. She is forty, and at forty, possibility feels increasingly behind her.

Blair kisses Chloe good-bye at the door and turns to face the empty house. Most mornings of the week, Chloe walks the four blocks to school with her best friend, Xavier. Blair must convince herself each time that she has made it there safe. That she isn't in the back of a pedophile's van. If her phone rings in the morning, the thought occurs to her instantly: it's the school, and she never arrived. This maternal worry is the resting state of her mind.

Upstairs, she puts her nose against the concave ceramic of the bathroom sink. She is searching for the smell of the spearmint toothpaste Aiden would have spit, had he been home this morning. There's only a hint of Chloe's fluoride-free berry. The white towel hangs dry on the back of the door, although this isn't unusual. He showers at the gym on the days he works out.

Everything can be explained if she wants it to be.

Everything can scream at her if she lets it.

She reaches under the sink for the bleach cleaner and sprays the tiles. She does not stop when the fumes sting her eyes. The questions anesthetize her. Who is he fucking? And how is he fucking her? And where is the fucking happening? The rivers of bleach race down the wall. The details of the affair feel more important than what the affair means, and this makes no sense, she knows, but the human brain has a way of desperately wanting to know how the very worst things happen. We can't accept someone's death until it's explained—how and when and where?

But this is also a way of distracting herself from the truth, one that scares her more than the possibility of the affair and what it would mean: that she would do absolutely nothing about it at all.

That she'll quiet the whispers and throw out the foil. She'll tell herself he's only at the gym, only in a meeting every time he doesn't pick up. She'll choose to live with this, the tinny white noise in the background of their lives, because she cannot accept the consequences of the alternative.

And nobody would have to know.

The aloneness she feels, it's humiliating.

She is staring at a spot of mold when she's startled by Chloe shouting from downstairs.

"Mom? Xavi isn't home."

"What do you mean?"

"I mean nobody answered the door. I waited forever."

Blair flies down the stairs, thinking of the time, of how Chloe will be late for school now.

Chloe's face scrunches into the watch she's just learned to read. "Am I going to miss the bell?"

"Maybe he's gone early for chess club and forgot to tell you."

But it's unusual. Whitney will have left for work early, and Jacob is out of town, but their nanny, Louisa, would have been there, she is always there, marching those kids through the day.

"It's June now, Mom, chess club is over. Can you text Whitney and ask her where he is?"

"All right, but let's start walking, I'll go with you."

She sends the text while she wiggles her feet into her sneakers, the laces still tied. She stomps the sidewalk with satisfaction—she was home, she was ready and available. Look at my value. Look at how our daughter still needs me. She likes to orate in her head the things she wants her husband to hear.

In the morning, the commute flows through Harlow Street like a parade. Parents herding toddlers to preschool. Hollering city kids on scooters. Twentysomethings on bikes dodging cars, on the way to the kind of underpaid marketing job she used to have. This eclectic part of the city was once full of young Portuguese families who couldn't afford to buy homes anywhere else. Now, they've turned their properties over to people paying prices they never dreamed of seeing fifty years ago. Like Blair and Aiden, who have a mortgage so high that the number no longer feels real.

They march past the houses lined like monsters' teeth, unmatched and crooked, million-dollar rebuilds wedged between leaning, unloved Victorians biding time with painted brick. *Vogue* had called it the next coolest neighborhood in the world, something people cited as though it justified two million dollars for a semidetached house with a rotting basement and original avocado-colored toilets. They turn right off Harlow, past the poorly aged bakeries and the few remaining stores that imported clothes from Lisbon. The long-standing leases are coming to an end, and one by one the storefronts have flipped to cater to the money. Low-rise hotels where the black coffee is three dollars a cup. Kitschy plant shops and vegan grocers and overpriced children's boutiques. Blair works in one of them twice a week, five-hour shifts, and this week her second shift is today. She'll open the store in an hour. She answers to a twenty-seven-year-old named Jane who covers operating costs with a loan from her parents that she will never pay back. They sell linen bonnets and wooden toys that the parents like more than the children do.

Jane was a camp counselor and thinks she knows kids, but she does not know mothers. Blair circles items in the buyer catalogs that will actually sell, shows the customers who walk in off the street something they don't know they need. She'd first thought about working there while browsing for Chloe's birthday gifts, thinking of how much she'd enjoy curating the shelves. How the store could deliver a better experience for customers. Matte-finished wrapping paper in pretty pastels with long whimsy ribbons for the gifts. Themes for the window displays and tables organized in color stories. Wide straw baskets filled with seasonal items that moms like her buy on a whim. It was one of those times when the words were coming out before she gave herself the chance to think.

I help her out, she has found herself saying to friends when they ask about the job, as though she is doing it for free.

I think it'll be good for you had been Aiden's reaction when she got home and felt the wash of regret. As though she were a nursing-home resident who signed up for weekly bingo.

Whitney had been more encouraging, clasping her hands together with more enthusiasm than is natural for her. *Isn't that great! She's lucky to have someone as experienced as you are.*

Blair hugs Chloe outside the junior school doors as the bell sounds, and is relieved to have gotten there on time. Until she sees a group of second-grade mothers she knows chatting together. One of them looks up and catches Blair's eye. She has no choice but to walk over. To muster a cheery hello.

They are wearing heeled shoes. They have blown their hair nicely. They wear coats on trend for the season. A lawyer, a psychiatrist, an executive vice president. One of them has lost forty pounds and now sells real estate after not working for a decade. She calls it her midlife rebirth, says she has never been happier. They talk about being in their prime and "owning their forties," their language like the flex of a bicep. Blair studies them, tries on pieces of their lives in her mind.

How are things? they always say. Things. There is nothing specific to ask her about.

Morning drop-offs and the occasional volunteer duty are all they can manage, unlike Blair. Blair is there for every pickup, every pizza lunch duty, every birthday party, every playdate, every concert, every book fair. Every fucking parent council meeting.

Being this involved seemed like a noble decision at first. And the care and attention it required of her had felt more satisfying than writing ad copy for chocolate bars and laundry soap. She didn't miss the buzzing open-concept office like she thought she would. She didn't miss a wardrobe that required hangers, casual with a hint of business. She couldn't remember feeling fulfilled by the intellectual exercise of work, although she knows she had been. She had once loved the mix of creativity and marketing, coming up with the perfect phrase, the bang-on concept. She had been exceptionally good at it. She had five campaign awards with her name on them. She'd felt, sometimes, like a genius—

her boss had used that word, had jumped up in brainstorming sessions and scribbled her idea in the middle of the whiteboard and circled it five times while she tried desperately not to look chuffed.

But that career didn't feel like her anymore, not once she'd become a mother. Only Chloe had felt worthy of her time and her energy and her focus. She felt high off the baby those first early months. She would breastfeed her at night and stare into the dark and wonder about how she could ever give a fuck about a tagline again. She was supposed to want it all. And have it all. She wasn't supposed to let motherhood yank her away. But there hadn't been room inside her for anything else except the baby.

It hadn't felt sacrificial at the time. Devoting herself to motherhood and the domesticity that came with it had made her happy, at first. And Chloe does make Blair happy. Immeasurably. It is everything else that has happened along with Chloe, the changes in herself and her worth and her marriage that happened so slowly they were imperceptible. Where she'd once felt motherhood had given her so much more than she'd had before, now she could only see it as having taken everything away. Now she cannot reconcile the love she has for her daughter with how confined she feels by the privilege of being her mother.

These are the feelings she hates herself for having. These are the things she'll never say aloud to anyone.

"We wish you could come," one of the women says to her, hiking her very nice bag up on her shoulder. They've been discussing a moms' weekend out of the city, in July. A rental in the Berkshires. Blair doesn't often go away without Aiden or Chloe, but when she does, the anxiety before she leaves is all-consuming—and then the freedom of being away from them is intoxicating. She is equally unsettled by both. The women will drink too much wine, they'll gossip about other people's kids, agree about every zeitgeisty thing in the news cycle. There was a time when Blair felt plugged in. Now she's found herself on the periphery of everything that matters to everyone else. She'll come home feeling shittier than when she left.

"I know, me too. But we've got a thing that Saturday, a birthday thing. Next time, though."

She's the first to leave the conversation, says something vague, again, about a courier delivery. She doesn't have the energy today to perform, to try earning their respect yet again. The stay-at-home mom of only one, the martyr. Sometimes she wishes she'd had more children to justify how little else she has going on in her life.

She checks her phone as she walks home, but there is no reply from Whitney. Busy, she is busy. Doing things working people do, her head full of big, lofty solutions to big, lofty problems in a stratosphere Blair does not pretend to be familiar with anymore.

And yet she always makes a point of replying to Blair's texts in the continual conversation they pop in and out of through the week. Checking in on each other, making plans for the next glass of wine. Blair has never liked drinking, but it's a way in. She senses Whitney let go of her usual intensity when they're in person at the end of the day, spending time together around the children. She feels Whitney slowly unfurrow. She begins to look more focused on the words Blair is saying instead of being elsewhere, and the noise of the kids eventually ceases to irritate her. It is the wine, of course it is the wine, but Blair would also like to think it's her company.

But being with Whitney has the opposite effect on Blair. Blair is not unwound when she's with her, she is fueled. The thought that Whitney might suspect she's the most exciting part of Blair's week is humiliating. And yet because there's not much to tell Whitney about, she makes piddly things sound like more than they are. She regrets it afterward, every time. Whitney doesn't care about who wrote what in an email that confused the treasurer on the parent council, and what Blair did to defuse the situation before the entire fundraiser was canceled.

It's insignificant.

But Whitney kindly pretends it isn't. She gives Blair the dignity of listening to her talk for an hour about a fucking bake sale that raises less than two hundred dollars a year.

Sometimes, though, while she's meandering, she can feel Whitney studying her. Like she's looking for an ingredient that she herself is missing. She isn't sure if this is true, or if she just wants to believe it is. But there are moments when she senses Whitney wants to know what it feels like to care about the things that Blair cares about. To look at her own child and feel the way Blair does when she looks at hers. She lifts her chin. At least she has that.

4

Mara

Mara Alvaro crosses her legs at her ankles and sits back in the folding chair on her front porch. Something about this Thursday morning feels off. Nobody was home next door when Blair's daughter knocked, not even the nanny, and she's usually there every damn day of the week.

But these mothers are all busy, she knows. Too much going on and yet nothing going on at all, creating urgency where there is none, rushing their lives away. They don't know how to just be. They make no time to think about what's right there in front of them.

How fast it can all be taken away.

And she also doesn't understand why Blair wears those hideous black leggings every day, and Whitney with that dyed yellow hair, wearing those masculine suits and carrying those big ugly bags. Not a feminine thing about them. It's a shame the way women their age are now.

She thinks about going inside to rinse the crumbs off her breakfast plate. She should clean herself up for the day, too, although that routine has become less effortful in the past few years. The last tube of Avon, the Toasted Rose lipstick she's worn for decades, ran out nine months ago, and for the first time she hasn't bothered to replace it.

What does it matter anymore? She's eighty-two. Unlike her neighbors, she has few friends left around here. Everyone is either dead, or in a nursing home, or one of the lucky ones burdening their children way out in the suburbs. There had been a time when she couldn't open the front door to get the newspaper without someone stopping to gossip on the porch. Now she's being swallowed by all the new: the new ugly renovations, the new flashy cars parking on her street, the new young families and all their noises, their stuff, their excess. They want big-city living, they want to feel relevant, but she's got news for them—they're all heading in the same damn direction.

She had done her neighborly duty as each of the families had moved in around her. She brought them pastéis de nata and made sure they knew about the garbage pickup schedule. For months, she offered to collect their packages and keep an eye on things if they went away. She offered her advice about their ant-infested peony bush. She dropped off homemade canja in the winter. She didn't say a thing about the unnecessary third story that now blocked the sun from her small vegetable garden, or the two years of sound pollution she's lived through given all the self-important renovating they've done. And the constant noise of those kids. The hollering about. The slam of that stupid back door.

They had all been kind at first, despite their obvious differences. They seemed interested enough in how long she'd been there, and *Oh, you must have seen so much change in the area over the years,* like it was a wonderful thing. No acknowledgment that the change was exactly the problem. Every service is empty at St. Helen's Portuguese Catholic Church on the corner. The remnants of a community painstakingly built by an entire generation of her people were now just eyesores in *their*

neighborhood. They're waiting to snatch up the few remaining properties owned by old people like her. Salivating for signs of the last import
grocers going under. They all want that goddamn mermaid coffee chain
within walking distance.

Since those early pleasantries, hardly anybody has asked anything
about her. Or her life. Or how she got there. It's only their children who
bother to wave to her. And Rebecca. She likes Rebecca. A doctor doing
good, dignified work. Naturally pretty.

So no, there's no need for doing up her face today or any other day.
Instead, she shifts in her chair, listens for the squeak of the canvas beneath her.

"Mara!"

"It's on the table, Albert!" she shouts back. Like it always is, she wants
to add. Every damn morning. Through the screen of the kitchen window behind her, she hears the chair drag across the worn linoleum. She
hates watching him eat that sausage, hunched over a greasy plate of food
that's not good for him, not with his heart problems and the high cho-
lesterol.

Instead, she'll sit in the cool air of the June morning, try to figure out
what's going on.

It's amazing what you can learn about people when you're more or
less invisible. It's the things they don't want you to see that tell you the
most.

5

Whitney

The Hospital

The tubes don't upset her like Rebecca said they would. The IV, the breathing tube, the wires, the tape that pulls angrily at his skin. None of it even registers. There is only a boy. Her boy. His beautiful face, his cheeks that always smell like fresh air. She feels relief when she sees him there. He is in the world. She had pulled away from Rebecca's hand and swiftly picked up his, and she has not let go, not yet.

The hospital where she gave birth to him ten years ago is ninety-five miles away in a building she hasn't thought of in a very long time. Had the walls been this color, this same sickly green? And weren't the curtains this same candy-cane stripe? His birth is a memory she doesn't reach for much. She doesn't walk down memory lane with a lump in her throat. She doesn't make keepsake albums and growth records or save tiny teeth crusted with dried blood. She doesn't engage in conversations with women topping one another's labor stories. She has no time for that. She has no time for the kinds of details and measures and particulars that seemed to matter so much to other women.

She isn't that kind of mother.

Although there is one thing she remembers clearly about Xavier's birth: he came out of her in three pushes. Three pushes were all it took to separate from each other for the rest of their lives. That thought seems absurd to her now, like she should have every right to put him back inside her with that same amount of effort. Three. Two. One. He is hers. She made him. She grew him and raised him. She is supposed to be able to protect him. And she wants him back inside her. She could do it all over, do it differently. Start from the beginning again.

She traces his name in the fine blond hairs that cover his forearm. The skin on his elbow looks like wax where the latest scrape is healing, for now. He'll rip it open again in the next few days. There is always some bleeding part that he barely notices himself, and she finds smears of blood on the kitchen table, the bathroom rug.

She runs her finger over his elbow and then the ripped cuticles on his right thumb. It looks red, like he was sucking it. Does he still do that at night? She'll put lotion on his hands after his shower tonight. She will send Louisa home early and she will take over this time. She will do it all by herself, every night from now on, the stories and the second glass of water and the endless questions, and she will learn how to enjoy that kind of time.

This is how she thinks about things that morning, as though there will be a chance again for him to fall off a scooter, to continue a habit. As though there will be another chance to find patience. And restraint.

Accidents happen. People will say this to her, even though they don't believe she deserves the compassion. But no, an accident is a glass of spilled milk. The split lip of an adventurous toddler.

Someone asks if she has an update about when her husband might arrive. They think she's incapable of answering questions, of making decisions as the parental guardian. And perhaps they are right.

Jacob. She will check to see if he's called again. Her phone seems heavy in her hand. Had it always felt like a brick? There is a text from him. He's on the standby list at Heathrow. He will come straight to the hospital when he lands.

He'll be traveling back in time.

She imagines Jacob catching their son as he falls. The weight of him, the grunt of effort as his body lands in the cradle of his arms.

She texts him—go to Sebastian and Thea first, make sure they're okay with Louisa. He won't, of course. He will beg for the taxi to drive faster, to run the red lights. But she is not ready to see him. He'll take one look at her and he'll know everything. She is sure of it.

She ignores the other barrage of texts and the small red bubble reading "27" on the email icon. The number changes to "28" while she stares at it. She's missed six calls from her colleagues. The world is waking up, it is motoring with hours that are billable. Meetings that seem important.

Her phone hits the hospital room floor. She leaves it there.

Rebecca appears again at the other side of the bed.

She does not lift her eyes.

What would it be like if I wasn't here?

He'd asked her this, a couple of months ago one afternoon in the car. They were on the way to a dentist appointment for a filling that Jacob was supposed to take him to, until he'd been offered a last-minute preview at a gallery. Whitney technically had a clear afternoon.

What would it be like if you weren't here? she'd parroted, like she does when she doesn't want to think of the answer. Instead, she'd thought of someone she forgot to call back before she left the office. She'd thought about calling from the waiting room while Xavier was in

the dental chair. She'd thought about whether she had the budget numbers handy she knew the client would ask for; she could search her
emails when she parked. *What do you mean? Do you mean, where would
you be if you weren't on earth? Explain yourself a little better, Xav.* And
then, *Shit.*

She'd missed the entrance to the underground parking.

She can't, now, remember how he'd answered, if he'd said anything
at all.

She traces Xavier's name on his arm, again.

6

Rebecca

She scans a patient's lab results for the third time. She doesn't like feeling distracted at work, but she's stuck on Xavier. And the conversation earlier that morning in the hallway, when Whitney asked her why she doesn't want children. She'd replied with something she's never said aloud before: "There's nothing in the world I want more than a child."

The words had felt exposing. There'd been no hiding the desperation in her voice. But she'd wanted Whitney to know that she'd still choose to be a mother, even if she knew it would end this way, in an ICU bed. She wanted to remind her in that moment that as of 2:08 a.m. on Thursday morning, she still had her son. He was alive. He was hers. There'd been something uneasy in Whitney's eyes before she blinked once, slowly, and looked to the double doors at the end of the hall. But then she'd reached for Rebecca's hand again.

Normally, the fragility of life isn't something Rebecca allows herself to contemplate at work. That awareness does not serve her constitution here. It is better to assume that every child who crosses her path will live, and that she is responsible only for the next fragment of time that will begin the rest of their long and meaningful lives.

But if that child doesn't live, she will, from then on, be the person who changed that family's life. Her words—*I'm so sorry to have to tell you this*—will be burned in their memory until the day they themselves die. She becomes a part of those broken people's histories. That is a consequence of the job, and she has gotten used to it. She can move past it. Today, though, has been different. She checks her wrist for the time—9:18 a.m.—and wonders if it's too soon to call the ICU again for an update. The social worker would be by to see Whitney soon, if they haven't already. And the police will be back. The nurse can tell she's unfocused.

"Sorry to ask again, but did you talk to the parents? The suspected cardiomyopathy?"

Rebecca nods while she scans discharge papers the nurse put in front of her face. "Very sweet kid. I paged the on-call too. They need a breast pump machine, can you find them one? What do you have for me next?"

She rubs the top of her forehead under her rainbow scrub cap and then bangs the sanitizing dispenser to clean her hands. She needs to wake up. To jolt herself out of this.

She usually thrives here in the emergency department, the pace, the unknown, the constant rotation of cases. Anything can happen on a shift, and she wonders how people with almost any other job get out of bed in the morning to face the guarantee of monotony. And yet she, too, finds comfort in her days. The comfort is in the new. New children, new families, new problems, and she can help most of them, most of the time. The not-so-sick ones go home, and the others enter the system in some capacity, upstairs to other doctors, oncology, neurology, nephrology, wherever they end up after leaving the cramped, curtained lineup of bays she does her work in. Some might never leave the hospital again, and when she suspects this, she finds herself surveying the few things from home they've got with them. The pilled pajama bottoms, the clutched teddy bears. Markers of the end that parents will carry, later, without them.

Rarely does she learn what becomes of these children unless she bumps into a parent in the parking garage or the line for coffee. She has become expert at looking engaged with her phone as she walks through the hospital atrium; she's not as recognizable with her scrub cap off, her dark, straight hair falling over her shoulders. She feels guilty about this part, but it's how she's able to push open the swinging double doors of the emergency department ready to work.

A nurse is briefing her about the two-year-old waiting in room 3. Recurring high fever, lethargy, loss of appetite. The girl's parents sit on either side of her gurney, watching her focused on the iPad on her lap. They straighten when she comes into the room, and Rebecca can feel their assembly of relief and tension: the doctor is here, but something is wrong. Rebecca scans the child's chart on the computer monitor, and it happens: 05/19/2017. The patient's birth date. She's been waiting for this. She breathes in sharply and rolls the stool toward her.

"Lucy? I'm Rebecca. Do you mind if I have a look at you while you watch your show? Is that Daniel Tiger?" She picks up the girl's hand and pinches the skin gently to check her hydration, presses on her tiny nail beds. She turns her hand over and slowly feels her smooth, chubby palm. She slips the stethoscope up the back of the child's pajama top to listen to her lungs. She thinks of the bedroom Ben painted two years ago. She thinks of pretty floral crib sheets. She moves the bell around to the girl's chest to hear her heart. She thinks of the pulsating mass of cells she and Ben heard in the very first ultrasound. The girl's eyes are on her now instead of the screen. Rebecca reaches to the wall for the ophthalmoscope and moves close to her. She can smell peanut butter on her breath as she looks at her retina. She pulls the instrument away. The girl is studying the parts of her face, her nose, maybe the mascara on her eyelashes. Rebecca touches the back of her head. She runs the fine, dark curls through her fingers. She touches her tiny earlobe. The softness of her warm, plump cheek. Her tiny chin.

The mother clears her throat.

Rebecca turns away. "I'd like to do bloodwork, if that's okay with you both?" She types in the order. Name. Birth date. The blinking cursor on the screen is hypnotic. She'd have just turned two, like her. She'd have been perfect.

7

Blair

Aiden had appeared at Blair's feet. It was the year they both turned thirty-one, at a mutual friend's party jammed in a studio apartment. She'd been about to leave. And she'd also been about to step on a piece of a broken bottle. Aiden had put his arm out to stop her as he dropped to his knees to pick up the shard, lifted it up in his wide palm like a glass slipper.

It was a bit of a charade, too dramatic for her taste. But when Aiden stood up, she saw the kind of man who wasn't often looking at her. She could tell immediately. It was the grin, the boyish mischievousness, his six and a quarter feet. The way everyone around them was watching him.

She came to crave the rush of being found by him in a room, of having his attention land on her, the one he wanted. He was loud, his voice deep and reverberating. She'd felt desired by men before, but not like him. Aiden's gregariousness made her feel vulnerable at first, like someone had ripped off her clothing in public. She wasn't used to so many eyes in her direction when she was with him, to his volume, to the socializing that came so naturally to him. He was magnetic. He was inarguably handsome. He touched her a lot. He held her tightly under his arm and he stroked her shoulder with his thumb when they spoke to other people. She liked that this gesture caught people's attention. She watched for them to notice, for their eyes to dart down to that touch.

There was a softness about him when they were alone, and that she was the only person privy to this side of him felt special. His sweet, slow doting on a Sunday morning. The noise he made when he smooched her cheek, successively, like she was delicious, like he needed his love for her to have a sound. Evening baths they'd have together, tangled and giggly, he far too big for the tub, damp hair in his eyes.

"Do I make you happy? Is this what you want?" He was always checking with her, always making sure he measured up to what she expected of him. She never thought he would cease to care.

When she had called her mother to tell her about Aiden, that he had a good job in sales, that he'd sent flowers to her office on her birthday, her mother had been silent. Blair had stared at the twenty-four peach garden roses in the cloudy plastic vase from the staff kitchen and waited for her to speak.

"Hello?"

"That all sounds fine."

Fine. Fine was always her mother's answer. Fine, like the excellent marks she got in high school. Fine, like the scholarship she won to her first-choice college. Fine, like the first studio apartment she rented in the city that she was so proud to afford on her own. Her mother had so few expectations as time went on, so little interest, but Blair tried to remind herself it wasn't about her. There was nothing she could say that would enliven a better response from her mother. Her dial was stuck at neutral. As far as Blair could tell, her mother couldn't feel anything anymore.

She had been different when Blair was younger, lively and fun. She worked three days a week as a secretary for her father's insurance business until Blair was eight years old. She'd bring her and her younger brother to their office in the summer where they'd make forts under the desks and spin in the office chairs until all three were too dizzy to stand. She'd loved how her mother's lipstick smelled like the tempera paint from school. She'd loved touching her long strings of layered pearls, hearing the clacking sound of the beads. They would blast the radio in the car on the way home, and from the back seat, she would mimic the way her mother's shoulders moved in front of her.

But somewhere along the way her mother had seemed to reduce herself, quietly and slowly. She left her job, and she spoke less to them. She stiffened in her father's hands.

Blair hadn't understood the burden of her mother's deadening until she moved to college and felt how easy it was to breathe. She found excuses not to go home when her friends would. The tension in the house had grown too much for her. By then, her parents only spoke to each other through Blair, like they could no longer register the sound of each other's voices.

Blair wonders, now, sitting behind the cash desk of Itsy Bitsy, if she and Aiden are really any different than her parents were. If that's what awaits. Misery served every night for dinner.

She's staring at the six-foot-tall stuffed giraffe they have priced at $249 when the door chimes for the first time this morning. She's about to force something resembling a smile, but it's Aiden who walks in.

He never stops by to see her.

"What are you doing here?"

"Nice to see you too. I finished a breakfast meeting nearby, thought I'd pop in."

He wanders to the shelf of wooden race cars. From behind, he reminds her of the Aiden from ten years ago, the thick flow of his hair at the back. His broad shoulders. They used to have so much fun together. Long road trips and scuba lessons in the pool. Lip-synching in the car. They used to crave being soaked in each other. Where had that feeling gone? Was it more than parenthood? Had she slipped too far away from who she used to be?

He lifts a car in her direction. "These sell well?"

"Not really."

He chuckles.

"You left for work early this morning," she says.

"I usually do, don't I?"

She lifts her eyebrows. She neatens the pile of courier papers on the desk. She is used to being on edge in his presence. This is how things feel between them now. Rote. And blunt. They don't talk about anything real anymore. Their conversations are an exchange of logistics and information. "Did you eat at the Egg and Bean?"

He nods. "I should have brought you a coffee. You want me to get you one?"

She shakes her head, but she does want one. His pleasantness irritates her. The ease of his days irritates her too. She would feel better, she thinks, if he worked harder for them. If he worked as hard as she works in her role, the thinking, the accommodating, the planning, the doing, the thinking again. She wants his head to spin at night with the things he must do the next day so that their lives are smooth, so that they float.

Has Aiden ever noticed that? The way they all just seem to float? That they are fed and cared for and have shampoo in their shower, and salt in their shaker, and gifts on the morning of their birthdays? That they have antinausea tablets placed in the palms of their hands the second the motion sickness hits? That is *her* doing. Her unseen value. That is worth more than the sixteen-fucking-fifty an hour Jane pays her.

Aiden sells software security systems to financial institutions, and although she can regurgitate that line when someone asks, she knows very little about what this entails. He is mostly on commission, and this means some years he makes really good money, and some years he makes an amount he can't possibly be proud of.

So they have to be careful. He complains about the credit card bills on a bimonthly basis, and when he does, she feels instantaneous fury. She says things like, *Do you want her to go to school with holes in her pants? Can you even tell me how much a loaf of bread costs? What did you spend on your fancy lunch today at the office? Do you think I* wanted *to fork out $134.36 to have the dishwasher looked at? Should I decline all the birthday party invites, then? Tell them we can't afford the gifts?*

Why are you always so angry? he will say, in a voice that is infuriatingly calm.

He's checking his email now.

"Did you come to spend time with me, or your phone?" She hates herself as soon as the words come out the way they do.

He apologizes, puts the phone on the counter. She senses the good intention he's come with is fading. This feels familiar, the chance he offers her to reciprocate his good mood, to have a moment of connection, and how hard it is for her to accept. She wonders when he will stop trying to offer the good mood in the first place.

"The store looks great." He looks around, maybe to remove himself from her stare. Maybe she's making him nervous. The foil wrapper, it's back in her mind. Never gone for long. Does he ever wonder if he's been careful enough? Does he wonder when she'll find out?

"I'll pass that along to Jane." But Blair won't. The store only looks great because of her. She wishes the moment felt different. She had a chance at finding comfort with him and now it's gone. The door chimes and a woman about the same age as Blair scans the store and makes her way to the bookshelves. Blair clears her throat to get Aiden's attention back, but she can't let go of the thoughts that consumed her that morning. Her heart races.

"Can I ask you something?"

He nods as he checks his watch. His patience is gone.

"Did you come home last night?"

He looks stunned. But not caught. This gives her a split second of relief.

"Of course. I slept in the spare room. I didn't want to wake you up."

She faces the wall and refills the stapler. There is never the satisfaction she thinks there will be in saying the things that eat away at her. She always feels worse.

She wonders if he might leave the store without saying good-bye to her. But she turns back toward him, and he's watching her with his arms crossed. His phone is back in his pocket.

"You know, Blair, sometimes it feels like you want me to disappoint you. Like you're hoping to find a reason to hate me as much as you do."

Blair shushes him to lower his voice, and she feels her face redden. She can tell him it isn't true. She can defend herself.

But there's truth to what he's saying. She wants to like him more than she does, but something makes that feel impossible. And now, she's got a piece of garbage she stares at every morning forcing her to face how weak she really is.

She wants to say she is sorry. She wants to tell him she feels unseen. And unimportant. And that she doesn't know what being loved by him feels like anymore, or if being loved is even enough. That she doesn't know how to fix any of this, and so she copes the best way she knows how.

There is no relief when he turns his back to her, only an aching sadness. He faces the door when he speaks. "I'll be home at six for dinner, all right?"

Is this what the end is like? Did she owe him more just now? Why has she done this again? One of these times, she might go too far. And the choice to stay in this marriage will no longer be hers.

Through the window of the store, she watches him walk away, hands in his pockets, eyes on the sidewalk. Sometimes his very presence makes her hate herself.

When Jane arrives twenty minutes later, Blair tells her she doesn't feel well.

And she doesn't. She feels very, very unwell.

She's halfway along Harlow Street, eyeing Whitney's lifeless house catty-corner to hers, when she decides she needs something to cheer her up. It's the one thing she's promised herself she wouldn't do anymore. But it's her only vice. And she feels owed at least one.

She digs in her bag for the keys.

8

Mara

Something about the way Blair stands for a minute at the end of the Loverlys' driveway makes Mara think she's not supposed to be there. But she's done this before, gone over when nobody's home, let herself in with a spare key.

It's nearly 11:30 a.m. and she hasn't seen a soul at that house since yesterday evening, when Whitney's car pulled in after work, just as the rain stopped. She hadn't spoken to anyone all day, and nobody had spoken to her, other than Albert grumbling about the temperature of the house, the fridge smelling sour, the garbage truck being fifteen minutes late. But that was more like background noise she just happened to catch as she moved around him. She'd waved to Whitney as she got out of her car, tried to get her attention. It was only six steps, maybe seven, from her car to the front door, but the woman couldn't take her eyes off that stupid phone.

There'd been noises last night, of course there'd been.

But that wasn't all that unusual living in the city.

It could just as easily have been a dream, something from her past knocking around again.

As a girl, Mara had been a vivid dreamer. She paddled her legs through the night as she ran from the devil. Her sisters stuffed cotton balls in their ears so they weren't woken up by Mara talking in her sleep. In the morning, she'd recount outlandish stories to her siblings as though what happened in her dreams was real, and they'd run to tell their mother she was fibbing again. And she usually was. But as she got older, there was more to the dreams than her overactive imagination.

When she was seventeen, she dreamed of handsome Albert the night before they met for the first time. He showed up at her family's house with his father, the refrigerator repairman. He was supposed to be apprenticing, but he spent the whole hour leaning against the lime-green wallpaper in the hallway, talking too fast to Mara, who sat on the third step of the staircase with her legs politely crossed. She could see that he was trying to be charming. She'd never felt the power of making someone nervous until then. She noticed him tap the wall with the knuckle of his index finger to punctuate the end of his sentences, sometimes once, sometimes twice. The young man in her dream the night before had done the same thing. Tap. Tap, tap. She had been there, in that moment with him, before.

The morning after she got pregnant, she knew as soon as she woke up that she had conceived. They'd been married for a year and only just started praying for that miracle to happen, but she had dreamed all night of the baby floating in the blue of her womb, her lining white and soft and wispy, like blankets of stratus cloud.

After dinner, she poured Albert a drink and casually told him he'd better call the travel agent to book their tickets for the move. He'd jumped from the table and spun Mara around in the cramped kitchen of their apartment, her feet knocking over a stack of blue-glass plates. He put her down and dropped to his knees and cried into her apron, damp from the dishwater, as she rubbed the lobes of his ears between her fingers.

Like most of their friends dreaming bigger things for themselves, they always said they'd leave Lisbon to establish life somewhere with more opportunity. Mara insisted. Portugal had nothing but agriculture, no modern economy or commerce, no industry set to boom. Lisbon felt left behind from the prosperity happening in the world, stuck under the thumb of a government opposed to change. Albert couldn't fathom repairing aging appliances day in and day out, not if his father's dull life was anything to go by, so he'd gotten a job selling fishing equipment and surpassed his quotas for the year in three months. Mara knew he could make a decent living as a salesman somewhere in North America if he learned English. They both watched the affluent tourists from the rest of the world flooding their beaches for holidays. They knew there was another way.

Everyone told Albert to go alone to America, to find a job and establish some connections first, but he would never have left Mara, and she never would have let him. They'd go as a family. He'd already saved most of every paycheck, she'd cut every unnecessary expense, and they talked almost every night about where they'd go, poring over books and maps from the library. The West Coast. Or Massachusetts. Or Toronto. They'd learned common phrases in English, quizzing each other over late, boozy dinners that ended naked in bed. They were ready.

"What did the doctor say? Lots of rest? A baby. A baby." He wiped his face with his hanky, chuckling at their unbelievably good fortune.

"I haven't been to the doctor yet."

"But then how do you know?"

"I dreamed about him last night."

"Mara!" He threw his head back, covering his eyes. "For God's sake, woman."

"Just trust me, Albert." She'd pressed her lips to the top of his head.

They decided on a patchwork pocket of a big city where they'd heard Portuguese were settling, where rent was cheap, and the houses were run-down, but there was talk of things changing with more families coming, people bringing siblings and in-laws, a restaurant and fish shop opening on the main street. Albert's English had become good enough to get a job selling soda machines for an American distributor, and they gave him a company car, a shining red Ford. He asked Mara to take a picture of him leaning on the hood, with their new Kodak camera, and he mailed the photograph home to his parents. He opened a bank account and they started saving for their first home. They hated the cold, and they missed their families, but there was a sense of community sprouting around them, parish clubs, a bakery with a queue on Saturday mornings, copies of the *Correio Português* landing on their porch. Mara loved to find opportunities to speak the English she'd been proud to learn, although she rarely needed to in her new neighborhood.

Everything was happening as they'd hoped, as they'd planned for, until Mara was nearly nine months pregnant and had the first vivid dream since she'd conceived.

She knew something about the child would be different.

When she pushed her son into the world two weeks later, Albert pacing in the hallway, she closed her eyes and listened for the silence. Deafening silence. But he screamed. Frantic and healthily.

"Here he is, a perfect baby boy," the doctor's voice boomed over his wailing lungs.

Her head shot up to look for her son, but he was already wrapped in the hands of the nurses. She needed to see him with her own eyes to be sure. Sometime later, after she made enough fuss about it, they wheeled her down the hall to the nursery, to his spot in the rows of glass bassinets. She unfolded the blanket slowly. She put her hand on his pink chest and thanked God. She could feel there was something special about him.

Albert proudly carried Marcus to the church on the corner, showing him off every Sunday as though nobody had ever seen an infant before. He held the phone receiver to the baby's tiny ear when his parents called to sing to him. Marcus was happiest when Albert held him over his head and whisked him around the room. He bought a vintage airplane from a secondhand store and hung it from the nursery ceiling with fishing string.

"He's going to be a pilot, Mara. I'll bet you anything."

The milestone months came and went uneventfully, and so the doctor glossed over Mara's concerns at Marcus's three-year-old checkup. Marcus was increasingly less verbal around everyone but her. He feared other children in the sandbox. He covered his ears when delivery trucks drove by, when a door closed. He wouldn't eat anything wet.

"Particulars, Mrs. Alvaro. That's all. Every child has them, some kids are just more sensitive than others. Get him exposed to more, it'll toughen him up." The doctor had opened the exam room door while he spoke. "And try being more relaxed around him. Children can sense when their mother is nervous."

As though it were her fault.

He was meant to outgrow it all.

There was an evening after she'd kissed Marcus good night that she worked up the nerve to ask Albert if he was ever worried about him. About how little his son spoke to anyone but her. About his anxiousness. His retreating. Albert didn't know much about children, but the other kids at church who were Marcus's age were climbing the back pews together. Their parents had to hiss for them to be quiet during the service and call for them to stop when they ran out the arched doors toward the road. Albert had to have noticed how their son cowered on Mara's lap, buried his head into her neck whenever he was spoken to.

Marcus wouldn't go to Albert at all.

She wanted money to take him to a specialist. She felt queasy saying this aloud to Albert. She knew before he answered that she'd made her concern too official for him. The examples too hard to refute. He wanted their son to be a certain kind of boy, beaming at the center of this life he had worked so hard for, and she was telling him now, with words she could not take back: our son is not that child.

He had left the room to have a cigarette and water the small back garden in the dark. They'd planted it together that spring, Marcus watching quietly from under a sun umbrella, uninterested in the dirt, the worms, the plastic containers that held the bulbs. They'd just bought the house on Harlow Street, a bungalow with cinnamon-colored brick on a strip of narrow property Albert could pace the width of in seven steps. He'd installed yellow-and-cream-striped aluminum awnings over the front porch and the front windows. He'd painted the low wrought-iron fence in the front yard a crisp white and tended the new sod with care. She watched him in the backyard from their bedroom that night, one hand on the hose, the other brushing his cheeks while his shoulders shook.

She brought Marcus with her everywhere she went. Sometimes he would hide in the footwell of the car and refuse to get out. Other times he would do all right until there was a certain clang, or the hairstylist at the salon bent down to offer him a lollipop. He would become stiff and stare, like an animal in the wild. Shy, everyone called him.

By the age of five, he only spoke to her in whispers.

She came to crave his warm breath on her ear, the sound of air passing through his teeth.

"Tell Mommy, why won't you speak to anyone else? What are you frightened of?"

"It's like I'm on the stage all day." He hung from her back, clung to her shoulders, never far.

"On the stage? What do you mean?"

"Like everyone's watching me at the theater. But I can't remember what comes next." The hot breath again. "They're going to laugh at me."

He amazed her with how smart he was, speaking both Portuguese and English fluently, completing adult jigsaw puzzles and memorizing every country on the map. He read softly aloud on Mara's lap if Albert wasn't home to overhear. But school was a challenge. He was often too anxious to make it through the day. Stomachaches and diarrhea led to one too many accidents. The children were cruel.

She decided she would teach him at home herself.

He became more a part of her than most children ever were of their mothers, although Mara had nothing to compare their unusual attachment with. She never ached for a moment without him underfoot, never shooed him away, even when she bathed or used the toilet. He lived on her like a layer of skin. He didn't smile in front of anyone else but her, but she knew he was happy. He was happy with her.

By the spring Marcus was seven, Albert was staying late at work almost every day of the week. He would come home long after Marcus's bedtime and wake up well before he rose. He occupied himself out of the house most weekends. Mara kept a calendar in a kitchen drawer, and she marked an X on the days when Albert didn't see their son at all. After an entire month was filled with her angry black ink, she made sure their son was asleep, and then marched to the sitting room. She banged the television knob and threw the calendar on his lap.

"Four weeks. It's been four weeks since you've laid eyes on him. He's the greatest gift you could have, and you're missing everything about him."

He looked past her at the screen. He was like stone.

"What's changed in you, Albert? What gives you the right to be so unhappy?"

His stillness infuriated her. He could ignore everything so easily. Their beautiful son. Their hardened marriage. The dangerous place they were headed. There were no other options for her here, no money, no family, no alternatives. He didn't blink. She wondered where he went, how he could just disappear from the room. How she could never allow herself to falter, not for any of the waking minutes in her day. How she was never not there. For them, with them, in spite of them.

"You're not the man I thought you were."

Now, Mara watches the Loverlys' house.

"What are you doing out here still?" Albert holds the screen door open. He's in his burgundy robe and the smell of grease lingers in the terry cloth.

"Nothing." She gestures for him to move out of the doorway, to make room for her. She's surprised to see a sausage left on his plate. He's never not eaten his breakfast.

"Not hungry today?"

"I guess not," he says on his way to their bedroom.

She tidies up the kitchen counter, puts his plate in the sink, soaks the frying pan. He'll want more coffee, she knows, so she throws out the soggy filter and replaces it. Scoops the grounds from the tin barrel. Fills the back canister with water. She waits for the gurgle; it doesn't always work properly, twenty years old it must be, but he won't replace it until he's convinced the damn thing is dead. She tries to recall what she was going to do this morning. The laundry. And collect the paper airplanes from the backyard bushes, because it's Thursday.

He comes back to the kitchen, buttoning his shirt, his fingers reminding her of the sausages. His swollen hands can barely make a fist anymore.

"Coffee's on," she says. "Come here, I'll finish."

He scoffs but he lets her do the last two buttons as he looks away from her. They haven't looked right at each other in decades, not really—not like they used to. She wonders if he sees too much in the glassiness of her eyes, the whites dulled long ago. Or maybe he sees too little. Are their lives supposed to feel fuller than this? Does he sometimes cry about this too? He smooths the wisps of hair at the top of his head and clears the phlegm from his throat. He rubs his chest. He tucks his shirt in and sits at the kitchen table.

"Where is it?"

She slides his empty mug across the counter toward the machine, gestures to the cream on the table, and goes downstairs to the basement.

9

Blair

She double-checks the time as she approaches the front door to
Whitney's home. Not quite noon. She still hasn't heard back from
Whitney today, but she knows Sebastian and Thea are normally at a library program with Louisa on Thursdays. Louisa posts a family schedule
in the kitchen each month, and Blair stealthily snaps a photo on a regular basis.

The massive windows at the front and the open-concept layout mean
that Blair, from her own living room, can usually see straight through
their house into the back garden. At least until midday, when the sun's
glare reflects her own tired house back to her.

Sometimes, on weekends, she watches Jacob make breakfast at the
wide kitchen island. His trackpants sit low. She has watched Whitney
wrap her arms around his bare shoulders and pluck fruit from his fingers.
Once, she slipped her hand down the front of his pants. Jacob had put the

spatula down while she stroked him, inches from the hot griddle, as the kids watched television in the next room.

That kind of thing doesn't happen on her side of Harlow Street. Blair's proximity to Whitney makes her painfully aware of this difference. She and Aiden live in a narrow patchwork starter home they were supposed to renovate five years ago. Her husband doesn't know where the waffle maker is kept. She never thinks to touch him in their kitchen. She never thinks to touch him at all.

But she wouldn't want everything about Whitney's life. She wouldn't like being consumed with work and absent for her daughter, divided and distracted all the time. Searching for the balance that eludes every woman. Balance isn't even a concept Whitney seems to consider.

And yet Blair envies her. She wants to feel about herself the way Whitney does, she wants to know what it's like to be in that echelon of women. The gratification of having made the right life choices.

The key was given to her as a spare for emergencies.

But there are never any emergencies.

She walks inside and punches the security code numbers. She turns the lock behind her and stands in the stark white entryway. An enormous abstract painting looms above, hung from wires like in a gallery. The mess of muted, mucky acrylics are as appealing to her as vomit, although she has pretended otherwise. She breathes in. There is a manufactured freshness to the air in this house, like a car at the dealership, like something newly unwrapped.

She slips her shoes off and walks toward the spotless kitchen, with its wide slates of black marble and knobless cupboards and quiet-close drawers. There isn't an item out of place. No sippy cup on the counter. No spoon in the sink. No oil stains on surfaces from peanut butter fingers. Louisa must have been there and cleaned up the mess of breakfast already. Peppermint and citrus diffuse from the ceramic cylinder on the island. Louisa sells essential oils on the side. Whitney says they give her a headache.

Stacked neatly next to the diffuser is yesterday's mail. She shuffles through the envelopes. There's a credit card bill she would have liked to open. Sometimes she takes them home with her, betting nobody reads them anyway. A statement from the insurance company. And a postcard invitation for a shopping event at a department store where Blair can only browse.

She pulls on the stainless-steel handle of the paneled fridge. Louisa does the groceries on Wednesday evenings. The full shelves are organized by food type and then container size and then expiration date. She takes a green apple from the drawer and has three sour bites. She drops it in the organic wastebin and notices it's empty—no soggy cereal, no strawberry tops. Like the kids hadn't eaten that morning at all.

She scans the built-in desk next to the pantry. It is meant as a place for the children to do homework, although she has never seen Xavier sit there. There is a cup of fresh crayons for the twins. She wiggles the computer mouse, and the black screen disappears to a sign-in page. She had regretted the advice the second it left her mouth a few weeks ago.

By the way, are all your screens locked? Do you have parental controls on? They're at that age now, they could find anything online.

She often mentions things Whitney won't have thought of. Measures only an attentive mother would take. Whitney doesn't waste energy worrying about what could go wrong.

She's disappointed she can't check the browser history or open Whitney's personal emails. She likes to see what Whitney keeps separate from the work account her assistant manages. She once found the confirmation for a breast lift Whitney hadn't told Blair about. But she takes the most pleasure in the exchanges she has with other friends. They are superficial and swiftly written. Those women don't receive the time and attention that Whitney gives to Blair.

She has been coming here for just over a year, every couple of months. Each time, at the bottom of the stairs, lit from the flat skylight above, she stops to question: What if she is caught? What if someone sees her through one of the many expansive windows and asks Whitney about it later? Mara's eyes have followed her across the street on several occasions.

She has a bank of answers prepared.

Desperate to pee, locked out of my house.

Thought I'd left my phone in your kitchen yesterday.

Could have sworn I heard your smoke alarm.

All plausible.

She doesn't always go up to the third floor, where Xavier's and Sebastian's rooms are. There's nothing interesting there, and it rests worst on her conscience to be snooping in a child's space. But she's particularly curious today, given the situation this morning. She opens Xavier's door first. Cool air hits her right away, which is strange. The window is open. She nearly steps in something dark all over the hardwood. Coffee, she can smell it. The splatter covers the back of the door and some of the wall. The white ceramic handle is broken off the mug on the floor. Her nerves accelerate as she imagines what kind of anger sent Whitney's coffee flying across the room. The duvet and the pillow are on the floor, too, in a heap. There are sheets of paper everywhere, pencil and markers scattered, an empty wallet. Several paper planes are folded and stacked together in a pile on the nightstand. And then something dark catches her eye—a black scribbled mess across the white wall. Paint. Or maybe ink. The room feels eerie now. Like she's witnessing something she shouldn't be.

She hates this about her friend, the frustration with her children, although she knows Whitney tries to temper herself around Blair. It's uncomfortable, the whipping of her voice when she speaks to them, being privy to her frustration. The sourness they're all left with in her wake. Blair's own heart races when Xavier or the twins get a little too out of control, as kids are meant to do, the escalation of their energy, the cacophony of voices, a scream and then a cry and then one blames the other—Whitney up, grabbing an arm, pulling a child into another room with a force Blair would never use herself. She doesn't like the thought of Chloe being around this when she goes over to play; she's grateful for the buffer of Louisa being there most of the time.

And then, of course, there was what happened at the backyard party in September.

She wonders if she should leave, given the oddness of the morning. But instead, she stops on the second floor at Whitney and Jacob's bedroom suite. She slides the door open, feeling the wooziness of doing something she shouldn't.

She runs her fingers along the steel gray grass cloth on the walls. The white linens are tucked at the bottom of the bed with precision, but the spot where Whitney slept is still crumpled. That's unusual—she's heard Louisa say she does the bedrooms first thing. She smooths the bottom of the duvet cover and marvels, as she always does, at how buttery it feels. She scans the room, but it's tidy, nothing else out of place.

In the walk-in closet, the clothing hangs from evenly spaced wooden hangers. Whitney's wardrobe is too extensive to deduce what she might be wearing that day. Blair feels the ends of the wool jackets and the hems of the structured dresses. The cashmere is folded and stacked, the whites on the shelves like the gradients on a paint chip.

Blair's favorite thing has slipped from the hanger and is puddled on the floor. A short silk robe with navy floral lace, something she would never think to own. She puts the robe on over her cotton shirt and leggings and ties the belt.

The robe mocks her in the mirror. Whitney has never looked better than she does at forty, despite giving birth to the twins four years ago. She wears clothing that shows off her back, her long lean legs, her smooth and unmarked skin. Blair feels juvenile in comparison. She is freckled in a charmless way. Her arms feel like inflatable swim floaties that need more air. Blair finds it hard to shift her eyes away from Whitney's perfection when they're together, especially when Whitney's head is turned away from her. She's become expert at consuming her swiftly, thirstily.

She puts the robe back on the hanger.

Jacob's things are casual, monochrome, unvaried. His shirts line the smaller end of the closet and share space with Whitney's handbags. She lifts the heavy cotton of his black crewneck to her cheek. She feels more uneasy touching his things than she does Whitney's. She doesn't think her attraction to him is inappropriate, considering how most women would feel if they saw Jacob. But she's most attracted to the things about him that others wouldn't notice right away. The way his stubble defines his jawline two days after shaving. The subtle dimple, only on his left cheek. That he's quiet only because he's a thinker.

There is a rush in the betrayal she feels, both of her husband and of her best friend, as she touches Jacob's things. She lifts a pair of his white briefs from the drawer and pictures him getting hard, filling out the slouched pocket of Lycra. The bit of dampness he would excrete on the fabric. Her eyes fall to the pretty wicker basket meant for dirty clothes. But Louisa has already done the laundry.

She opens the top drawer on Whitney's side of the closet. Her bras are structured and fresh. The shapes are still intact, the elastic straps still taut. She puts her hand on one of the firm cups, as though she's holding Whitney's breast.

In the second drawer, each pair of panties is folded into tiny squares and arranged like a box of chocolates. They are black and silk. Blair thinks of the pair she is wearing now under her own leggings. Pilled, once white.

She puts her hand toward the back of the third drawer, past the expensive scarves and pantyhose. She pulls out the soft blue shoe bag with two vibrators inside. One is small and red and firm and turns on with one click, the other malleable with various speeds and frequencies. She lifts each one from the bag to her nose. Sometimes the scent of Whitney lingers on the velvety-smooth rubber. Sometimes it's the rosemary soap in the master bathroom.

She stares at the larger one and imagines Whitney arching on her back as she pushes it inside herself. Lying on their king bed as Jacob watches her from the chaise across the room. She knows they like to do this. Whitney told her so at the bottom of a second bottle of wine last summer. Blair loved possessing this confession, this titillating thought in the back of her mind when she saw them together. She's hoped for more from Whitney, more uninhibited throwaways about her sexuality, but the topic seems to extinguish their conversation lately. Like maybe Whitney knows she said too much before, although Blair is naturally the more prudish one. Sex with Aiden is a performance she can barely bring herself to do anymore. But here, in Whitney's bedroom, the arousal comes easily. She runs her thumb down the silky rubber of the larger vibrator and then places them both back in the bag.

Next, she opens the drawer where Whitney keeps the fancier lingerie. She lifts the navy lace bodysuit that matches the robe she had on earlier. She notices the slit in the fabric of the crotch. She slips her fingers through and thinks of Jacob doing the same and feels herself warm. Before she can change her mind, she undresses. She steps into the bodysuit and pulls it up. The high-cut bottoms are too tight and her breasts too slight to fill out the wire cups.

She lies on the end of the bed and reaches for the opening in the lace. She can't remember the last time she has felt like this. She doesn't touch herself often. But now, she thinks of Jacob and Whitney there with her in the bedroom. Of Whitney watching as Jacob moves closer to Blair. They have invited her, they have asked her to do this for them. She is worthy of them. She is desirable. He enters her.

Seconds later, she unfurls. She stares at the blown-glass pendant above her. The boldness leaves her much faster than it came. She peels off the bodysuit and places it neatly in the drawer.

As she washes her hands in the en suite bathroom, the marble warm under her feet, she's reminded of what Jacob would really see. She turns away from herself in the mirror, the endorphins gone. She could never let another man put his fingers where her own have just been. Or his face, in her wiry hair and her loose folds. The intimacy of even a kiss feels repulsive to her. She doesn't know when this change happened.

In the cabinet behind the mirror, Blair surveys the thick green glass vessels of skin-care products. Regenerating cleanser. Reparative moisturizer. Restorative eye cream. Resurfacing serum. Rejuvenating face clay. Redefining body balm. Revitalizing body oil.

She picks up the package of birth control pills. There are unpopped foils throughout the month again. A few weeks ago, she had slipped and mentioned them to Whitney by mistake. The topic of vasectomies had come up. Jacob would never do it.

But don't you worry when you forget to take your pill?

Whitney had looked at her curiously. She'd never told Blair she was on the pill.

I've been taking it so long that I never forget, was all she had said.

Blair puts the package back on the shelf.

Yeast infection suppositories. Yeast infection ointment. Aluminum-free deodorant. Sensitive-enamel toothpaste. A spool of mint floss. Hemorrhoid cream. Smoothing hair cream.

The transparent orange cylinder with the label peeled. She takes off the white lid and shakes the tablets into her hand to count them. There are only six left in total. There were twenty-three last time she was here, almost two months ago. She likes to keep track of how often Whitney needs them, although she's never mentioned to Blair that she has the prescription. Blair had looked up the pentagon-shaped tablets online and found out they're Ativan. For anxiety. Insomnia. Trouble sleeping.

She drops her eyes to the marble tiles under her feet. She thinks of the coffee all over Xavier's floor. Has there been anything off about Whitney lately? Something she might have missed? She tries to recall the last few times they'd been together with the kids. They haven't seen each other as frequently as usual, but Whitney's had dinner meetings and cocktail engagements.

She looks down at the dish of fine jewelry that Whitney rotates through most often and is surprised that her wedding rings are there, the emerald-cut diamond between baguettes and the solid gold band. She almost never takes them off, not even when she sleeps. Blair puts them on her right-hand ring finger but can't move them past her knuckle.

She picks up a diamond pavé bracelet instead. She slips it on and admires her wrist in various positions, in the way one does at the counter of a jewelry store. This is something she does every time. A ritual that isn't about her admiration of the pieces, but about feeling like a different kind of woman. A woman who has the confidence to wear expensive things. Who can buy expensive things for herself. She drops it back in the dish without the delicacy with which she'd picked it up.

She dresses and takes her phone from Whitney's bedside table. She notices the time on the screen and realizes Louisa will be home soon.

But there is one place she's forgotten to look. She sits on the bed and opens the drawer of the side table. Earplugs. Scented pillow spray. A cuticle pusher. The usual things. She unfolds a birthday card from the kids that Louisa had made. Xavier had signed his name in cursive with a heart dotting the *i*.

She puts down the card and sweeps her hand to the back of the drawer in case there's anything she might have missed. She feels something that hadn't been there the last time she checked the drawer. She slides it forward to see. A small, pink satin pouch with something in it. Something cool and metal. She opens it, shakes it into her hand.

A key. She turns over the tag on the silver loop and then she recognizes it. The keychain is Blair's husband's. His initials are embossed in the leather. A. P.

10

Whitney

The Hospital

Whitney tries to figure out what day of Xavier's life it is. 3,680 is the answer she comes to after a long time of adding the numbers in her head at the side of his hospital bed. She likes the reprieve of the math. She says this number to herself over and over, so she doesn't forget: 3,680 days. How many times has she felt the weight of him on her, on her hip, in her arms, on her back? 3,680 days. How many times has she told him she loves him? This number feels important. Tombstones should be etched with total number of days lived instead of dates, she thinks; the dates mean nothing. And then she shakes the image of wet, gray granite from her head; the thought was a betrayal. She whispers the number. She wants to count each day one by one now. To feel the weight of 3,680 in her mouth.

One. Two. Three . . .

. . .

Two days after Xavier was born, they had brought him home from the hospital propped and padded in the car seat, handling him with the delicacy of live ammunition. Jacob wanted Whitney to spend the day in bed with the baby.

"I gave birth, I didn't have open-heart surgery."

But he insisted. He brought her coffee and toast and Advil and opened the windows wide for an early spring afternoon sunbath.

He wrapped the baby in a blanket, not so much swaddled as packaged, and placed him gently beside her before he slid onto the other half of the bed. The baby lay examined between them like a rare species. They leaned on their elbows and stared. He yawned, the tiniest of yawns, and their eyes darted to each other. A yawn! She touched his matted hair, the folded tops of his ears. Jacob left to get her a glass of water. When he came back, she was inconsolable, and she didn't know why. He took her head between his hands and rubbed her temples with his thumbs. He handed her a tissue and nodded, although she had not said a thing. Everything, they both knew, had changed.

When she stopped crying, the tears gone as easily as they came, he went to the store to get groceries for dinner. She remembered, then, about an email from her boss she hadn't responded to before she'd left for the hospital. She'd gone into labor two and a half weeks early and didn't have the last details at work sorted out yet, although she'd been promised nobody would encroach on her role. Senior director, human capital group. Eight to twelve months until they had the partner conversation, that was her plan. And if that didn't work, she'd go out on her own.

But she knew how these things worked, and so she wouldn't be taking much time off. She wouldn't sit around for months, anxious she was being displaced with her clients. She'd feel calmer staying in the mix, knowing she hadn't lost any ground. She could manage to keep an eye on things remotely until she was ready to be back in the office in a few weeks' time. She and Jacob had started interviewing nannies but hadn't found the right person yet. Her friends with children said she was unrealistic. *Yeah, we all thought we'd be back to work quickly too.* She'd heard that kind of refrain almost as much as she'd heard *What a surprise, I didn't think you wanted kids.*

And she hadn't thought so either, for a long time. But soon after she turned thirty, it seemed as though everyone around her was pregnant. Even the friends who had been in child-free solidarity. Each of those new babies was treated like an accomplishment, and this had surprised her, that they considered motherhood that way. Their sudden air of superiority. It was around that time when she started to feel the tug.

That, and she didn't want to regret not having a child. The decision had been simple when she thought of it in those terms. And Jacob, of course, had wanted what she wanted.

She ambled out of bed and pulled her phone from the hospital overnight bag. The battery was drained. She found the charger and winced as she squatted down to plug it in near the bed, feeling another clump of blood slide out into the swath of rough cotton between her legs. She couldn't bear to think of what had happened to her body. She hadn't wanted to know, to touch, to feel any of it. The nurse had asked her to reach down, to feel the baby's head crowning, and the thought of it had made her feel faint. *Just get him out of me. Just close my legs.*

She stared at the black screen waiting for the battery sign to disappear and the home screen to load. *Come on.* The familiar pang of anxiety, of needing to know who was trying to get in touch with her and why. The screen lit up and there it was, the calmness of holding the phone in her hand. The lifeline. The messages filled the home screen, the number climbed on the in-box icon. The news alerts, one after another. The satisfaction of all of it being there, unread, unchecked, the consumption of information she had ahead of her.

And then she remembered, suddenly, about the baby.

The baby. She had one. He was here, outside of her now. She felt even better about this fact than she had hoped she would. Everything felt as it should.

She put one hand on her ballooning breasts, growing hard as rocks, and then looked back at the screen. She rolled away from him and faced the warm breeze of the window. She answered her boss's email. She answered another. She scrolled through the barrage of texts. She sent a message to her assistant checking in. She scanned the news and then texted her large group of friends a picture from the hospital, one where you couldn't see her bloodshot eyes and puffy face straight on.

> He's here! Xavier Wesley James Loverly. 7lbs on the
> dot. Baby and mom back home in bed, doing great,
> awaiting first glass of champagne.

The replies came in rapid fire, ding, ding, ding. More email. More responses. More questions after her responses. Did this budget range work for her? Was it okay if they sent the latest version of a proposal? Could she look quickly at an email they'd drafted for a client? She was sure not to answer with more brevity than usual. She was needed. She had authority. Nothing had changed. She checked her stocks. Twitter. She scrolled more headlines and raced through an article about toxic masculinity. She replied to a few more texts. She checked her email again.

"I'm back. How is he?"

Jacob's voice from the bottom of the stairs surprised her. She fixed her eyes on the ceiling before she turned herself around to face the baby again. She put her hand around his entire tummy. He was warm and pulsing. Jacob poked his head in the room. He looked as though he'd been holding his breath since he left.

"Have you been staring at him this whole time?"

"I have."

She lied without even thinking about it. She shouldn't have been distracted from him, not for work, not for anything. He's been here for mere hours, he is a miracle, look at him! How could she have taken her eyes off him? She smiled and said it aloud. "I can't take my eyes off him."

Jacob sat at the side of the bed. He pulled his glasses from his face and touched the thick black frame to his lip. He wore the same kind of shirt every day, he had ten of them, and she reached to touch the black cotton sleeve, to pull him closer to her. He made her feel safe. From herself. And the potential she had to fail them.

"I kept thinking to myself at the store that we'll never get this day back. His second day of life. Look at his skin, how thin and pink it is." He lifted the baby's hand and touched his papery nails. She couldn't recall ever seeing this level of pure elation in another human being, and it made her hurt; she wanted to feel the way Jacob felt too. She was already missing so much with that screen in her face.

Jacob left the room and she held her phone out beside the bed and dropped it on the floor. She then reached down and shoved it under the bed frame, out of reach. She rolled back to the baby, to the second day of his life. His eyes opened a sliver. She read somewhere that a mother should look at her baby with genuine delight, a nourishment as valuable as milk. She tried her best. He stared at her stretched-open face. He was hers, they belonged to each other. She had never understood that sense of ownership over a child before, that egoism that parents have. But yes, now there lived a piece of herself, right there.

Someone speaks from the open door behind her now at the children's hospital, and it's like the overhead music in a department store. A familiar tune, some version of a song she might know. She ignores what they're saying, pretends those concerns, those tests, those medical acronyms, are for another mother to hear. She nods, she answers their questions with few words, the words that will make things easy for her. That will make them all go away. Instead, she wants to feel all the parts of his body again.

She uses her finger like a pencil and traces the shape of his eyebrows, his nose, his gagged open jaw, down his swollen neck, along his collarbones. She can't feel the tape, the tubes, the brace, the plastic. She circles his small shoulders, his thin upper arm, circles again around his elbows. She stops on his forearm and squeezes.

The squeeze feels so familiar to her, the feel of his skinny bone like a branch she could snap. Did she often grab him like this? Did she squeeze him hard, tug him toward her when he wasn't listening, when they were meant to be out the door five minutes ago? Did she tighten her grip around that arm when he wouldn't look her in the eye as she spoke to him, sticking his tongue out at his little brother instead? Would the rage wallop her so quickly that she'd twist his arm just enough that he would protest, but not a split second longer?

And now, she's done something much worse to him.

She steadies herself on the railing of his bed. She pulls down the sheet covering his chest and kisses him lightly all around, in between the stickers and wires, down his stomach, up his sides where he once liked to be tickled. She imagines each imprint of her lips making him better. Taking away the fear and everything that hurts. And then she pulls his freckled forearm to her cheek, and she smells his skin again.

11

Blair

Aiden's keychain. She stares at it in her hand, willing the growing panic to slow. It was a gift from his parents, with a matching wallet. He'd used it for years, for the key to his office. But she doesn't know if this is that same key on the ring she holds now. Or why Whitney would have it. Hidden, at the back of her drawer. In a pink satin pouch.

She can't think of an explanation with the urgency she needs. She sits on the floor with her back against the bed. The weight of what the key could mean creeps through her, uninvited. It's impossible. Unfathomable.

She thinks of the foil wrapper. Of Whitney and her endless freedoms. Of her avoidance lately. Of the way Whitney sometimes looks at her like she's studying her. Or trying on the betrayal. Trying on the guilt.

She'll never find out. She has no idea. She can hear exactly what those words could sound like in her husband's voice.

She grows hot, nauseated with humiliation. She thinks of Chloe.

She rubs her tightening chest. She lies on her side.

She wants to see nothing behind her closed eyes, she wants to fade to black, but now the wide-open thighs held open with her husband's hands are Whitney's. She imagines another kind of woman driving through red lights, interrupting her husband's sales meeting. Demanding answers. Phoning her friend over and over and over until she finally picks up. Throwing clothing. Packing suitcases.

But she feels shrunken. And scared.

There's one thought she hangs on to: would Whitney do this to Jacob?

She knows it's pathetic that she can't say the same thing of her own husband.

She could have lived with denial, before. With the quiet knowing in the back of her mind, something nobody had to know. If it was anyone else but Whitney.

The queasiness is back, she needs to get out of Whitney's house quickly. Her footing slips twice coming down the staircase.

She can put an end to this tonight, invite herself over when Whitney gets home from work. She'll suggest they open a bottle of white like they usually do, casually ask as she pours if she's seen a key Aiden lost, that he thinks he dropped it last time they were over. She'll get the logical explanation she needs, and they'll move on.

She'll throw out the foil wrapper when she gets home.

This anxious spiraling isn't good for her.

She needs to make this go away.

She locks the Loverlys' door behind her and turns to see Ben watching her from across the street. Her mouth is warm again with stomach acid. He's walking toward her as she jogs down the driveway. He lifts a hand ever so slightly, as though he's about to do something she needs to brace for. She stops and swallows down the burn.

"You okay, Blair?" He slows and crosses his arms gently.

"Yeah, I'm fine. Why?" She shields her eyes from the midday sun. Ben looks confused. He turns toward the Loverlys' house and shakes his head, like he cannot believe what he is about to say next.

Time stops. The anticipation of what he might share feels exhilarating, the split-second high of knowing something bad has happened, but not knowing what. A worst-case scenario. Car crash. Aneurysm. Homicide. Outlandish thoughts, but nothing ever turns out to be what she thinks it is. Not the key, not the affair. Not the hurled cup of coffee in a child's bedroom. And knowing this, she indulges the pleasure of imagining Whitney in a short-lived moment of struggle. The workday interrupted. The money with less meaning. The trajectory of her accomplished life a little less certain. Blair's simple existence looking not so bad after all.

"I'm sorry, Blair, you . . . you were just over there, you looked like you knew." He pauses. "Something terrible happened."

She can only make it halfway up her staircase. She leans against the spindles. Her eyes shift to find something to focus on. The spot on the wall where the paint stroke shows. A magenta sequin from Chloe's craft box that's stuck on her sock. Thread, unraveling from the edge of the carpet runner.

Aiden was quiet for too long when she called him a minute ago from the sidewalk to tell him about Xavier. She didn't want to analyze his reaction, the pace of his breathing, his pause, but she had. He asked, first, about Whitney.

"You need to go to the hospital to be with her," he'd said. "Jacob is away, isn't he?"

She hadn't mentioned before that Jacob was away. But the two men are friends. Casual friends. Maybe he told him, maybe he saw him leave the house for the airport.

"I need to think for a second."

"Blair, she shouldn't be alone. You have to go, it's already past noon."

"I will. I just . . . I need some time to process this. My God, how will we tell Chloe?"

But Aiden hadn't seemed worried about that. He'd seemed worried about Whitney. She'd nearly told him, then, about the state of Xavier's room. The spilled coffee. But she'd stopped herself just in time. She can't tell him she was in their house.

She wants the key gone. She doesn't want the key ever to have existed.

She thinks of throwing it into the pond at the park. Or a fountain. Of how it would sink, become camouflaged among wishing coins.

She burns with shame when she thinks of what she did before she looked through the bedside drawer. Of how it had felt to orgasm on Whitney's bed. Of how foolish she was to imagine herself in that way, given everything she knows now.

She pulls herself up, holding the railing.

She can't let herself spiral.

Xavier will be okay, he'll recover.

It's just a key, she tells herself. A piece of metal.

It's just her unoccupied, idle mind.

12

Rebecca

It's half past noon when the charge nurse on coffee-run duty lifts a cup in Rebecca's direction. She thanks her, but turns her attention back to the computer screen to see what lab results have come in. From tab to tab to tab she can feel the sting behind her eyes, but she's still on call until tonight. She's normally not fighting the urge to put her head down on the desk this early. A third resident is there now; he is getting the rundown from a nurse, and she's relieved to have his help. She needs to peel the lids from her eyes, fight through the cripple of exhaustion, and convince her brain to find another gear. To get to the next hour, and then the next, until she is through to the other side of tired. She drinks a cup of cold water to wake up and then fills it again at the cooler as one of the mothers she met with earlier puts two baggies of her pumped milk into the patient fridge.

She calls up to the ICU again to check on Xavier. No change. Mom still not speaking much, brief answers for the social worker, the police officer—they'll speak with Dad when he arrives. She'll go up at the end of her shift to see if she can help with Whitney, but right now she needs to step outside. She asks the nurse to page her for anything urgent.

She's putting her hip against the heavy door of the hospital entrance when someone calls in her direction. "Excuse me? Excuse me?" There's a tightness in the voice. She turns to see a woman with an infant on her shoulder, bouncing him, like she's trying to keep him awake. "How do I get to Emergency?"

Rebecca starts to give her directions, but the woman looks confused. Rebecca asks if she can touch the baby and then puts the back of her hand to his forehead, runs a finger over the fontanelle. He is okay, he's cool and hydrated. She puts a hand on the woman's shoulder and makes sure she can see her eyes. But she is crying now like the baby, she is trying to pass him to Rebecca.

"I dropped him, I dropped him when I was coming down the stairs. Something's wrong with him, I can tell." There are people staring, people slowing down, people pretending not to listen. Rebecca takes the baby, looks at his eyes, feels the back of his scalp for bumps. She looks for a volunteer and spots a teen in the green hospital vest handing out pamphlets. Rebecca asks him to show the woman to the admissions desk. And then she passes the baby back and puts her hand on the woman's arm.

"I know you're scared, but it's going to be all right. We'll get you sorted. We'll make sure he's okay."

She will ask the woman the difficult questions later. Who was responsible for the child at the time? What happened immediately after? How long did she wait to bring him in? She will focus on the facts. Lacerations. Swells. Fractures. No parent wants to be in her emergency department with their child, but it's her duty to make sure there are no inconsistencies, that the child is safe—and that is all. She reminds herself of this at the times when she feels the ugly pull of judgment. That kind of judgment is not her job.

But had she pressed Whitney enough? As much as she will this woman?

She makes a mental note to follow up about this with the team in the ICU. To make sure the proper diligence has been done. A matter of protocol, and that's all.

The fresh air feels cleansing in her chest, and she has the rare feeling of not wanting to get back to work right away. There is something else she needs to do.

Sometimes she does it in the resuscitation bay on a slow shift, or the back stock room of the operating theater in the middle of the night. But this afternoon she takes the elevator down to the dim hallways of the basement, where they keep spare machines in the old clinics. She chooses a room at the end of the corridor.

The moment the door closes, she lets the fear consume her. Of what she might not find. Or of someone walking in to find her. But there is a sense of excitement, too, and the anticipation of the relief on the other side, as fleeting as it might be; the uncertainty will win again, it always does.

She lies on the table with her eyes closed while the machine warms up. She pulls down the top of her scrub pants and squirts the cold blue jelly on her abdomen. She takes the Doppler and reaches to tilt the screen in her direction.

The mass of cells are now a shape she can recognize. Feet and toes. A head. A brain. A brain that will develop the function to love her. The fetus jostles under the pressure of the wand while she listens through the static for the sound she came for. And then she finds it. The womp of the heartbeat. She lets it fill the room, until it sounds more like a constant, distant siren.

And then she looks away from the screen. She doesn't like to remember the shape. She's better off moving through her days assuming that what was confirmed to be alive inside of her soon won't be. Matter that will expel. There is security, at least, in the constant state of disappointment. There is less threat for her there.

She wipes the jelly from her skin and stuffs the cloth in her pocket. She swings her legs around and sits up to check her phone. There's a stream of texts from her husband. She'd called earlier to tell him about Xavier. *My God*, he kept saying. He's asking now how she's doing. Telling her he loves her. They are trying to be better. They are trying to move on. He's asking about the trip to Oregon again. He wants to take her to the Willamette Valley, tour the wineries on bicycle. He knows it's been a tough day, but has she finally scheduled days off work, midautumn? He needs to book their flights.

The baby is due in October. But he doesn't know this.

She opens the photos. She finds an album she's created.

They are the photographs of women she doesn't know. Mothers she has had in her emergency room over the past couple of years. The ones who have children she doesn't think will make it in the end. She began taking their pictures without letting herself think about what she was doing. A quick and silent tap from the corner of the room while she was meant to be doing otherwise, sending an email to another doctor or looking up a dose. She flips through the photos. Some are side profiles, lips bit, a hand on a temple. Some are distorted from motion. In others, the women are looking right at her. They're all pallid, and tired, and hunched. None of them is aware of what she's doing.

This is a breach of privacy she could be fired for, and she has promised herself she will delete them. But for now, she needs these faces, in case this baby leaves her too. If her uterus cannot hold on, as she's been told it likely will not. She needs them to remind her that despite how much she wants it, becoming a mother is the most foolish thing a woman can do. That a love like that will inevitably hurt her more than she could possibly imagine. Bludgeoned, like the mothers in the photos, like Whitney, three floors above her. Or cut over and over during the long years of motherhood, a dull heartache following everywhere she goes.

And yet she wants it all so badly. Somewhere along the way she has become frighteningly desperate for it.

13

Whitney

I t is the morning before she'll sit guard at her oldest child's hospital bed. Whitney stands in the conference room with her back against the wall, trying to look as though she is enjoying the baby shower brunch she's throwing for her most valuable senior executive, who has asked her for an extra six months of maternity leave. Whitney agreed to the time off because she doesn't want to run her company like the men who run the competition. She wants to be supportive of the women she employs. She wants to be liked by them. But she was disappointed when Lauren asked her. Whitney had thought Lauren was more like her.

They are passing around soft newborn sleepers and patterned gauzy blankets. There are still more gifts to open and croissants to eat and mimosas to drink for everyone but Lauren. There are a few young fathers on her staff, but Lauren will be the first mother other than Whitney, and so the women are talking feverishly about babies with only secondhand authority, a friend who co-sleeps with twins, a sister who gave birth in her bathtub. She doesn't like that babies and marriages are the only things in a woman's life celebrated like this. She'd refused to let anyone throw her a shower. Someone passes around a card in which they're meant to write well-wishes and advice, but Whitney has none, despite the three kids. Nothing that Lauren will want to hear. She writes, instead, that she will miss her.

She slips back to her desk to think about the presentation tomorrow morning. The pitch deck was final five days ago, and they've rehearsed every word, performed mock questions and answers; they have prepared for this meeting for three months. She likes this stage in the process, the perfecting. The small but critical details. Quietly practicing her delivery, the right words, the moments of emphasis. Visualizing the success at the other end.

The outcome of the meeting is pivotal to the future of the growing consulting firm she's built over the past seven years. If she wins this business from the bank, a huge change-management mandate for a global merger, the firm's revenue will more than quadruple. It will put them in new markets. She'll open an office in London. It will attract top talent from her competition. It will set them up for a different level of acquisition, and she'd have the clout to retain part ownership. She'll be elevated.

She wants this win more than she's wanted anything.

She's going through the proposed budget for the fourth time when Lauren knocks on her door. "Whitney! That was far too generous of you, as always. You're the best."

"You deserve it."

"Are you sure you don't want me to come to the meeting tomorrow?"

"Don't even think of it. You're officially done. Go get a pedicure or something, enjoy the day before it rains."

Whitney doesn't know what this feels like, to equate slowing down with enjoyment. But she can feel Lauren's body soften as she hugs her good-bye, she can feel her relief at the mere thought of leaving work behind. Lauren's husband makes a lot of money in commercial real estate, more than Whitney can pay her, although she earns the highest salary on her staff. Lauren might not come back to work, Whitney knows this. There's a high probability that she'll push the baby down her birth canal and be convinced, like most women are, that giving is the most important thing she can do. Her milk. Her sleep. Her self-worth. The more she gives, the more she'll be praised. The selfless mother. Look at how good she is with that baby. That's how it begins.

Whitney knows not every woman believes what she does: that independence, in all its forms, is the most important kind of power. That the world is made up of the enviable and those who envy. She made the decision early in her life that she would never be the kind of person who just perpetuates the sense of power the most enviable live with—instead, she would be one of them. And every decision she makes is a choice to remain at the higher end of that balancing scale.

She saw few other options for herself, if she was to have a different kind of life than the one she grew up with. Unfairness lived on her father's lips—the rules were unfair, the government was unfair, the world was unfair. But she couldn't understand why he never did anything about it. Why there was never a plan to make anything better. He worked for the town on seasonal contracts, cutting grass and salting roads, but pain in his hips put him on disability from time to time.

Don't insult your father, her mother had said, smacking her on the side of the head when she asked why he didn't just get a different job, why they didn't have more money. And then she had kissed her, and rubbed the spot where she'd just knocked her. She did this often, followed her aggressions with affection, like one erased the other. *We're just ordinary people, Whitney, doing our best. And one day you'll see for yourself what that's like.*

She's been getting up every day at 4:00 a.m. for nearly a decade. An unordinary hour. The hour when her whirling mind wakes her, and there's nothing to be gained by the futile attempt to fall asleep again. There is no value in allowing her inner dialogue to wander, creating problems where there aren't any. There is no value in simply being *busy*—everyone these days is busy. There is value in focus. In the satisfaction of control and the productivity of lucrative work.

She leaves the house most days before Jacob and the children wake up. Louisa arrives by 5:45 a.m. to pack the kids' lunches and handle the morning routine. Whitney tries to be home in time to say good night, or by dinnertime when Jacob is traveling. But she knows what Louisa and Jacob don't tell her—things run more smoothly when she isn't there.

She doesn't submit to the social contrivances that cause other working mothers so much guilt. She doesn't let herself think about what's happening at home when she is not there. For her, it's a matter of what she enjoys, and she enjoys working more than she enjoys spending idle time with her children. She cannot find gratification in those hours. She cannot recognize herself as the warm body leading their routines, the person marching everyone along, responsible for school forms and extra clothes and the application of sunscreen. The onslaught of demands, the whining, the constant changing of their minds after she's made what they want, given in to what they want, bought what they want.

She needs windows of time with them, not stretches. Small, orderly windows.

And then there is the matter of Xavier. He adds a tension to it all that she has never been able to cope with. There is a frequency to him that clashes with her own. The irritation feels nearly electric in her at times, and she doesn't like this about herself. The ease with which he threatens the control she thrives on is unsettling. She doesn't know where the anger comes from. Why it's always there, lying in wait.

She and the twins have more tolerance for each other. Her experience of them is distinct from her experience as Xavier's mother. Their built-in companionship, their fixation on each other's plump and happy faces, the way they seem to need each other more than they need her. She is the roving mother figure. The mother who is not Louisa. She feels, sometimes, like they accept her limitations in ways that Xavier cannot.

She loves all three of her children, of course she loves them. But she is not always the best for them. And they are not always the best for her.

Jacob calls her from London, her focus on the spreadsheet interrupted again. It's 3:00 p.m. there, but that won't matter to him because he never adjusts to local time when he travels. She puts the phone on speaker. He sounds stressed, again. He's been away for work a lot this year, and these trips overseas make him anxious. He tells her about the art he was shown that afternoon, and she is listening in the way she does, which is to be multitasking, to be answering the emails that require only brief replies while she feeds him advice that he has not asked for.

"Can I just interrupt, honey? For a sec? Did you bring up exclusivity, at least?"

He is an art dealer. But he does not have all the qualities of a successful art dealer. He is in London for four days to scout pieces for his clients, who are wealthy individuals without the time or interest or inclination to find their own art. They like Jacob because he is an intellectual, the son of two Yale humanities professors. He will, reluctantly, stand in their opulent homes and drink their finely aged wines while he teaches them everything they ought to know about the contemporary art world, his PhD distilled into ninety generous and well-spoken minutes, in exchange for the one piece they might bite on over the next five years.

But the money in art dealing is not based on knowing about value and trends like he does, or being able to recite every record-breaking sale at the New York auction houses like he can. It's about the volume of sales and the commissions on those sales, and Jacob is uncomfortable with exploiting either of these measures, despite Whitney's loving and voluntary coaching.

He knows this. He doesn't care about this. They both understand that he mostly humors her need to interfere. As much as it galls her, he doesn't have the same hunger for success and money and status that she does. He hasn't been working and investing since he was fifteen years old like she has, he doesn't have the MBA she has earned on nights and weekends while excelling in an executive role, and yet *he* is the proximate one to the real wealth. She envies how naturally he fits that echelon of society, how bred he was for a world he doesn't want much to do with. He has the privilege of having nothing to prove. In that same kind of room, she would be acting. And more self-conscious than she would ever admit.

"You know what I'll say, Jacob. You can't undersell and overdeliver in your world, it's too finicky. It's about hype, right? You've got to do a harder pitch up front, or you'll lose his interest from the get-go."

But she's not threatened by Jacob's intellect, because there's no power in holding court over a glass of wine. There is power in her own income. In her own financial security. In a padded investment portfolio and a growing business with eight-figure revenue. It is her ambition that has given their family the life they have, that allows him to stroll the grounds of an international art fair for four days and return with nothing to show but inspiration. She has afforded them the three children, the house on a double lot, the multiple vacations a year, the on-demand nanny, the sought-after art he has chosen for their own walls. There's nothing ordinary about any of it, thanks to her. Still. She'd like him to contribute more. To take some of the pressure off her for once.

She knows most people recoil at the idea of women like her pursuing wealth with the same vigor men do all the time. Even if they don't admit it. That it's off-putting for a woman to want more money than society thinks she's worth.

"My advice is to get the commitment from Pearse on the thirty percent first. You've gotta be firm. Much firmer," she tells him.

Her assistant, Grace, is in her office now, mouthing something as she puts bound copies of the presentation on her desk. She sticks a note beside it.

"I've got to go, but call me tomorrow, okay? If you want to talk anything through? The pitch should be done by noon."

The pitch, he says, of course, he hasn't forgotten about it. He can't wait to hear how it goes. He knows she will nail it.

But sometimes she wonders if he's as happy for her success as he wants to be. If he's ever hoped, in a weak moment, for her to fail, just once. There's a tautness to his words sometimes, although they are exactly the words he's supposed to say.

Try to leave at a decent time tonight, he tells her.

She doesn't say anything.

Maybe I shouldn't have gone, he says.

She stiffens, turns her back to the open office door.

"Why would you say that? What do you mean?"

He is quiet.

He doesn't know. He feels far away. He misses the kids, he's tired. Never mind.

She doesn't like him this way, wishy-washy and anxious. She looks at the sticky note from Grace. The name and phone number of Xavier's teacher. She doesn't mention it. She folds the paper and slips it into her breast pocket. She doesn't want it lingering in her periphery.

She tells him not to be silly. That everything is fine. The kids will be fine.

She waits for him to say he knows she's right. But instead he's quiet.

And then he says something about a taxi, he's got to run. She tells him she loves him. He says nothing, and then a car door closes, and he's gone.

There's a text on the screen of her iPhone when she hangs up.

Hey 🙂 Still good for tonight? 11pm?

She sits back in her chair and undoes the gold button on her milky white blazer. She tries to make sense of Jacob's uneasiness. She doesn't like how it feels. She taps the phone against her chin. She breathes in sharply before she replies, and then swipes to delete the conversation.

14

Rebecca

She's just entered the stairwell when the code blue is paged overhead. Third floor. Room 3103. She's not on the response team, so she continues scanning her emails while she takes the stairs slowly, careful not to trip without her eyes on the steps, but then it registers—third floor.

Room 3103.

She tries to remember what room Xavier is in, it's 31, 31-something, 3108, 3111? She's pumping her arms as she runs up the stairs, one more flight to the exit on the third floor. Room 3103, it's too familiar, it must be him. She nearly cuts off the crash cart in the hallway, but then jumps back to let them through, and follows the team's steady march to the corridor at the right of the nursing station. Xavier's hallway.

No, no, no. She wills them to stop, his room is nearly three quarters down that hall, but they're jogging too quickly already, they're nearly at his door and she can see it's open now. She imagines Whitney in the corner of the room, being told to leave, to get out while they try to restart his heart. Two doctors rush past her, an elbow knocks her hip, and she stops.

It's the room next to his.

She folds, her hands on her knees. Her throat is tight. She steels herself. She should clear the area if she's not helping. She'll come back to check on Xavier later.

She isn't herself.

She needs to get a few hours of sleep before she makes a costly mistake.

She's usually driving against traffic when she comes and goes from Hospital Row downtown. Her life flows in a different direction than most people's and she has felt this her whole life. She likes watching the cars build in the opposite lane. She likes going home to bed when everyone else's day is already under way. She doesn't need to take these long on-call shifts as often as she does, but it's a way of separating herself from the routines she can't have. This way, she doesn't have to walk through her own front door to a quiet dinner with only Ben, on a bench that is upholstered with washable, stain-resistant fabric. The kind made for families with sticky fingers.

The children at the hospital are different. Those children need her, and she can, usually, fix them. It is the not being needed when she leaves the building that she has come to find so difficult.

The way Ben needs her has changed in the past few years. It might only be the march of marriage, the way early love melts slowly into a form less nectarous. But she has felt less precious to him ever since the losses began to feel like something other than bad luck. Since they learned they've been dealt a definitive mechanical failure. That she, the machine, is broken.

She has a mind for statistics, for probability, for outcomes that can be predicted by treatments. But that kind of thinking doesn't work for reproductive biology. There aren't straight lines. She and Ben are not in the category of no possibility, but the odds no longer seem to favor them. Recurrent miscarriage. Three years. Model sperm. Thirty-seven-year-old eggs. An inhospitable uterus with an endometrial lining that isn't lush. "Yours is a bit flat," is what they had said. "We prefer it to be fluffier." Her body wasn't responding like it should. Their language is a language of failure.

The problem isn't the kind that can be fixed. "We don't know" is the answer to most questions she asks, as if this vast hole of medical knowledge is acceptable. The only treatment she was offered was no treatment at all. To keep going, if they are willing, if the disappointment is something they can bear. After the doctor had left the room at their last appointment, the nurse, a young woman whose ovaries were probably teeming with good sticky eggs, whose uterus she imagined to be ripe as a tropical fruit, had said the word she least wanted to hear: "miracle." That they see miracles every day.

But Rebecca is a scientist. She had never believed in hope being an influential power. She had never believed in miracles before.

During her first year of pediatric residency, a staff doctor told her the best thing she could do for parents in the hospital was to keep the space between their expectations and reality as close as possible. In other words, the feeling of hope, the thing everyone was searching for, was not necessarily a good thing. This had made all the sense in the world to her. She had been trained for thirteen years to believe in evidence. To make decisions rooted in her knowledge about how the body works. But about her own body, right now, she has almost none.

.   .   .

She parks on the street outside her home with four bedrooms and three bathrooms and a mudroom with bright yellow hooks at a height meant for the reach of young arms. They gave the builder their down payment three and a half months after her first positive pregnancy test. They'd had the privilege, then, of certainty.

Inside, Ben will be making her a sandwich for lunch, brewing her fresh coffee. He took a leave of absence at the school this year, a decision that had surprised everyone, including Rebecca. He'd always loved teaching. He loved the kids. He'd had a job for years at the middle school ten minutes away, one of the reasons they bought a house in this neighborhood. And they liked that it was still mixed income, mixed ethnicity, even if the school was overrun by a small, privileged group of parents who were too involved.

But he'd come to want a break from the routine of the day, from teaching the same curriculum year after year. His friend had a tech start-up, a homeschool app for parents, and he was looking for an educator to consult full time. They're still paying down Rebecca's medical school debt, and the job paid twice the income of a teacher. Ben was excited about the idea of trying something new, so he took the eight-month contract, mostly working from home. And he agreed to coach a softball team for the junior school a few blocks away, as a favor to a colleague. He'd seemed relieved with the change.

She wonders if he really left because being around children all day was too hard. If the reminder of what they might never have had become too much.

It was Ben who had always wanted kids.

She met him on a last-minute date set up by a friend at work, who thought she should get out more, change into nice jeans and heels for once. It had been almost a year since her last relationship, short-lived like they'd all been—he was in plastics for the money and hid a vaping habit from her. She'd been reluctant, but when her friend said Ben was a teacher, a genuinely good guy, she figured there was no harm in a late dinner. She was surprised when Ben stood from the table to reach out his hand. He was tall and fit, like her, and looked more earnest than in the photo her friend had showed her, shirt off on the dock of a lake.

She liked him immediately. She was charmed by the way he touched a knuckle to his top lip when he laughed. He talked about his seventh-grade students with the pride of a parent. But he had mostly wanted to talk about her. The things she liked and didn't, the places she had been and wanted to go. Her running. Her work. Her research. Her childhood, growing up an only child to a struggling single mother, who did everything she could to ensure her daughter became successful.

And then when the table was cleared, when they'd already laughed so hard that the people next to them were annoyed, when they'd had a handful of moments staring at each other but saying nothing at all, he signaled to the server for one last drink. And then he'd asked her: *Do you want children?*

She didn't notice until the glass was tipped at her mouth that her wine was gone. She placed it back down, conscious of the seconds that were passing.

Yes. I think so. And then, to reassure herself, she tried again: *Yes. I want kids.*

He'd looked down, he'd touched his knuckle to his mouth again as he smiled. He'd heard the answer he'd hoped for. Everything between them was unfolding exactly as he wanted, she could see it.

She was thirty-three. She had always felt sure of what she wanted, and what she didn't want, but motherhood felt like a topic for other people to discuss. Not her. Nothing about the idea excited her. It had been a source of contention between her and her mother for years—her mother desperately wanted a grandchild. She wanted Rebecca to know the kind of maternal love she knew. And although Rebecca felt indebted to her mother, and couldn't stomach the thought of disappointing her, she had never envisioned her life with a child.

But she liked the exhilaration she felt on the walk back to her apartment that night, having said those words aloud to Ben. Something had started to shift. Something was beginning to feel bigger than herself. Maybe, she wondered, the maternal urge had been there inside her, but she hadn't wanted to listen for it. Her ambition was loud, and the science was consuming. The infinite knowledge she tried to absorb, the extraordinary hours she had to work. She couldn't have known what lay underneath that for so long.

She thought of her mother, alone. Of the years that were going by, and of the way Ben had kissed her outside the restaurant, like it hadn't been about the kiss at all. It had been about possibility, and sometimes that's how love begins. She called him when she got home to say she was safe, and they talked for two more hours.

They were married a year and a half later, a small family ceremony at the farmhouse where Ben grew up with his two brothers and his sister. Rebecca's mother walked her from the freshly painted white porch of the farmhouse to the altar of stacked hay barrels and steel buckets stuffed with hundreds of sunflowers. There was much talk, after, of the babies who would one day be joining the nine other children in the family. Rebecca had watched Ben's nieces and nephews chase one another through the tall grass in the ginger glow of the early-evening September sun, and had turned to see her mother watching too. Her mother hadn't been able to give her everything, but she had got her there, to that moment. Accomplished and respected and secure. A life her mother could never have had herself.

Ben had then come to the porch, had stood beside his new mother-in-law. He put his strong arm around the shoulders that had carried more weight than any of them could comprehend and whispered something that made her laugh. They looked back at the children in the grass. Ben winked to Rebecca and she smiled with cheeks that ached from the joy of the day. She would have thrown off her satin shoes and run with him into the fields if he asked her to, let the bottom of her dress be soiled with dirt, raced against the sinking sun.

Somewhere between those beginnings and now, Rebecca traded her disinterest in motherhood for an obsession she can't articulate. She was wary, until she wasn't. She didn't want a baby, until it became the only thing she needed.

And yet most of the time, she's angry at herself for being hostage to the longing. The desperation feels like her greatest weakness. She can't find the discipline to escape it, despite how tightly she can focus every other part of herself. Every other thought she has.

When she walks in the door, she sees his laptop open on the dining-room table, his earphones dropped next to it. He calls to her from the kitchen.

He pulls her near and rubs his thumb over the red mark on her forehead where her scrub cap fits too tight. It's the gesture of a parent, wiping ketchup off the corner of a mouth. There's a muted energy to their marriage now. He worries about her lack of sleep, the ache in the arch of her feet, if she eats enough when she's at work. He slides the plate and a coffee across the table and takes a seat, waits for her to sit down too. His chin is in his hand, his elbow on the table.

"How is he?"

"Well, it's hour by hour, but he doesn't seem to be improving yet.

The longer he's in the coma, the less chance of making a recovery. They're going to text me with any updates."

"Jesus." He shakes his head. He can't imagine.

"I know. I couldn't believe it was him this morning. I mean, these kinds of things happen every day, but right across the street, to a family we know. It's just . . . it's awful."

"Let me get you some water."

She watches as he moves around the kitchen. The display of concern, the constant attempt to nurture her. Like he's convincing himself that caring for her, and not their baby, will be enough for him. Trying to silence the bitterness that might win, eventually.

She knows he wants to love her. But love can change. Love is based on an idea about who the other person is, and she isn't wholly that idea anymore.

"Why don't you go for a run," he says. She used to run all the time. Miles after a long shift, shaking off anything that lingered, doubt about how she'd handled a case, niggling worry she'd sent a child home when she shouldn't have.

Maybe, she says. She lifts the water to her lips. He turns around to wipe his hands on the dish towel. A little longer than he needs to.

He's asking now about the days off work for Oregon. She promises to sort it out.

He asks why she doesn't want the coffee.

She looks down at her untouched mug. She tells him she's had one too many at the hospital.

She can do this now, lie to him so fluently. Like the words aren't really hers. Like none of the dishonesty counts because it will have happened in the Before. And everything will be better in the After. She only cares about the After.

She goes upstairs to sleep and makes sure her ringer is set loudly. She has less than three hours before she has to go back, unless the resident needs her sooner. In their bedroom she slips off the pants that are too tight around the waist. And then she listens to make sure his footsteps still come from the main floor. She lifts her T-shirt up and looks at her middle in the mirror on the back of their door. She has never made it to one hundred and twenty-nine days. There are weeks, maybe only one, until her shape will be too obvious to hide.

He can no longer bear the burden of so little hope. But she cannot live without it.

15

Whitney

The Hospital

S he puts the tip of his right index finger between her teeth and gnaws at the nail until the thin strip pulls off. She keeps the crest between her tongue and the roof of her mouth. She touches the exposed pink skin on his fingertip and wonders how much he can feel now. Her touch? Her presence? Has he heard her say how sorry she is?

Everything about him at ten years old feels so familiar. A part of her. But they are nearly at the time when this begins to change. He has been growing away from her since the day she gave birth, and soon she will start to feel it, physically, in the way a child no longer seeks comfort in the gesture of a mother's affection. Soon, he will love her less than he once did. And then soon after that, she will begin to feel irrelevant to him. He will become more uncomfortable when she is around than when she is not. And then, he will not think of her much, or think much of her either. They'll only touch for a quick hello, a cordial pat good-bye on the strong, round shoulders of a man.

Isn't that how it goes, with sons?

If he lives. If he doesn't remember what happened.

She runs her finger under his eyes, as though he has tears to wipe. She puts her hand over the ventilator that covers his mouth. She imagines she is the one filling his lungs with air, that it is only she who can save him.

His laughter comes to her mind then. She can imagine the lift of his cheekbones, the stretch of his jaw, but she cannot hear how he sounds. What sort of pitch is it? How is it possible that she can't remember how he laughs? Might Jacob? Might Louisa?

Does he ever laugh when he is around her?

She doesn't remember laughing much as a child herself. The only laughter she recalls is through the wall from the television set in the apartment next door. Her father would bang every once in a while for the guy to turn it down, and her mother would complain about the banging being worse than the noise of the television, and her father would say that if she didn't like it, she was free to leave, though everyone understood she would never do such a thing.

But Whitney knew her mother kept a single bus ticket hidden in her interior coat pocket. Good for any weekday, no expiration, direct to the national terminal three hours away. She can hear this exchange perfectly, still, and there is even a sense of comfort she can remember in the predictability of it all, in the way he'd flop back down in his chair, wincing at the pain in the aching hip that had taken away his livelihood. And his ability to back her mother up against the wall, his words spewing. He'd hum a verse or two of Johnny Cash to soothe himself, not any more than that. But she cannot remember any of them laughing.

And so, no, maybe there isn't enough laughter in the Loverlys' house, at least not when Whitney is home. When she is home, there is a lot of her phone, and a lot of shoulds, and a lot of tears when the behavior isn't what she needs it to be. There is not a lot of room for spontaneity. There is not a lot of time.

She tries to think of when she last played with him, LEGOs or a board game or chess, or one of those plastic spinning things he collects that she can't remember the name of.

She doesn't really like to play. In fact, she hates to. There is no productivity in play. She hates the plastic bins full of toys, and hates sitting on the floor. She hates making the noise of a car and pretending to be a cougar. She hates the mundanity. She hates trying to sound light and cheerful and surprised when she isn't. She hates feigning interest in things that aren't real.

Will you play with me? When can you play with me? Can we play after dinner? Can you build something with me? She must close her eyes and brace herself for the whining, for the fuss, when she tells them: *I'm sorry, but I can't right now. There are a few other things I have to do.*

Does she always have something else to do, or does she always *find* something else to do? She thinks of the schedule on her phone, that color-blocked, chock-full calendar that she lives or dies by. There is no color assigned to him or the twins. There is no color assigned to Play.

Had they ever lain together, in the sunshine, and looked at the clouds? Had they made up stories together, silly songs, silly words? Did they know the kind of unique joy they're supposed to?

She isn't that kind of mother.

A mother like Blair. Who has made different decisions than she has.

She picks up Xavier's hand and puts his nails to her lips again. She once threatened, offhand, to rub onion on his fingers every morning if he kept biting them relentlessly, something her mother used to say to her. He hadn't thrown his usual excuses at her. He had only asked if she could please stop talking about it. That chewing on his nails was sometimes the only thing that made him feel better.

Better about what? But he didn't have an answer. She left him alone. She knows what that's like, doing something you're not supposed to because it gives you the thing you need most. A sense of relief. A sense of control.

There is a doctor in the room now. She can't listen to this person, she can't pretend to know what he is saying to her. She wants to shush him, to cover her ears. *Go away, go away, go away.* She smells alcohol. And then latex. She squeezes Xavier's limp hand because it feels good to make sure he's still there, that there are tissues and muscles and bones. That he isn't a memory.

Memory. The doctor says this word now just as she's thinking it. Xavier's memory. Trauma. There is some kind of scan. Swelling. The words "plate" and "skull" and "blood supply." A jumble of numbers with decimals.

She opens her eyes to see him. She's heard other mothers say they often catch a glimpse of what their child will look like when they're older, that a certain expression moves their imaginations forward in time. This happens, sometimes, with the twins. But Whitney never thinks about Xavier in this way. With him, she could never see past the day, the hour, the boy he is in that very moment. Needing, wanting, challenging. Pushing her right to the very brink.

16

SEPTEMBER

The Loverlys' Backyard

The rawness in her throat is familiar, but she can't swallow it away—this time it's shame, sour and thick. Whitney pulls herself up from the bedroom floor and stares at Xavier, who is staring at her. They both look to the open window above the backyard party. She clutches her breasts as though she's been exposed, as though someone has ripped off her clothing and left her bare. Her face is burning now, her brain clocking the options that could make this better.

She can pretend he was about to ingest something poisonous.

She can lock herself in her bedroom for the remainder of the afternoon.

She can feign illness.

But she knows she must face a backyard full of people who have just heard the most monstrous part of her come alive. They will have widened their eyes, felt their own hearts race to have experienced this display of her rage. They will feel the heat of her humiliation when they see her. Why has she done this? Why does she snap so easily at her son? They are cookies, they are just cookies. He is just a little boy.

It's the alcohol, she can say. It's one drink too many. They've all got a glass in their hands.

But it won't be enough for what she's done.

Her fury parts for the remorse. She puts her palms on either side of Xavier's messy face. She feels queasy as she comes down from the familiar high of the rage.

"I am so sorry. I didn't mean to yell. You can stay here in your room."

But what she means is, do not come downstairs. Do not make this any worse than it is.

She closes the door behind her.

Her legs are weak taking her down to the kitchen. It will be better to get this over with. You can do this, you can do this. She will look for Blair; Blair will pretend that this has not happened. Blair will carry on as though she hasn't a thing to feel bad for. She sees Jacob coming toward her, baffled and red, and she smiles, she tries her best. She touches his arm, feels he is tense. She says everything is fine and they will talk about it later, and she keeps moving to the backyard, her long silk dress flowing behind her with an elegance she has betrayed.

Outside, she feels eyes averted, guests evading the uncomfortable sight of her. Conversations have slowly resumed, but they are restrained. The disgrace she feels is staggering. She stands on the rainbows Blair's daughter has drawn on the patio, and she can't seem to move her feet. She knows she must say something to someone, but she doesn't see Blair. She needs Blair. Blair can make this feel better. She turns to three mothers from school who forge smiles. She winces.

"I'm so sorry about that. Xavi's having some serious challenges lately. Mental health problems. I won't go into it now, but we're worried." She pauses. She needs to give them more. "He's seeing a behavioral specialist."

It isn't the truth, but it might make the height of her anger seem warranted. Necessary, even, if their minds go to the worst. They will think he had something dangerous in his hands. They will think he was going to hurt himself with that something dangerous. They will understand the explosion, reframe it as concern, they will feel sympathy. Please, feel sympathy.

And they seem to, they all speak at once. Of course. We get it. Don't apologize.

There is a beat that feels more like minutes. And then, "We were just talking about the city's plans for the new playground, and do you think—"

Blair is watching her now, and Whitney glances just slightly toward her, like she can feel her staring. Blair has heard the lie about Xavier. She is crouched with the children to hide from the discomfort, and her knees are aching, but she will not stand up. She smooths her daughter's ponytail, patters her fingers up Sebastian's arm to make him giggle. She imagines herself going upstairs to check on Xavier, to cheer him up, but Whitney won't like that. Instead, she finally stands, politely interrupts the group of women with an offer to help clear the paper plates, the paper cups. Can Whitney remind her where the garbage bags are kept?

Whitney is grateful for the deliberate reprieve. Blair knows exactly where they are under the sink. She bends to pick up Thea and kisses her playfully, three, five, seven times. She spins her once and Thea laughs. She hopes everyone is watching this. She does it again. Thea asks for Zags, the twins' nickname for Xavier. He's fine, Zags is up-stairs, he's fine, Whitney says and puts her down. She asks Blair in a lowered voice if she and Aiden can stay after everyone leaves. She knows Aiden will have more drinks with her, he'll lighten things up. There is a chance Blair will feel put off by what's happened, but Blair says of course. Of course, they'd love to stay, and like that, they pretend the incident is inconsequential.

But the other women will talk, as though they've never screamed at their kids themselves.

I mean, sure, we all lose our patience, but that poor boy.

They will replay it in their private conversations about how terrible the moment felt, how completely unexpected it was. They will even use the word "frightening." Because Whitney is the kind of mother with whom other women try to find fault.

Whitney knows this. The judgment of her priorities is something she can normally quell, because the judgment is laced with envy. But this afternoon, on her own beautiful turf, she has diminished this envy, and that loss of control will humiliate her every time she thinks of it.

Blair can see this realization unfold on Whitney's face that after-noon. She's never observed Whitney in this weakened position be-fore, and it makes her physically uncomfortable. The other mothers from school are retreating by inches, they are talking about rounding up their children. They are checking the time on their phones. Blair wants to ease this for her, for them both, so she talks about how great the magician was. What a good time everyone is having. How lovely the cheese plat-ters are. She can look away from her friend's maternal transgressions with an unsettling ease. She is complimentary and upbeat, and she might even have another drink.

. . .

B ut Whitney is scanning the guests, making a catalog of every
person who heard her lose her shit. The faces that will consume
her for the next several weeks, or for however long it takes for the
shame to dissipate.

She nods as Blair talks, looks past her, across the backyard to
Aiden, to some woman who is laughing at whatever he's saying now. She
looks to the fence, to Mara's shape moving between the slats of wood,
and then up at her son's bedroom, to the wide-open window, where she
thinks she just saw him look out. She jumps at the touch of Jacob's hand
on her shoulder.

S omething in the way Whitney has just flinched at the touch of her
husband makes Blair feel anxious, and then she hears the toying of
Aiden's voice behind her. Her cheeks grow hot as she tries to diagnose
his tone. And then on the other side of the fence, the back door of
Mara's house slams a little too firmly, as though she's heard quite
enough. Whitney and Blair catch each other's eye. After the party, these
few tense seconds will cross their minds again, but neither of them will
understand why. Not for many months more, on a Wednesday night in
June, when everything will begin to implode.

T wo hours later, the backyard crowd has thinned, and most of the
small children have been shuffled home for bed, and Whitney's
dress has slipped down so low that Blair can see the valley between her
breasts. She's taken her bra off at some point and her nipples are sharp
under the silk. Her feet are bare now, too, the strappy sandals tossed
onto the lawn. Blair adjusts her own plain cotton shirt. It's new, the

white is still bright. She straightens the cuff of her pleated olive-green shorts, ones she bought with the shirt. They remind her, now, of something her mother would wear. The good tequila has been opened, and although she doesn't like to drink tequila, it was Jacob who'd handed her the glass, so she took it.

Aiden and Jacob come over, and Whitney tells Aiden to take a seat on the backyard furniture, to stay and have some fun, and then she asks Jacob to turn up the music. When he comes back, they click salt-rimmed glasses and the men talk, again, about how much of the summer was rainy, about the water levels of the Great Lakes, and then Whitney, uninterested, pulls Blair to dance.

Blair says no, she is stiff and resistant, and the party has exhausted her, and there are still too many people there. The thought of dancing makes her flush even more than the tequila. She hates dancing and Whitney knows this. She hates how incompetent and foolish it makes her feel. She hates being made to feel like a wet blanket when she won't join. Redness creeps from her chest up her neck.

But Whitney is impossible to say no to. The music is like something in a Miami beach club. Blair watches the way Whitney moves and tries not to think too much about what her own body is doing. And it starts to work. She feels a rare kind of freedom, an unfamiliar sense of fun. And then something akin to pride. She is relieved to have more alcohol, she takes another sip. She reaches her hands above her in the way other people seem to do, loose, snaking, and she swings her head to the side. And then the other side. Her eyes lose their focus. She can still surprise herself. She can still feel alive.

Jacob stands then, and she thinks for a moment that he might dance with them, too, and she's jerky, she begins to lose her rhythm. But then he touches Whitney's hips and moves past them both into the kitchen. Blair reaches for Whitney's hands and copies how she's moving again, and she can feel her confidence recover. She turns her face to where

Aiden sits back, watching, his leg crossed, hand on his ankle. He'll like this, his uptight wife having a good time for once. He'll see that she can be loose. She can be fun. Maybe he'll feel a little aroused. She puckers her lips a bit. She thinks about how they could have sex tonight. She could instigate things for once. Slip her hand into his underwear while he's brushing his teeth. She feels herself swell between her legs and she's surprised herself again. She lifts her eyes to meet his.

But her husband isn't watching her. He has a glassy look she recognizes. A hunger. He is fixated on Whitney's body, her breasts, the bare back of her dress. The tip of his tongue trails his lower lip slowly. Blair stops moving. The tequila burns hot in her chest. She is not there at all—she never is.

17

Rebecca

She wakes up from her nap to the sound of the television downstairs in the living room. She takes a few seconds to place that it's only midafternoon, she's still on call. The image of Xavier in the trauma room comes back to her. Ben is watching last night's baseball game, he is clapping and hollering, forgetting in the excitement of bases loaded that she's asleep upstairs.

"Come on. Come on! YES."

He'll be wearing his Yankees hat backward. He'll be having a light beer. She will slip beside him on the couch and put her head on his lap for another twenty minutes before she goes back to the hospital for the last few hours of the shift.

But first she picks up the iPad from the floor beside her and clicks on the link to the forum she has saved in her bookmarks. She hasn't let herself do it yet, not in this pregnancy. She finds the page for the month her baby is due, October, beautiful, crisp October, and she begins to scroll the message boards. The selfies in bras and underwear that track every change in shape, the questions about the color and scent and texture of discharge, it all fascinates and embarrasses and thrills her, like it had all the other times she allowed herself the indulgence. She won't let herself fall back into the habit of consuming the details, but she allows herself five minutes, just today.

She hears Ben clapping again as she comes down the stairs afterward. He jumps when she touches his neck from behind the couch.

"You're awake. Is the game too loud? One more inning and then I'll get back to work, I've got a few calls later this afternoon."

He is reaching his arms up toward her, he wants to hold her. She thinks of how it would feel to pass an infant into those arms, fed and tired. She sits beside him, lowers her head onto his lap, in the glow of the bright screen. His hand is on her side, above her hip, and she stiffens—he might reach around, might feel her swelling middle as he pulls her tighter into him. But he so rarely touches her there now, given all that has happened.

W e need to stop trying for a baby," he'd said. They were sitting at the foot of their bed five and a half months ago. He had held her hands and fiddled with the rings on her finger, the rings he had given her. There was exhaustion in his voice. He didn't want to be thinking this way. She shook her head no—no, they would not have this conversation right now. No, they would not have this conversation ever.

"Are you serious?"

"I don't think I can do this anymore."

"Do what? You want this, Ben! You want us to have a baby."

They were supposed to want the same things. The same future, the same house, the same family. She had pulled his hand to her mouth, to make sure he could feel that she was right there beside him, the lips of the wife he loved. He stared at her toes. He couldn't have meant it.

"It's too hard. For us both," he said. His voice was flat at first. "We need to accept that this isn't going to happen for us. We can't keep making babies and losing them like this. All the wanting and the failing, over and over and over. And for how much longer? When will this end, what's the number? Six? Ten? Fifteen? One of us needs to make this decision, or we're going to destroy ourselves. Can't you feel it happening already?"

"You're just scared, Ben. You're giving up because you're scared. What if we wait a bit this time? We can take this month off and you'll feel better after a break."

She needed him to hear the desperation in her voice. He was silent for too long, and then shook his head slowly.

"So, you're just . . . you're done? No baby? Just like that?"

He said he was sorry, that he loved her. That he needed her to understand. He was quiet while she let him hold her. But she hated him.

Another woman might have felt relief. Or pounded her hands into his chest. Might have screamed that it wasn't up to him. Might have convinced him that they should not give up hope. Recited the stories on the message boards, the women who try for years and years and years, who are told it is impossible, and then it happens. Magic, it was kind of like magic, and if she of all people could make herself think this way, couldn't he? The word—"miracle"—it's all around her, it floats through the hospital corridors and is whispered at the fertility clinic, and everyone says they happen every day, and so, where is hers?

She could beg him. It feels like the only option left.

But Rebecca wondered if he meant something else when he said, *This isn't going to happen for us.* Us. What he meant was, this wasn't going to happen because of her. He had to accept that he had chosen a life with damaged goods. The nieces and nephews he flew across the country to see four times a year, the nursery he had already painted in a color called Calamine. He had wanted a child more than she had at first. And now he was giving up? Now the hope was too hard to feel? Now that her obsession and desperation has worn her threadbare? This should have made her angry, but it only made her scared. Keep me, she thought. Don't throw me away. She was ashamed of these weak thoughts, but there they were.

They were so far away from siblings chasing one another through the field at his parents' farmhouse. From filling their mudroom with raincoats and mucky boots.

So she agreed with words she could barely get out. They would stop trying. There was sound reason to what he was saying, and the rational part of her brain that she trusted in every other hour of the day could accept this. But she was trembling in his arms.

The defeat wasn't a respite, it was excruciating. She cried quietly into her pillow every time she was alone in the bedroom. She could barely bring herself to answer when her mother phoned. She moved heavily through her shifts at the hospital feeling more barren than she had before, although nothing had technically changed. She had been holding on to more hope than she'd realized.

Ben had been especially tender with her in the days that followed. Doting and soft. But then he seemed to find a kind of lightness for a while. Relief, it must have been, until the weeks marched on and the emptiness was palpable again. But she had never felt anything close to relief. She found herself drifting away from him when he was near, leaving the room, putting in her earphones even though she wasn't listening to anything. She started running again to get out of the house, but every pound on the pavement felt like a punch, a reminder of the broken body she lived in.

Three weeks later, after she felt the dull ache of her ovary releasing an egg as it did exactly every twenty-nine days—the compliance of it almost cruel—she couldn't help herself. She felt for him under the blanket on the couch as the credits rolled on the television screen. She acted ravenous for him again. Him, and not his sperm, for the first time in a long time. They hadn't had sex since he told her he wouldn't try for a baby anymore.

"I'm not ovulating," she had whispered to reassure him. And then softer, more convincing: "I just want you. I need you."

She had clutched his hips tightly to her while he came.

On the day before she took the pregnancy test to confirm what she already knew, she asked him one last time. A Hail Mary that could change what she'd done.

"Do you still feel that way? About trying?"

He had pulled her close, put his chin on her shoulder. She could feel his chest sink, every bit of air gone before he spoke.

"I can't go through it again, Rebecca. I'm grieving that future. I'm moving on. And you need to move on too."

There is a crack, another home run, and she is jolted as Ben claps his hands, speaks to the players as though he is standing on the baseline. He settles, twirls a strand of her hair around his index finger. He leans to kiss her head and fast-forwards through the commercial.

She will tell him tonight. Tomorrow she will be five days further along than she was the first time. She has never had to admit to a lie before. And maybe this is more than a lie. The outcome might make this an unforgivable, unthinkable betrayal.

She, Dr. Rebecca Parry, has separated herself from the irrational woman who has been hiding the pregnancy from her husband for four months. Who didn't tell him, because soon it was likely to be a lie that no longer mattered. But now that other woman, the one who was certainly going to lose her baby, who had only been hiding something the size of a pea, and then a berry, and then a grape, and then a plum, has finally found hope again, and the lies are not moot at all. They are missiles. *I need to tell you something, Ben. I need you to hear me out. This could be the time it works. This could give us everything.*

A hit. He pumps his arm, he swigs the beer. And then he leans back and is quiet. His laptop is closed on the table. The sun is moving behind the house now, and the room is shadowed and cool. She finds him here more and more now in the afternoon, asleep on this couch when she comes home.

She knows he won't survive another loss.

But she's not sure if they'll survive without a baby.

Maybe it's her time for the miracle. Maybe she has saved them.

Her phone glows on the table, a new message from her colleague in the ICU.

> Xavier's status getting worse. Mom still won't speak.
> Can you help?

18

Blair

She paces the kitchen, trying to think of what she should bring to the hospital for Whitney. She's felt immobilized for the past twenty minutes, since Rebecca called to ask if Blair could come. She looks across the street at the Loverlys' house, but she can't go back in there to get Whitney's things, not right now. Instead she goes upstairs and packs her only cashmere sweater, a gift from Whitney that always felt too nice to wear. A travel-size toothpaste. A spare phone charger.

She places each item in the bag with the same thought: she's been lied to. She's been made a fool. But now Whitney needs her. She calls her again, although Whitney hasn't answered her phone all day.

Xavier. It doesn't feel possible that he's unconscious. She sits down on her bed to hug the duffel bag, her chest aching. She wants to see Chloe. She wants to run to school and rip her from the classroom and keep her safe from everything. She worries, she worries constantly, and this is why. Bad things happen. When Blair holds out an arm against a child in the car, shouts up the street to be safe, questions whether the barbecued chicken is too pink, Whitney floats her hands down through the air as though quieting the orchestra. *Stop worrying so much.* As though Blair's worrying is a fault and not the natural state of mother-hood. A wasted emotion. As though it doesn't serve a purpose at all.

At the hospital, Whitney won't be stuck in catastrophic thinking, she'll be taking charge. Demanding the doctors do everything to save her son and accepting nothing else. Whitney is the strong one, the con-trolling one, the one who gets exactly what she wants at all costs.

The last thought unsettles her. Blair zips the bag with shaking fingers.

She must compartmentalize right now. She must do what Rebecca asked and go to the hospital.

When she leaves the house, Mara calls her name from her porch.

"I'm so sorry, Mara. I have to go, I'm running late." Blair speaks as she jogs, she barely turns her head on the way to the car parked on the street.

Whitney and Aiden fucking. The deceit was almost inconceivable. Almost.

Stop thinking about this, she tells herself, starting the car. It's not the time. She shouldn't have been snooping in the first place.

She shouldn't have seen the smashed coffee cup in Xavier's room.

Or that prescription, so many pills gone.

The backyard party in September wasn't the only time she's heard Whitney lose her temper with Xavier. There could have been an argu-ment. A misstep. The recklessness of rage.

The impulse of a person to lie when they have a lot at stake.

But, of course, accidents happen.

A few weeks ago, Blair had gone to the Loverlys' backyard to get Chloe for dinner. Whitney had just come home from the office. They stood together talking, Whitney's heels in her hand. Blair liked these opportunities to fasten herself into the rhythm of Whitney's day.

Blair asked about the vacation she and Jacob were planning to a place in the Caribbean Blair had never heard of, although Whitney referenced the island like it was Target. Blair was hungry for more details than Whitney shared—how much it cost, what kind of room. If they'd be flying business class. But she was careful to quell her curiosity. She didn't like to highlight the disparities between them.

She'd kept one ear on Chloe, who had been inside, playing upstairs with Xavier. They were jumping on the bed in his room, squealing, fits of giggles floating into the backyard.

The bed was under the window.

Blair wanted to interrupt Whitney, to ask her to hold her next thought for just a minute so she could shout up for Chloe to be careful near the open window, but then Chloe leaned out and yelled down, "Hey Mom! Come see our gymnastics routine!"

"She can almost land a flip! She's incredible!" Xavi's head and shoulders popped out beside her.

"GET INSIDE! BE CAREFUL!"

The next second, Blair reddened at the panic in her own voice, the mad waving of her arm.

She had asked Whitney about it several times before, the disastrous potential so obvious of a bed under a third-floor window without even a screen. Could Whitney not see this? She had said she would handle it, put a lock on, although Blair hadn't ever seen her take care of anything like that. Things just happened around her home. Help always at her fingertips, Jacob always finding the solutions, whereas Aiden couldn't even see the problems. There were no lists, no afternoons of back-to-back errands that kept them all functioning. Whitney was a conductor; Blair was a grinder.

Whitney had barely lifted her eyes up to the window. "Close it, Xavi!" But she'd sounded apathetic. She was dismissive. "Don't worry. He knows to be careful."

And then she had checked the phone in her hand as it chimed. An email she was waiting on. Blair stared at Whitney's face, concentrated on the screen. Sometimes it was like the children weren't there at all. Not until they irritated her enough to snap at.

Her jaws clench. She can't question Whitney about the key right now. Perhaps it's fair game, though, given the circumstances, to wonder how a little boy falls from a third-story window in the middle of the night.

19

Whitney

The Hospital

A voice behind her says they have good news: someone is finally on the way to be with her, they'll be here in ten minutes.

She hears Blair's name. And nothing about that feels good.

They hadn't known each other well for the first year of living on Harlow Street, beyond a hurried and casual hello when they happened to be outside at the same time. They'd moved in a month apart, the Loverlys to their beautiful new home that had taken eighteen months to build, and the Parks to their semidetached fixer-upper across the street. Xavier and Chloe had been too young to take a genuine liking to each other yet.

When the twins were two weeks old, Jacob caught an awful flu and was bedridden for three days, barely able to keep fluids down. Louisa couldn't come; she lived with her grandmother then, who was in frail health, and Louisa couldn't risk bringing germs home. Whitney had been coping okay until that point, recovering from a caesarean and working from bed, often with a twin on one of her breasts. She planned to nurse for six weeks. She couldn't do what she did with Xavier, who had wanted her breast at night for far too long. She wanted to get back to work. She wanted to get away from the multiplying children. She'd been ambivalent herself about having more, but Jacob was right that a sibling, one sibling, would benefit Xavier, and they could afford more help this time around.

She'd tried to disassociate herself from the overwhelm of twins the second the doctor told her; they felt more like a concept than two additional children. And then, they offered a peculiar relief: she could be a naturally divided mother, understandably distracted from focusing on one or the other in the way she'd been expected to with Xavier.

It was midmorning after two sleepless nights when Whitney realized something was officially wrong, that the babies couldn't suck from her without all three of them being in excruciating pain. Her breasts were engorged. Two throbbing, dripping taps. The twins were screaming for what had been hours, and Sebastian was slightly feverish. Jacob had taken Xavier to school and went straight back upstairs to sleep, his side of the bed soaked in sweat.

She called Louisa to beg, but it went to voice mail.

The exhaustion made her face hurt, her jaw ache. Three children were too many children. She wanted to give one away. She wanted to keep pushing the stroller to the farthest edge of the city, where the concrete met the deep dark lake. But she could barely walk without grimacing, her incision still oozy when it shouldn't have been, but the outside air was the only thing that seemed to calm the twins for more than forty seconds at a time. She had counted those seconds. She managed to get the twins in their new double stroller and together they moved slowly up and down the same stretch of the block, from stop sign back to stop sign, her incision growing hot. She winced as her shirt rubbed against nipples that felt like newly exposed nerves.

She passed the agony of time by imaging how it would feel to sleep. To wake up in the morning and think of only herself. To be freed. She could leave the children. But they would still exist. They would haunt her like ghosts. Their burden would never go away, no matter how far she ran, no matter how many days or weeks or years it took for her to come back, if she came back at all.

She thought she might throw up right there on the sidewalk. Wipe her mouth with her sleeve and lie down on the road to close her eyes, leave the mess for a dog to lap up.

She didn't notice the woman from across the street walking toward her until she heard her name, twice, three times.

"I'm sorry, have I got your name wrong?"

She couldn't remember exchanging names before. The little girl held the woman's hand and stood shyly behind her.

"Is their racket bothering you?" Whitney said. "I'm sorry."

The woman laughed. "Not at all! I remember these days. Chloe, aren't they cute? She's been excited to meet them." She lifted her daughter onto her hip and Whitney pulled Thea's blanket lower so they could peek at her screaming face.

"Ah." The woman looked closer. "The white on her tongue. Do they have thrush?"

Thrush? Whitney thought. Is that a word? Is her brain broken?

"Do you know what it is?" she said. "My daughter had it. You'll need an antifungal prescription."

They all watched as the babies' faces grew redder. Whitney couldn't fathom having the energy to get in a car and drive them to a doctor right now. She couldn't fathom having the energy to walk back to her own front door.

"I'm Blair, by the way. May I?" Blair put her toddler down and took the receiving blanket from the bottom basket of the stroller and draped it over her shoulder. She lifted Thea and placed her on it gently. "Aw, there you go, sweetheart. Sometimes they do better when they can't smell Mom. See, Chloe? Babies liked to be bounced a little, like this."

Whitney was not a crier. But she held her hand over her face and hadn't an ounce of energy left to stop the tears. She was mad at herself for feeling this desperate so quickly. She was incompetent. She was useless. She should be better, this was her second time around, she was a high-functioning, enormously privileged thirty-six-year-old woman with help at her fingertips. The problem wasn't that she didn't know what to do. It was that she didn't want to do it. She didn't want them anymore.

"You know what?" Blair said lightly. "We've got no plans this morning. We'd love to help, if you're comfortable with that."

Blair got Thea to doze and insisted she walk with the babies for an hour while Whitney went inside to get some rest. It might have seemed foolish to trust a stranger with her newborns, to put a container of formula and two clean bottles in her hands and leave. She knew Jacob wouldn't like it, but this woman was a mother, and lived across the street, and she seemed perfectly kind. Whitney didn't have the capacity for worry. She didn't care if this woman sent the babies on a shuttle to the moon. She'd had enough. She'd lain on the couch in her living room with her jacket and running shoes still on. She slept for four hours, until she heard Jacob's voice asking where the twins were.

The next day she'd felt embarrassed. She couldn't believe what she'd done. She sent Blair a two-hundred-dollar bouquet of flowers. Blair came over in the afternoon to thank her and see how she was feeling. The doctor had confirmed the next morning that it was thrush; Blair gave her tips on how to get the full dose of medication onto the babies' squirming tongues. Whitney watched her studying the babies, her genuine interest, the kindheartedness in the squint of her eyes. There was something quietly cool about her, her bluntly cut bangs, her army-green jacket, her white canvas sneakers. She spoke to her toddler so patiently, asking her fully formed questions, crouched down to her eye level, waiting intently to hear how the child answered. Nothing was rhetorical or hurried. Whitney could try this with Xavier, she thought. She could pause, and listen, she could try to really care. Like this new friend did.

Whitney had never had mom friends the way other women did. She hadn't had the time with Xavier. She'd felt the pang of missing out on these social connections when she'd go for business lunches and see a group of mothers at the next table over, enjoying their wine and salads while their babies, the size of Xavier, slept in car-seat buckets at their feet.

And now here was Blair, and she seemed eager for Whitney's company. There was something appealing about being neighbors, how simple and wholesome that was. How simple and wholesome Blair was. A reminder, right there, across the street, of how motherhood could feel. Whitney was excited about the idea of being friends.

"Can I come by to help you tomorrow? I don't mind at all. I've got nothing going on."

But Jacob was starting to feel better, and Louisa would be back. "How about just for a glass of wine? Your daughter could play with my son after school?"

"We'd love that." Blair took Sebastian from her arms and knelt so Chloe could let him grip her finger. "What a nice mommy you have, you lucky little boy," she said.

Whitney had smiled, and then she had turned away.

There was nothing lucky about it at all.

20

Blair

Blair stands alone in the hospital atrium holding two lattes, waiting for Rebecca, who texted that she'd meet her around now. She's nervous to see Whitney. She'll need to be comforting and reassuring. She'll need to put what she's learned to the side for the sake of Xavier. She'll be expected to help and they'll both need her.

Rebecca rubs her hands briskly as she comes around the corner. She looks commanding in her crisp white coat, the badges around her neck. Seeing her outside of Harlow Street feels strange. Blair puts the coffees down and they hug.

"I should have brought you one, too, I wasn't thinking."

"No, no, I'm fine." Rebecca puts her hand on Blair's shoulder. "I'm so sorry. I know how close your families are. It sounds like things aren't looking any better. They've just told me there's some concern about his blood pressure now. Still no signs of responsiveness."

"Do you know anything more about what happened?"

"Not yet, other than he fell sometime between eight p.m., when he went to bed, and midnight, when Whitney found him."

"God, it's unthinkable, an accident like this. Right at home," Blair says, shaking her head. She wonders if that's the word they're all using—"accident." She watches Rebecca for a reaction, but she only nods. And then she motions for Blair to follow. She's quiet in the elevator and on the way to the ICU, glancing at her phone. And then, without looking up: "Blair, I know you're close friends, so can I ask you—has Whitney been okay lately? I mean generally speaking. Nothing that would concern you, nothing out of the ordinary?"

Blair shakes her head, she scans the panels of lighting above them. An affair—an affair with her husband would be concerning. "Nothing I can think of." She shakes her head again. "Why?"

"She's been really out of it, that's all. Not speaking to anyone." Rebecca glances at her and then swipes her badge to open the double doors. "But this can happen, this kind of shock. I think having you here will help."

She talks quietly to the doctor at the admissions desk and signs Blair in. Blair grips the cups too tightly and foam erupts from the lids, drips on her hands. She'd convinced herself earlier that Xavier would be okay, that this would be a temporary crisis, but everything feels precarious now. She looks down the hall of closed doors as Rebecca clips a visitor's pass to the bottom of her sweatshirt. None of this feels real to Blair. That they're on the critical care floor in the children's hospital. That Xavier is in one of those rooms. She takes a seat in a row of cinnamon-colored chairs and waits.

Hundreds of hours she must have spent with the Loverlys and their children over the years they've lived on Harlow Street. The idle time that fills family life, the daily back-and-forth that makes one privy to the rhythm of another's week. What the other family orders on pizza night, the ringtone on each other's phones, how the latch on the side fence works. Their children's favorite pajamas. That's what makes her and

Whitney's friendship so special—this familiarity of the mundane, the comfort of being witness to each other's interior lives.

It makes it all so much worse—Whitney and Aiden. Her eyes well up.

She opens her phone and scrolls through photos of Xavier and Chloe together. Of the tea party the two of them set up for the twins' birthday, all of their mouths stained with grape juice. The last time Xavier was over, he had brought his chess set. Blair had noticed, once again, that the brightness he'd had as a younger child was fading. He's become so sullen, she'd thought, as he'd set up the chessboard for them.

"Do you like doing this with me?"

The skepticism in his voice had sunk her. "Oh, Xavi, of course I do! I'm having so much fun with you as my teacher."

He'd taken a moment to process whether she was being truthful, smiling only after she smiled. Blair had wondered then how he saw himself. How he was usually made to feel. He'd set up the rest of the pieces carefully. Slowly. Buying time with her.

Her phone dings three times in her hand.

How is she?

Any update on X?

You doing okay?

Blair stares at Aiden's first text and her insides roll again. She needs to occupy herself with useful tasks to keep focused.

She will check the status of Jacob's flight.

She will offer to make phone calls to whoever needs to know.

She will ask a nurse to set up a cot for Whitney to get some sleep.

She will drive home to get her a soft blanket and a feather pillow; she should have thought of this.

"Thanks again for coming," Rebecca says, startling her.

"Of course, it's the least I can do. Ben said you were the one to help Xavi when the ambulance brought him in."

Rebecca folds her arms. "Yeah. It was a shock to see him."

"I'm sure this is tough for Ben too. Seems like he'd grown close to Xavi lately," Blair says. Rebecca looks confused. "All of those hours playing catch in the backyard, I mean."

"Right, yes." But Rebecca seems like this hadn't occurred to her. "Come. I'll take you in."

T he hair at the back of Whitney's head is kinked from the rain yesterday. This is the first thing Blair notices. It takes her a moment to force her gaze away from her friend to Xavier on the bed.

His head is small and fragile compared to the mass of medical equipment surrounding him. He looks like an experiment. His face is bloated and gray, and his eyelids are glossy, his lips thick with petroleum jelly. A brown bandage stretches tight across the bridge of his nose and over a mass of clear tubes. The air is stale and aseptic, and although the room is dim, he's lit with the soft light of an overhead lamp. A steady beep. Speckles of fluid catch somewhere inside him. The room feels both calm and chaotic, dozens of electrical sockets, boxes of gloves on the walls, posters with warnings, bags of liquid hanging from his bed, from poles. There's a cart of supplies, straws and syringes flagged with labels, sterile water containers, wipes, clamps, Glowing lines of orange and red crawl across the monitor like city traffic at night.

Whitney doesn't move. Her hand is on her son's. Her long legs are crossed, her feet in slide-on sandals. Her toes are purply. Blair knows she hates to be cold. She should have brought socks. Behind her, she hears Rebecca leave the room.

"Whit," Blair says softly. But Whitney doesn't move. She doesn't seem to hear her at all. "Whit," she tries again.

She touches her back. Whitney is shaking, or maybe shivering. Blair drapes the cardigan she brought over Whitney's shoulders. She fixes the sleeves so they hang nicely. The way Whitney would want. She puts her hands on her shoulders and leans down so their faces are close. So their cheeks touch. Whitney is scentless, stale.

When she pulls away to look at Whitney's face, she sees her lips are dry and picked apart. Lip balm, Blair thinks. Lip balm and socks. That's what she'll bring her tomorrow. Lip balm, socks, her pillow. Lotion. The nice face lotion from the cabinet in her bathroom that smells like garden roses.

Blair glances to the floor. Whitney's phone is facedown, discarded under her chair. She thinks of the texts she sent that morning, unread, asking where Xavier was. All the emails from work. Everyone trying to get ahold of her.

This is not the woman she expected to find here, taking charge, demanding second opinions, searching Google on her phone to corroborate everything the doctors say. She looks hollow.

There's a gurgle from somewhere in Xavier and Blair inhales audibly before she can stop herself. But Whitney is unmoved. She's never seen her so silent and still before. She's always in motion, always engaging with something or someone or thinking of a new idea.

She wonders if she's praying. If she's begging some higher power to save her son. Blair isn't a religious woman either, but it's what she'd be doing if Chloe was in that bed. The pain Whitney must be feeling. She puts her hand on her shoulder again.

But Whitney flinches. She leans forward in her chair, away from Blair. Blair holds her breath as Whitney shakes her head.

"I know, Whit. I'm so sorry this has happened. I can't believe it." Her words are strained. She doesn't want to cry again.

But Whitney shakes her head again. "No . . . no, I can't have you here."

Blair is stunned. She looks around the room.

"You want me . . . to leave?"

Whitney cups her hands around her face, shielding herself from everything that is not her son. And then she nods. She sniffs through the phlegm in her throat and exhales steadily through her mouth. She does not want Blair there. She won't even look at her.

"All right," Blair's voice shakes. She doesn't want to comply. She doesn't want to accept what this means. "But if there's anything I can do—"

"Please. Just go."

Blair turns to face the door. They are best friends, loyal friends. The ugly rumors that will swirl, the conclusions everyone else will jump to about what happened to Xavier. Doesn't Whitney need her? Who else does Whitney have?

And yet. At a time like this, it would be hard to look in Blair's eyes if she's fucking her husband. If Blair's very presence at her side reminded her of the horrible person she was. Unworthy of the miracle she needs right now.

Rebecca calls her name from the hallway as she leaves, but she walks faster and faster away, until she's jogging to the elevators. She pretends she cannot hear. Pretending is what she is best at.

21

Whitney

She's at the office, on the other line, when Xavier's teacher calls her cell phone again. And again. The urgency makes her uncomfortable. She puts her client on hold and answers hastily.

"Nothing serious, Whitney, I should say right away. But Xavier isn't having a good week."

Whitney stands; she paces her office as the din of rain on her tenth-floor window begins. Not a good week. What does a good week look like? It's only Wednesday. There was a math quiz the day before. He studied with Louisa. He'd been fine when she got home last night, his usual—tired from the day, grumpy. He's said nothing concerning. Louisa hasn't mentioned anything.

"He's been increasingly quiet, very withdrawn in class. And there was an incident at recess this morning, with some name-calling from other kids. The kind of thing we don't tolerate, we can assure you."

Whitney asks her which kids. She is hot now, her stomach clenches.

She pulls the blazer from her armpits. But the teacher can't say who it was. Instead, she assures Whitney the children were spoken to. That things were dealt with.

"With the summer break starting in a few weeks, though, I wanted to suggest you might work on strengthening Xavier's friendships with the kids in his cohort. Find him a buddy or two for some playdates this summer. For a nice strong start to sixth grade, socially. I can send you the names of some parents—"

But no. Whitney does not want the names of more parents. She does not want the teacher's thinly veiled criticisms. She understands exactly what the woman is telling her: Your son has no friends. He's a loser. There's only so much time left to turn things around for him. Does she think Whitney doesn't know? Does she think Whitney can't see this about him? He is her child. She is his mother.

Her throat is tightening. She doesn't want to sound emotional. This shitty public school Jacob insisted on, she knew it wasn't good enough. This school doesn't have to answer for anything. Xavier deserves better. She will find him a private school for September, one with nicer children; she will get on the phone first thing tomorrow afternoon, and they'll call in every favor they can, and she'll donate whatever she has to. His academic performance alone won't be good enough to get him in, but she'll make it happen somehow.

She thanks the teacher. She tells her how much she appreciates the call. She wants to drive there now and take him out of class, get him away from those fucking kids. She imagines the girls in the cafeteria making fun of him while he eats at lunch with his mouth open—he's told her this before, that sometimes they point and whisper, and he doesn't know why. She's reminded him a thousand times to close his lips while he chews. It breaks her heart to think of him being teased like that. Being made to feel repulsive.

The names of some parents. She thinks back to the barbecue in September. How little she's heard from the other fifth-grade mothers since. The gossipy group chats she's been dropped from. How it stings. She'd been waiting for an invitation to something at some point, for one of them to reach out. But there'd been nothing but silence.

And then she thinks of what Jacob said on the phone earlier that day. That he shouldn't have gone to London. Like she wasn't good enough. He doesn't voice his judgment about her often, but it's there. In his cool silence after she loses patience with the children, the way he pulls them into him, wraps his arms around their heads while he looks past her, like he's wishing in those moments that she was not there.

Like he doesn't think she can be trusted.

She should, to be safe, cancel her plans tonight.

She slams her phone on the desk.

Outside her office door, Grace lifts two fingers. Two minutes until her last meeting of the afternoon. She collects the agenda, her notepad, her phone. A crack has grown across the screen, across a photo she took last year of Jacob and the three children on the beach. Their matching striped bathing suits. The salty curls in their hair. She leaves it on her desk. She won't think any more about her family right now.

22

Mara

Mara has become good at reading lips. It's a skill of the lonely. But Ben's back was to her as he spoke to Blair on the driveway earlier today, right after she left the Loverlys' house. And her hand was cupped over her mouth. In shock, it seemed like. Something is going on next door, and she's satisfied to have had a hunch all morning. She's annoyed she missed Rebecca's car leave while she was making Albert a snack—that was her ticket.

She should get out for an hour to take her mind off it, or this will consume her all day. Pick up some potatoes for dinner and give her legs a proper stretch. The thing is, if she leaves, she might miss something again, and it's not like anybody will come over later to tell her what's going on. She'd better stick around. She'll finish the laundry in the basement and then she'll get back out there, to the porch, to watch for them all to come home.

She thinks, while she folds, about the time in her life when she'd felt tethered to her house in a different way. To the family inside who needed her. For years she was the referee in a boxing ring, the opponents unfairly matched. Only one of them knew how to throw a punch, although those punches were never physical. Somehow that made it worse, though. It was much harder to protect her son from Albert's words. From the way he made Marcus feel. But she tried.

She can't, now, remember how it felt to be throttled by that responsibility. By the endless obligation. She touches her neck, thinking of how hard it was to breathe sometimes. How her chest would ache. She pulls at loose skin that doesn't feel like it could possibly be hers.

She had sat outside on the porch then, too, when it had all been too much. In the middle of the night while they slept, she would wrap her housecoat snug and light one of Albert's cigarettes. Something about the first inhale gave her a kind of permission. She could indulge the ugliest part of herself, the part she couldn't face when her son's sweet breath tickled her ear or when she smelled the custard left in the corners of his mouth. She was never lying when she spoke to others about how blessed she was to have the son she did. About how he lit her up. He made her feel whole.

But there was another truth, too, that burned at the center for all those years, and that was the truth she never said out loud. That she felt angry. And resentful. For having a son who needed her in the way that he did. For the kind of mother he needed her to be. Thinking of it now chokes her up. The exhaustion of carrying that every day, whittling away at the resilience she relied on to survive, while she gave and loved and listened desperately for his voice like the wind whistling through the trees.

She stopped looking Albert in his eyes back then. She was terrified about what he might recognize in her. Unlike him, she didn't have the luxury of hardening into stone.

The love she'd felt for Marcus could bring her to her knees. And it did, some nights, right there on the porch, on the varnished planks of pine. Some nights the love and anger and the unfairness of it all hurt so much that she could swear someone's hands were gripped around her neck. She'd reach up to feel for them. She never allowed herself the relief of tears.

N̲ow, she ambles up the basement stairs with the basket of folded laundry on her sore hip. She hoists it onto the kitchen counter next to the stairs, and notices the pot is missing from the coffee maker. But she smells the strong waft of coffee. She turns around. Albert is lying on the linoleum floor, his pants soaked in a pool of brown.

She crouches and places her hands on either side of his head. He's conscious, but his eyes go through her. She smacks his cheeks, unsure of what to do. His upper body looks tense. She fumbles to reach for something, to do something, but she can't think of what. She scrambles to the phone in the other room.

"An ambulance, for my husband. He's on the kitchen floor, he can't speak."

She can barely understand what the operator is saying to her, something about staying with him, about checking his breathing, but the panic takes over, and she can't make sense of what to do next. She puts the receiver on the side table and goes back to him.

"Albert? Can you hear me? An ambulance will come. I don't know what else to do."

She wets a dishcloth and wipes the sweat from his forehead. She kneels next to him, her arthritic knees burning, and lifts his head onto her lap. She can hear a voice from the receiver in the other room, but it's too faint to make out. She tries to think if it's been minutes or only seconds since she called 911, when she'll start to hear the sirens, if the front door is unlocked. Will they be able to get a stretcher up those stairs and through the doorframe? Will it be wide enough? Will they carry him out there themselves?

His eyelids are lower now. She puts her hand over his mouth and then her finger under his nose and she can't be sure if she can feel anything. She can't be sure.

Her mind jumps from the static noise from the phone receiver to the weight of his head on her lap to the smell of the coffee. She'll never brew a pot again. She closes her eyes and doesn't open them again until she hears the sirens. She stares at the door and waits for something to happen. There's a knock before it opens and the floor shakes from the weight of their steps, their huge black boots coming toward her. She falls back, away from Albert, she moves like a slug to the corner of the kitchen floor. She doesn't know how to answer their questions. They cut his shirt with scissors and put paddles on his skin. She thinks about ripping his shirt into rags for her cleaning, like she does to all their tattered clothes. The sopping squares of flannel absorbing the spill after they leave.

It feels like they're standing over him for hours. And then minutes. There's a calm in the kitchen she can't make sense of, so little fuss. It's all nearly perfunctory. They sit back. One of the paramedics asks if anyone else is home. She shakes her head. There is nobody.

"Do you have someone who can help you right now? Any children, or . . . ?"

"No," Mara says. "No family."

"A neighbor, maybe?"

She shakes her head.

They stand close together so that she can't hear them speak. One of them seems to be trying to convince the other of what they'll do next, he is gesturing to Mara on the floor, he is looking around the kitchen. She feels embarrassed all of a sudden, like they can smell her loneliness. Like they can see the misery of their life together in the stained countertop, the table with only two chairs, the bare fridge door. No photos. No magnets. The other one walks outside, speaking into the radio on his chest. The first paramedic kneels where Mara is slumped against the kitchen drawers.

"There's nothing left we can do. I'm sorry." He keeps his blue gloves on. He wipes his brow with his forearm. Mara nods. He helps her up into the kitchen chair. "We can call the medical examiner, and then you'll have to make arrangements with whatever funeral home you want to use. They'll have to come get your husband. Which can take some time. Probably all day." He looks around the kitchen again, at the mess all over the floor. "Or, we can take him to the hospital, likely Sinai. They can deal with things there. We aren't really supposed to transfer in this situation . . . but if it would help you out."

The medical examiner. Albert, damp, stained, growing cold on the kitchen floor. She wonders if they'll cover him with something if they leave him here. If he'll come back to life. If he'll begin to smell. If this has all really happened.

She says the hospital would be best.

He asks if she'd like to come, if she'd like to go collect her things first.

"I think I'll stay."

The other paramedic is back now with the stretcher, and it fits easily through their door, and they're tucking in straps and moving levers. She doesn't watch as they take him away. She sits at the kitchen table, and she listens for the sirens again as they leave but they don't turn them on this time. He was here, he was alive. Just thirty-five, forty minutes ago. The refrigerator is still humming. The kitchen window is open and the echo of the city floats in. Albert is gone, and she's the only witness to the end, and it all feels impossibly unremarkable.

Nothing like the day she lost her son.

23

Rebecca

She stands outside the door of Xavier's room and watches Whitney with her son, and wonders why Blair left in such a rush. A nurse, Leo, who normally works with her in the ER, is covering the intensive care unit this week. His shift is almost done. He stands beside her, slowly rubbing the sanitizer into his hands. She likes Leo. He'd noticed when she was pregnant for the first time, that she'd begun letting the coffees he brought for her sit until they were cold.

When she'd returned to work two days after the first loss, with pads in her bra to absorb the watery leak from her nipples, he'd greeted her at the start of her shift like he'd done for weeks: *How are you and baby feeling?* She could only shake her head as she watched her fingers type her password to log in. No, please don't ask me that question. No, the baby is not here anymore.

She'd tried to stop her forehead from crinkling. She thought she'd be okay. He had understood right away. He'd put a gentle hand between her shoulder blades and made sure it was the last time she had to ac-knowledge to anyone what had happened. Nobody said a word to her. He'd had the best of intentions.

Her colleagues might have noticed she was pregnant the times that followed, but nobody said anything, and so how could she? *How's my day? Fine. But I was pregnant yesterday, and now I am not. How are you?* The three-month rule of silence takes away the language for that kind of loss. The pregnancies weren't supposed to matter, not enough to jus-tify everyone around her being uncomfortable.

Now, outside Xavier's door, Leo tells her that he heard Jacob's plane should be landing soon.

"Do they think he might have jumped?"

His voice lowers for the last word. Jumped. Fell. Lost his balance. Rebecca isn't sure what they're considering. She's no longer in his circle of care, so she's kept at a distance, although she's also made it a point not to know more. Yes, he is a ten-year-old, and devastating accidents hap-pen to kids more frequently than anybody would like to think. But par-ents also lie. They protect themselves because they think they've learned a lesson and they won't do it again.

The yelling, the screaming that she has heard from the house. And Jacob being away last night. She wonders if the police in the emergency room hallway would have agreed to come back later if the white mother with her head in her hands had looked different. One who isn't drip-ping with every kind of privilege. And yet Rebecca had been the one to lift a temperate finger to the nurse, to make a sympathetic face so the officers would merely nod and walk away down the hall. Decide that, yes, it can wait, it is fine.

"I think it was just an accident," she says to Leo. "A boy who couldn't sleep. Testing the limits of gravity." And it likely was exactly that. She has no factual reason to speculate otherwise.

She calls Ben as she walks back down to the ER. No improvements, she tells him. She's not hearing anything positive from the team. Whitney still isn't speaking. Like she's grieving him already. More than a decade into this, and it's still hard to understand how parents do it.

"Ben? Are you there?" She wonders if she's lost service. He hasn't said anything.

"Yeah. Yeah, I'm here."

She's thinking of it, too, their childlessness. She always is. She has never asked him, *Does it cross your mind every day? Do you look the other way when you pass the swing set at the park? Do you hear my cries echo from the floor of the shower while you wait for the water to heat up every morning?*

He tells her he loves her.

She says she has to go.

24

Blair

Aiden's voice booms for Chloe from the front door, but she'd already leapt from her chair when they heard the knob turn. Blair heats up his plate, trying not to be irritated that the sauce will be pasty now. There are more important things happening than a ruined dinner. She's been checking her phone every few minutes, anxious for an update about Xavier. Or a text from Whitney, apologizing—offering an explanation for turning her away, other than the one consuming Blair's every thought.

The key is upstairs in her drawer, the weight of it palpable above her.

For the sake of the evening with Chloe, she needs to put everything aside for the next few hours. She is expert at veiling this internal confliction, going through the motions while thinking the worst of Aiden. She is counting on a reset with him after his visit to the store that morning. He normally lets things go so easily.

But now, he's barely making eye contact with her. He's only focused on Chloe. They've agreed not to tell her about where Xavier was today, not until the morning, in the hope they'll have more information. He throws questions to Chloe about her day in rapid fire. They love this energy they get from each other. *And then . . . and then . . .* There is always more Chloe wants to tell him. He loves being the receptacle for her endless exuberance. He loves the easy parts.

Chloe begins to cough, and Aiden pushes out his chair.

"I'll get you some water. Daddy's got it," he says.

Blair is standing right next to the sink. She feels him move around her, the plastic cup changing hands, the reach for the tap. He doesn't run the water until it's cold, like Chloe likes it.

They'd gone to Mexico last March. They couldn't get three seats together on the plane, so Blair sat with Chloe in the row behind Aiden.

She entertained her for two hours with card games and rounds of I Spy. With thirty minutes left, Chloe asked if she could sit with Aiden. They swapped seats and Blair finally closed her eyes. Sometime later, she woke up to hear Aiden's cheerful voice behind her: "Here you go, sweetheart. Daddy's gotcha covered, don't I?"

Blair thought of the flight attendant microwaving the small pizza. Walking it to their seat, running his card through the payment machine for him. She'd wanted to flip around and shove her head between the seats. *No. You've never got it covered. You took a nap and played poker on your phone and you packed nothing but your own carry-on suitcase. You don't take care of her. I do! I am the one who does everything. You ordered a fucking pizza from an in-flight menu!*

But instead, she'd stared at her reflection in the black digital screen on the seat in front of her. There is never any point. They had six days of vacation ahead. She'd once heard a therapist on a podcast say that someone's partner should calm their nervous system. She never stopped thinking about this—the way his very presence made her hold her breath.

. . .

N ow, Chloe drinks the lukewarm water at the kitchen table. Blair puts Aiden's dinner plate on the place mat in front of him.

"Mom. Aren't you going to say hi to Daddy?" The tone of Chloe's voice is changed.

Blair feels chastised. She lived through years of her own mother slamming down plates of cold chicken in front of her father. It was the tension she'd chewed through every night.

"Of course!" She smiles. She leans down to kiss Aiden on his stiff lips. "How was your day, hon?"

"Excellent." He doesn't look at her. He moves his chair closer to the table and smiles at Chloe instead, whose eyes are on Blair. Then the two of them resume. Blair tidies the counter and listens.

She doesn't want to know a life in which she no longer overhears them together. Chloe laughs differently when he is home. She sings more. She is sillier.

She slips into a scene that could be their future. The overnight bag she would pack for Chloe. The sound of the knock on the apartment door when he's there to get her. Having to see his new clothes, his new haircut. Having to confront the happiness he's found without her, there in the frame of her dismal apartment doorway. The deadbolt lock women use when they feel nobody will protect them. The crushing repetition of chronic loneliness, the deafening silence of hours upon hours alone when she does not want to be alone. Chloe's laundry smelling differently when she comes back from his place. Chloe's careful answers to her prying questions. What people will think of her. How shrunken she will feel.

She's not sure she would be any less angry than she is now.

They are calling for her. They want to tell her a joke they've made up. And then Chloe asks for ice cream with sprinkles.

Blair runs the scoop under hot water and listens to them negotiate how many rounds of hangman they'll play before bedtime. The steam fogs the window above the sink. She packs the ice cream neatly into the cone. She shakes the rainbow sprinkles on top.

Her husband's mouth over Whitney's nipple. The rush he would feel staring at the darkened pinch of her asshole as he fucks her from behind. Not wanting to leave each other when they have to go home. Feeling more pity than guilt when they see Blair, with her stretched-out jeans. The sandbag breasts under her shirt. Her cluelessness.

She delivers the cone to Chloe and then makes another for Aiden.

When she puts the carton back in the freezer, she notices Aiden's phone on the kitchen counter. She turns her back to them.

Her heart races every time she puts in his password. Nothing about this ever feels good to her. This collision of fear and anticipation. She doesn't want to find something she can't unlearn. She doesn't want this to be the last second in the before of their lives. It is terrifying and it is addicting and she can never talk herself out of it.

She scrolls quickly, looking for Whitney's name in his sent texts and then his email and then his messaging app and then his recent calls. He'd be calling her, texting to see if she's okay. But there's nothing but innocuous chatter with his friends.

She puts the phone back on the counter and pulls her shirt away from the dampness in her armpits. The relief is an anesthetic, for now.

Chloe is calling her. Blair needs to be with them. She needs to take a turn at the game.

She tries again. She stands behind Aiden and puts her hands on his shoulders. He pulls her lower so that her head is next to his. He rubs his face against hers and she feels the scratch of the day's growth against her cheek, smells the remains of his aftershave. He lifts his cone to her mouth, an offering. She feels Chloe watching them. Almost suspiciously. Blair licks the ice cream.

Can Chloe feel the foundation underneath her cracking? Will she wake up one day and no longer feel as safe as she has for the last seven years? She thinks of her unspoiled, impressionable heart. Blair cannot do that to her. She is desperate not to. She owes her more, and she will assume any cost.

Both things can exist at the same time: the resentment, and the comfort. The despair, and all that love. She pecks Aiden on the corner of his mouth. And then again. She sees the satisfaction in her daughter's face, and then she lowers her eyes to the hanging man.

25

Rebecca

I t's only 7:00 p.m. but she needs to find somewhere to lie down. She can feel the tension in her back after just a few hours of standing. Every little ache makes her nervous now. *Go away, go away.* She lets the resident on her shift know she'll be back in twenty minutes, and she finds an on-call room where she can rest.

Rebecca can see her sometimes when she closes her eyes. The first one. She was the size of a pomegranate, the app had said, the week she left her, although she had looked bigger in her hands. They measure in utero from crown of the head to the bum, as though the baby's twiggy legs, fully formed with every bone, with ten tiny toes, do not matter yet. She thinks of the hand towel she had wrapped her in, soiled with the makeup she had washed from her face a few hours before, at the end of a nineteen-hour shift. Of how it felt for the baby to come out of her. The physical sensation of the bulge passing through her. She cannot let go of that feeling.

They hadn't decided on a name. And nothing had felt right after she saw her. It's hard to choose a name you love that you will never get to say.

She doesn't want to let herself think about this now, not in the middle of a shift.

But this is the thing about miscarriage. It is not an event, something that once happened and has ended. Miscarriage goes on and on, follows a woman through her days and her dreams, and then she will have blissful split seconds when she forgets, when her brain can still feel the gratification of having that baby, until she remembers the baby is not hers anymore, and hasn't been for days or even weeks. There will be blood that soaks her sheets and odor she can't recognize. There will be appointments where they prod her, make sure she's spat everything out, because if not, what's left from that life could kill her. She will think of herself as a vessel that can only expel, that will never find pleasure again in being entered.

Rebecca had lain on her bed after it happened the first time and could feel only the heat of anger. Cheated of what she had thought was hers for nearly eighteen weeks. She hadn't known how badly she wanted the baby until she couldn't have it. But there was nobody to shout in the face of, to convince she should be given back what she was owed. And when the wrath subsided into sadness, she could think only of her mother. How unbearably hard it would be to tell her the baby was gone.

Ben had been crushed, but then he'd been optimistic. Bad luck, he had called it the first time, almost casually. We'll try again. Like a mulligan in his golf game.

The second fetus had landed in the toilet bowl in a mass of tissues. She had been dreaming of the baby's limbs hanging from her in the hallway of a dark labor and delivery ward, when the sensation of contractions woke her out of sleep. The cramps grew over the hours that followed as she crouched in her nightshirt in the shower, until she could feel it was time.

Afterward, she lay, wet, on the cold tile floor, until Ben came into the bathroom and brought her back to bed. She asked him not to flush the toilet and he had shaken his head, he wouldn't.

Once he fell asleep, Rebecca cupped the fetus out of the pink toilet water. It felt like a goldfish in her palm. She touched it with her finger, the slimy beginning of life. She put it in a plastic sandwich bag and tucked it under the bathroom sink on a stack of toilet paper rolls, and she waited, sleepless, for the morning. She was on day shifts that week. She showered and dressed, and as the sun was coming up, she brought the bag to the sparse backyard of their new house, the yard they were meant to clutter with tricycles and sandbox toys. She dug a hole as deep as she could by the fence made of pine, the wood still blond and fresh and smelling like the forest, and placed the plastic bag with her fetus inside. She covered it with dirt, packed it firmly, and then drove to work, her soiled hands on the wheel of the Prius. She scrubbed clean in the steel sink of an empty operating theater when she got there.

The third one left her in the staff bathroom during a busy shift, at the same point in her pregnancy as the second. It was fast, like a bowel movement, as though her body were getting used to ridding itself of any life that wasn't her own. She had spotted the day before, but the cramping was so light that she convinced herself it was her tired back, a strained muscle. For two hours, maybe three, she could believe that was all the discomfort was.

She put the mass, wrapped in toilet paper, into a specimen bag from the supplies room, and slipped it into the pocket of her white coat. She walked back to the nursing station to ask where she was needed next. Room 11. She pulled back the curtain but couldn't smile.

"So, tell me," she had said, putting one side of the stethoscope into her ear. "When did the fever first begin?"

On the way home in the morning, she had stopped at the fertility clinic and waited in the parking lot for them to open. They would test the fetus. The results showed no genetic abnormality. The life had a chance, just not a chance inside her. At home, she went straight to the backyard and stared at the spot where she'd buried the first one.

Ben watched her come through the back door and asked why she was out there. She hadn't answered. She'd gone to the fridge and taken out a loaf of bread and grabbed the first utensil she saw. While she tried to spread the almond butter with a fork, she calculated the dates in her head to figure out when she could get pregnant next. She could ovulate again in fifteen days, it is technically possible, she would test herself every day with the ovulation kit. The days between the losses and when she can try again are long and empty. They are meaningless to her.

Ben had asked her a second time what she had been doing outside. She'd only shaken her head. And then she'd shaken it again. She wanted rid of the milestones she'd let herself plot on the calendar, again, like a fool: late September, when baby would arrive, and the air would be perfectly cool for strolling. December, when they'd spend the holidays at the farm, walking the snowy fields with the cousins, the baby bundled in a carrier on her chest. February, when she'd begin a slow return to work, three days a week, maybe four. July, when they'd have their first family vacation to the coast with her mother. Long naps under the sun umbrella with Grandma. Chubby feet in the tide.

Ben pulled her away from the counter and took the fork from her hand.

"Is it the baby?"

She never could bring herself to answer, but he knew. He cried quietly into her neck, but she couldn't cry with him. She couldn't find any emotion at all.

The fourth time she was pregnant, Ben had only nodded when she showed him the stick. Nothing felt like a joyous miracle anymore. Every day felt perilous, living on the edge of a knife. She begged time to move faster.

They had twelve days to go until the eighteen-week mark, when she saw the smear on the toilet paper. She was scheduled for a dilation and curettage nearly a week from then, the soonest they could take her, and for those five days, her breasts were sore and the fatigue of pregnancy consumed her. Her body was confused, or maybe couldn't bring itself to let go.

She wanted it out of her. It was all she could think of as she went through her days. She looked forward to the IV needle in her hand, to the blissfully unconscious state of the operating room. The slit of indistinguishable eyes between cap and mask, cold steel tools, blinding lights, the biting smell of iodine. The scraping clean of every last unviable cell. The relief of not having to see, this time, what she had been growing inside her.

"You seem so calm," Ben had said to her quietly, shifting in his seat in the pre-op waiting room. What he'd meant was that she wasn't crying, like she was supposed to. Like the woman two rows in front of them. "I guess you're a doctor, you're used to this stuff."

But no. It was because she had tried on the disappointment over and over and over so that she was prepared. She had already lived the very moment they were in.

She had only nodded. Yes. My cold, clinical heart is used to this.

When she didn't want to talk about it, she only wanted to scream about it. But there was nowhere to go, no empty void to hold this kind of anger.

Ben had been so quiet in the days following each of the losses. He never asked her about what happened to the babies who left her. And so he didn't have to keep count in his head like she did in hers: one in their own backyard, two in medical waste bins, and one in her bottom dresser drawer in a small plastic bag from the crematory.

The fetuses were lost. But so was the way she had come to understand herself as they grew inside her. As a mother. As someone new. She loved that woman—that woman was who she wanted to be.

26

SEPTEMBER

The Loverlys' Backyard

Aiden's eyes dart from Whitney's breasts as she dances, to the ice bucket that Jacob puts on the table. Blair is punctured. She moves slowly as the air seeps from her body. She slinks backward to the patio sofa and clears her throat. She hates this about him, that he's always looking at attractive women the way he used to at her, probably imagining them naked. It's piggish. She cranes her neck to look for Chloe and Xavier, to buy time for the humiliation to leave her face. The tears rise to her lids.

Aiden seems to sense her turn of mood. He motions for her—come here, come sit on my lap. Like they're teenagers. Like they're in love. Like it's Blair he wants to fuck. Well, fuck *you*. She wants to say it out loud. But Jacob and Whitney are both watching her now, too, so she goes to him like she should. She puts a stiff arm around his neck and thinks of how much she hates him. She hopes the tears don't spill.

And then a woman Blair had noticed before, tall and lithe, with comically massive sunglasses and shorts like underwear, comes over to ask Whitney and Jacob about the caterer. Aiden seemed to have registered the woman's presence when she came into the backyard earlier, like a dog smelling something in the air—chin lifted, head slightly to the left, attention pulled away. Does anyone else see the thirst on his face that she always does?

But this was how Blair lived when it came to her marriage. On alert. She had trained herself to spot danger everywhere she looked. *You're overreacting*, he would tell her. *You're being insane.*

I'm not your father.

Whitney is oozy and overcompensating with the woman, who is the girlfriend of Jacob's college friend. They don't live in the area, and this bothers Blair, this infiltration of a neighborhood barbecue, that they've stayed so late. She suspects the couple invited themselves. The girlfriend is young and tight and speaks loudly, and there is too much shimmer in her makeup, there is maybe even glitter. Like the kind of makeup Chloe would want. Blair feels a sense of superiority over her. She seems to make Jacob uncomfortable, too—he's turned away from her—and Blair likes this kinship with Jacob, this bristling toward the same tawdry vibe she can't stand.

Blair listens in but it's not enough to distract her from her rage toward the man she's sitting on top of. Her throat burns. Her eyes burn. She wants to punch Aiden in the side of the face, his freshly shaved cheeks patted with aftershave; she wants to shove her foot into his scrotum over and over and over.

His hand moves to her back, and she arches away from his touch.

"Don't."

He doesn't ask her what's wrong.

She looks around again for Chloe. She's at the fence with Xavier now, he's finally come out of his room. They're talking to Mara, who is slipping violets through the wooden slats for Chloe to put in her hair. Blair would normally interrupt, stamp herself on the conversation, make her all-knowingness concerning the children obvious. But she stops herself.

She thinks of what Rebecca told her and Whitney two hours earlier, just before leaving the party. She had gestured to Mara's yard, stepped closer, and lowered her voice.

"Is she not coming?" Rebecca had asked.

"It's too much for her on our side of the fence, with the kids and the noise. And the fun," Whitney had said. Blair had chuckled. "How long until she sells, do you think?"

But Rebecca only twisted her lips and looked away from them, and then finished her glass of water. Blair had watched her eyeing the clusters of mothers earlier, as the servers kept topping them all up with wine, more wine.

"I'm not sure how much you know about Mara. But she and Albert had a son. They raised him there in that house. He died quite young, from what I understand." Rebecca pauses, and then says: "He was just a teenager."

Blair had looked at Whitney. They hadn't known. Whitney was quiet, but Blair watched the change in her eyes as she stared into Mara's backyard. "Do you know how it happened?"

Rebecca shook her head. "She's never said."

"Jesus," Blair whispered. "And they never wanted to move back to Portugal?"

"I asked her if she'd ever leave. They were the only ones in their family who immigrated here," Rebecca said. "They could live comfortably back home for the price they'd get for that property. My guess is there's too much of her son's memory tied to the house. Might be hard to leave that behind."

Whitney, who had a response to everything, who had been running full tilt all afternoon, had only raised a hand to her clavicle. Blair had touched her shoulder.

"Makes you see her a bit differently, doesn't it?" Rebecca had said. Blair wondered if it was judgment she heard in Rebecca's voice—of course they have empathy for Mara, even though they don't sit and chat with her on that porch like Rebecca does. She and Whitney are the mothers, Blair thought. Rebecca can't possibly understand like they can.

Mara is gone from the fence now and Chloe is sitting on the grass, tying the flower stems together for a crown. Blair moves off of Aiden's lap and watches her, wondering if she should have gone to the fence to say hello. At the very least.

"Hey, you okay?" Whitney puts a drink in Blair's hand, but Blair can't have another. She'll dump it down the bathroom sink so Whitney doesn't see. She will find the remote for the outdoor speakers and turn down the volume of the goddamn music; the twins should be in bed. She wishes Whitney would put a bra on. She hates that she feels homesick when she's seventeen steps from her own front door. She wants Aiden out of that backyard. She wants him to fix the drain in the laundry room and then clean the grill of their barbecue and then sit with Chloe for the last of her weekend homework. She wants to see something wholesome in him again. Something to pacify her.

Blair hasn't answered Whitney's question, but Whitney doesn't seem to notice. Blair turns back to find the woman, the sparkly cheeked girlfriend, to relish a sense of dominance she feels entitled to on this turf— but first, she sees Jacob and Aiden together, and they are looking at the woman too. They watch her run her finger under the hem of her little shorts, pull the denim from the wedge between her round, firm ass cheeks. Her finger stays there, inside her shorts, for a second too long, an inch too far not to notice. Aiden turns slightly as his stance shifts, so now Blair can't read his lips, but Jacob is grinning at whatever off-color comment he's made.

Blair looks away. Something about the moment is telling her, calmly, rationally: this marriage is going to end. And then she thinks about how it would feel if Aiden was dead. About the relief she would have if he was really gone, rather than just gone from her.

27

Mara

Her front door is still propped open from the paramedics, and from the porch, she can hear the phone ringing again in the living room. There's a dullness to the daylight now, the sun getting lower. They've been calling her all day. The hospital, she assumes, or the morgue. They'll want her to make decisions and probably pay them something. She thinks about Albert's wallet, about the bank, about what to do next. They'll want her to collect his damp clothes. His watch. How long can she wait? What do they do when there's nobody to call?

She's been out here for hours, trying to decide how the aloneness feels. She doesn't notice Ben until he's right in front of her.

"How are you?" he asks, but he doesn't wait for the answer. "You're probably wondering what's going on." *With my husband's body?* she thinks. *With his soul? Do I believe in the pearly gates of heaven anymore?* But, no, he's talking about next door. About the boy. He's saying there was an accident last night. He's mentioning Rebecca being at work and something about the father on a flight from London and something else about brain surgery. He has no idea that Albert is dead. That the ambulance took him away today. That tiny fraction of time can be erased in one rub with the end of a pencil. Mara only nods. She's thinking of how small her kitchen felt with the stretcher in there, like a dollhouse. And then it's like Ben is floating away, off her porch and into his own home. She can't remember what she said to him.

That poor child.

And then she realizes she forgot to check the backyard this morning for the paper airplanes, although they might be damp from the wet ground last night. She must not forget to look. They're important to her.

She holds her hands in front of her. They're trembling.

She wants to be downstairs, in the basement. In Marcus's old bedroom.

She pulls the cord on the bedside lamp. He'd always left it on at night, although she'd tell him to turn it off for the sake of the electric bill. But she'd liked to come down once he'd dozed off, to study his face when he slept. Sometimes she sleeps here when she's restless at night and thinking in circles about him. She imagines how it would feel to see sixty-one years on his face beside her.

She'd set up this room in the basement for Marcus when he turned thirteen. She'd hoped some physical distance in the house from Albert would help him feel less anxious. Albert never even saw the room. He only stomped around above, his footsteps like a drumbeat that raised her son's heart rate while he read comic books under the covers. The airplane models are still on the dresser, sky-blue paint on the walls. She never cleaned out the dresser drawers. In the closet is a box with his favorite things, some trinkets, a rubber-band ball, a Hardy Boys book. *The Great Airport Mystery.* There was a die-cast airplane in the box for years, but that was the only thing she gave away.

He had loved airplanes as a child and asked Mara every day when he'd get to go on one himself. When he was ten years old, Mara decided they would fly back home, even though the cost was stupidly expensive. The possibility had sat with her for years, but if they were going to spend that kind of money, she wanted to make sure he was old enough to remember it. She decided to tell Albert rather than ask him. Their parents were getting older, and his mother was ill with a cancer that would never go away, so she knew he'd reluctantly agree.

She left the invoice from the travel agency on the kitchen table one evening, next to his warm plate of glazed ham, with a number to call the agent in the morning about the payment. He folded the invoice and put it in his back pocket and said he would take care of it.

Mara filled an entire suitcase with gifts for their families. She had a nice sport jacket made for Albert by the tailor down the street, knowing he'd want to look sharp for his family. But he wouldn't even try it on. She could sense his reluctance about the trip, and knew it had nothing to do with the cost of the flights. It should have been easy for him to describe their son's difference to other people: he's just like other children his age, but he doesn't speak to anyone except his mother. He has anxiety. There was nothing wrong with him, nothing to fix or heal or hide.

She'd once overheard Albert use the word "slow" when speaking quietly on the phone to his older sister. She wasn't sure if he came up with that himself or if someone else had put the word in his mouth, but either way it wasn't accurate at all. That word described traffic at rush hour, not her sensitive, perceptive boy. Nobody could hear the things he whispered to her, so they didn't know about him at all. They had no idea.

But Mara didn't care what Albert thought of Marcus anymore. She didn't care what anyone thought of him. She couldn't wait to take him on an airplane. He had never anticipated something with so much excitement before, and she loved seeing this part of him come alive.

The Saturday morning of the flight she woke up early to wash and set her hair in curlers. She wrapped a small gift she'd bought her son for the trip: his own small die-cast airplane that said American Airlines across the side. He would love it. She put it next to his cereal bowl and dressed herself while Albert slept. At nearly nine o'clock, she shook Albert's shoulder and said it was time for him to get up and shave; that their taxi would be there in half an hour, that he hadn't even packed his things yet, that she was about to wake their son for breakfast. He had rolled over and told her to close the curtains.

"But we've got to be at the airport by—"

As soon as those words left her mouth, she knew they were not getting on the airplane. She wasn't even sure he had the tickets. He had changed his mind. He couldn't go through with the trip home.

When he got out of bed an hour later, she was drinking her coffee, waiting for him at the kitchen table. Their son was in the other room, playing with his airplane, sulking. He'd cried when she told him the trip was canceled, asked if it was a problem with the jet engines, because he couldn't fathom any other reason they were no longer getting on that plane.

"You call them all, Albert," she hissed. "You tell them why we aren't coming anymore."

He didn't even lie to her. Didn't give her the decency of an excuse.

Later that evening, he stumbled through the front door when he came home, his elbow gone straight through the window screen. She didn't ask where he'd been. She'd never seen him so drunk. Marcus was in the living room doing a puzzle on the floor. She stood up to go to him, to move him into his bedroom where she could shut the door. She had a feeling. But Albert held her back with his arm, walked ahead of her.

He slurred vicious words in their son's face, his angry, red nose pressing into Marcus's soft cheek, his stinky spit wetting his thin neck. Words she never wanted to hear again for as long as she lived. Words she had no choice but to convince herself had never been said at all.

She hurried him to his bedroom and then held him as tight as she could to stop him from shaking. Albert followed them, filling the doorway. She covered her son's ears and begged her husband to leave.

"Look at you two, like little girls whispering in each other's ear all day. You've made him this way, Mara. You've ruined him."

The next morning, her son wouldn't speak to her at all. She put her ear to his mouth, rubbed his back, coaxed him to say what he wanted for his breakfast. "He's gone for the day, it's just you and me. Tell Mommy, are you okay?"

But she knew he wasn't okay, not anymore. She had not let herself think of the possibility that this day would come. She knew then that she had heard him speak for the last time. He only shook his head. He whispered not one soft word to her, not ever again.

28

Whitney

She's called Jacob three times as she's driven home from work, the rain letting up. She knows he'll still be awake, but he's not answering. She pulls into her driveway. Her hand is about to open the car door when she looks in the rearview mirror and sees Blair toss a bag of kitchen garbage into the can at the side of her house. But she doesn't look up, doesn't notice the red glowing taillights on Whitney's car.

Tonight, she's relieved Blair doesn't spot her before she turns back into the house. She has too much on her mind. The new business pitch tomorrow morning. The school's concerns about Xavier. But Blair has left the front door open, she must be getting the recycling bag from the kitchen. Whitney waits.

Time with Blair is normally a welcome reprieve. Blair is grounding. She is like warm milk. She helps Whitney meet the quotient of hours she must spend thinking like a mother. But sometimes, being with her makes Whitney unspeakably envious. This way Blair has about her. How Chloe is so effortless to enjoy, their love synergistic. Sometimes Xavier feels to her like a gift given by someone who should know her better; something meant for her that feels nothing like her. Her heart hurts in that same way sometimes, of being misunderstood.

In the driveway, she cuts the engine and watches Blair's house in the rearview mirror, waiting for her to finish with the garbage and go back in. She thinks of the conversation they had last week. About Aiden and how little they see each other lately. Blair tends to cast the topic of her marriage like bait, wanting to talk about it—but not really. A futile exercise. But Whitney usually complies so that Blair doesn't suspect anything.

She knows Blair speaks in half-truths, testing how uncomfortable it feels to share the problems in her marriage, before she inevitably retreats. This seems to satisfy her on some level, the proximity of being almost candid with Whitney without having something to regret. She wants them to be confidantes. But she doesn't really want Whitney to *see* her.

The front door opens wider and Blair's back with the recycling. She flips the lid and pushes the bags down to make room. Whitney is careful to be still so the motion lights don't come on.

Blair has changed over the four years they've known each other. They've grown close in a short time, closer than Whitney has been to any friend since college, closer than the circle of well-dressed women she connects with professionally. And she has no contact anymore with the moms from school, not since September. But in those four years, she has felt Blair shrink. She sees the way Blair looks around her well-appointed home, the way she hungrily consumes the exchanges Whitney and Jacob have. And if Whitney is being honest with herself, this power dynamic between them is something she doesn't want to lose. She has the upper hand in their friendship, like most parts of her life. Although she isn't proud to need it, she does.

A different friend might push Blair to be confessional. *Are you sure there's nothing on your mind? Everything okay with Aiden?* A different friend might put a hand on Blair's knee, insist that she can tell her anything. Say that all of them—women of their age—have moments of realizing they no longer want what they used to, but now it's too late. Whether they admit to it or not.

But Whitney doesn't have the space for that kind of obligation in the tight operation of her life.

And there are other perilous matters.

Matters Whitney, herself, has complicated.

She shifts in her seat. She calls Jacob again. Voice mail. She texts him. She wants him to know that she's home. She wants to end on a better note. Reassure him.

Blair pushes on the lid a few more times. The front door closes firmly behind her, and Whitney is safe.

In the foyer, she hangs her trench coat and listens for where the children and Louisa are. They are late getting ready for bed, especially the twins. She wants quiet, she wants space to think. She wants tired children in pajamas. But it's only seconds until they surround her, there are hands on her leg and clumps of clay in her face and reports of hurt knees that look perfectly fine. Louisa calls the children back, but they don't want to hear Louisa tonight, they want Whitney to give herself over to them, to say things like "Wow, good for you!" and "You're so brave!" and "Yes, it looks just like a tetradactyl!" But Whitney is thinking about what an empty house would feel like. About the meeting in the morning. About her plans later that evening. She should cancel. She should.

Xavier comes in the kitchen with his socks slid halfway off his dragging feet.

"Those socks are filthy. Please take them off."

He ignores her. She bends to pull them but he won't lift his feet, and when she grips his ankle, he makes a noise like an animal, a whimper, like he is wounded. She yanks the socks from him. There's a hole in one of the toes and she throws them into the garbage.

"What are you doing? Those are my socks!"

Her chest grows tight. "How was school?"

"Did you know your phone's cracked?"

She takes it from his hand, and sees her last message to Jacob is marked as read. But he hasn't responded. He hasn't called. She flips it over on the counter. She peels the cellophane off the plate Louisa has saved for her. The twins are in her periphery, on the white carpet in the adjacent living room, where they aren't supposed to be with blue clay in their hands.

"Did anything happen today at school that you want to talk about?"

He picks up her phone again, he digs his nail into the crack. "Can we play chess before bed?"

She wonders where Louisa is. "Not tonight, sorry."

"Please?"

"Xavier. It's late."

"When's Dad coming home? I miss Dad."

"Not for two more days."

"Fine, then Lou will play chess with me."

"I said it's late. You've got to get ready for bed."

"But *she* said she wants to play chess with me."

"Xavier."

"But she said she really, really wanted to."

"She's being polite."

"No, she isn't."

"*Yes*, she is."

"At least she's nice to me."

"And so am I. But it's late."

"No, you aren't. You aren't nice to me." His voice curls. She looks up and sees he's trying not to cry. "You don't like me very much."

She would have rather he'd yelled, thoughtlessly, that he hated her. She would have rather he threw a tantrum like he was three years old. It is the softness in his face when he said the words—*You don't like me very much*—that makes her stomach tighten. She thinks of the phone conversation with the teacher. Of how a child is forever changed by the way they're treated.

"Xavi, honey, come here." She puts a hand behind his head to pull him into her chest.

But then his palms push into her stomach, he is shoving her. He is shoving her away from him and into the handle on the fridge. And then he turns and sweeps his arm across the kitchen island. The glass fruit bowl wobbles across the floor and the oranges roll like marbles. He kicks a banana and mush bleeds from the split in the peel. He stomps his bare foot in it and flings a glob onto her pant leg.

Whitney reaches out to grab him, the instinct as flammable as gas. He ducks away from her. "Get over here NOW!" She lunges for his arm, but he's too quick for her, and now he's on the other side of the island. She feels her temper rise in her throat. "I am WARNING YOU!"

But Sebastian is at her feet now, there is fear in his crying, and he wraps himself around the leg splotched with banana. She picks him up and holds him tight against her thumping heart. She smooths his hair. She kisses him.

"I don't like when you yell at Zags," he whines into her ear, an assault of wet breath. "Daddy said no more yelling."

Xavier glares at her and then he leaves the kitchen, calling for Louisa. Who will have heard it all from the next room, thinking of how Whitney has only just come home, she hasn't been with them for hours on end, she hasn't earned the right to feel suffocated by their very presence. Thea wails for Whitney from the floor where she's now splayed.

The resentment tightens behind her shoulder blades, it moves up and wraps around her neck. She can't be with the children. She can't do this tonight. She puts her son down on the floor, but he clings to her, every limb and finger a tenterhook. She unlatches him as he cries. Thea calls for her again as she leaves. She walks up to her room with her laptop, away from them all.

29

Blair

Aiden slips his head into Chloe's room as Blair is reading the bedtime story.

"I'm going out for a bit, okay?"

She looks back to the page. Everything inside her heightens, like
there's a threat in the room instead of her husband.

"Where are you going, Daddy?"

"Just out to see some guys from work, sweetheart. It was my friend
Lin's last day today."

She settles back into the nook of Blair's arm. She waits for Blair to
read, but Blair can't. How could he socialize on a night like this, when
their friends' child is in the ICU? She thinks of the shower he just took,
the aftershave she can smell. Perhaps he won't be socializing at all. She
wonders if Jacob has arrived at the hospital yet. Or if Whitney is alone,
waiting for Aiden to meet her there.

She feels insane. Or is this a whisper, speaking to her? She imagines herself looking back on this moment with the shame of idiocy.

He doesn't step out of Chloe's doorway. He is waiting for her to say, *Have fun. You won't be too late, will you?* But she can only formulate the words that are in front of her on the page, until he interrupts:

"You'll be all right? I'm sorry, the timing's bad given . . ." He nods his chin down to Chloe. "Just call me if you get any updates, okay?"

She stares at the book.

After they hear the front door close, Chloe looks up at her. "Are you mad at Daddy?"

"Mad? Of course not. Why?"

"You're always mad at Daddy. You don't love him anymore."

Blair feigns surprise with a wide-open mouth. "Chloe! That is not true at all, and you know that. I love Daddy very much. He's my favorite person, besides you."

Chloe looks away from her, back to the page. "Okay. If you say so."

"Baby. Everything is absolutely fine. Please, don't worry."

But there is skepticism in Chloe's small face. She knows. And Blair has just told her that she is wrong. That her intuition isn't valid, not when it's uncomfortable. No, darling, we pretend. This is how the life of a woman looks.

Blair swallows and finds her place on the page.

These decisions she has made—this marriage, this daughter, this life—she has made them just like everyone else does. With promise. With the belief that she was a different kind of woman than her mother. That she would be happy enough.

When Blair was eleven years old, she'd gone to her grandparents' house with her father one Saturday in the summer. Her mother hadn't wanted to come with them, but Blair hadn't minded; she liked when she and her father went places just the two of them. When they left home, her mother was in the kitchen, pulling the elements off the stove and soaking them in the sink. Blair noticed her wiping her eyes with her sleeve, her hands in yellow rubber gloves that were supposed to smell like lemon. The black marks on her shirt could have been from the charcoal caked under the coils. Or maybe she was crying. Blair hurried past her and called good-bye from the front door.

Not far from her grandparents' small bungalow, on the way home, her father stopped the station wagon outside an apartment building that had only three floors and bricks the color of hot mustard. A woman shouted through a small square window that she'd be down in a minute. Her father left the ignition running and said not to touch anything. The woman opened the door to the building, and then he was gone.

Blair bit all her nails, waiting for him. She unbuckled and lay down across the hot vinyl back seat and pretended she was naked in the cabin of a sailboat. With Ian Mackenzie from school, who seemed to have the superhuman ability to see straight through her. She pressed her hand between her legs and squeezed herself over her underwear.

The whole car shook when her father flung himself back in. He pulled out the cigarette lighter and blew smoke at his face in the rearview mirror.

"Come sit up front if you want."

He never let her ride up front. He smelled like her auntie's hair spray, but it wasn't her auntie's apartment.

A half hour later she had to pee, but she didn't want to ask him to stop for a bathroom. He hadn't said anything after they pulled out of the apartment parking lot, but then:

"Your mother, she's a good woman. You know that, don't you?" His voice was different. She had to watch his lips move to make sure the words were coming from him. "She puts up with a lot. A lot more than she should."

He sniffled. And so she sniffled, too, to make it seem like it wasn't a big deal. Like people sniffled all the time. Like she hadn't even noticed he was crying.

She was hot, too hot, and rolled down the window. She wanted to be home with her mother. The good woman. She wanted to be eating grilled cheese at the kitchen table, while her mother made a casserole and listened to a rerun of *The Young and the Restless* blare from the other room. She wanted to lie on the carpet in the spare bedroom and watch her mother's right foot work the pedal of the sewing machine under the desk.

But when they got there, being near her mother didn't feel like she wanted it to. She didn't feel like being nice to her. She didn't want the smell of that other woman's hair spray in her nose.

"Why didn't you come today? To Grandma's house?" she'd asked her.

Her mother sighed. She'd slammed the oven closed. "Oh, I don't know."

She'd turned her back. She'd placed the oven mitts on the laminate counter and she just stood there until they heard the toilet flush from down the hall. Blair's father came into the kitchen, buckling his belt. He put his mouth to her mother's neck and held her shoulders firmly. Sweet darling pie, he always called her mother, although she hated pie. She hated anything too sweet. He said dinner smelled good. He said he was hungry. Blair watched her mother stiffen. She watched her head turn to the side, away from him, and slowly close her eyes.

The good woman.

30

Whitney

The Hospital

It is a younger Jacob who is trying to stop the smoke alarm from beeping in her dream. He is teetering on the leg of a chair in the kitchen of their first home, like a circus act, fiddling with the buttons overhead to make the noise stop before the baby wakes up too soon from his nap. She is hissing for him to hurry up. She still has so much to do. So much to finish before the child is lying on her again, sucking from her, testing her. She rattles the chair he stands on. She smells toothpaste.

And then she's awake.

She opens her eyes in the hospital chair and sees there's no rim of light around the window blind she's staring at. It must be evening. There's a nurse cleaning Xavier's mouth with a mint-green sponge, and another changing the vial of medication on his beeping IV machine. Or machines. There could be three, there could be ten, there could be fifty.

She won't look at them. She pretends the nurse is not there and studies Xavier's hand again instead. His skin is hot from the fluids coursing into his vein. There's a brown bandage across the tiny tube, and the smell reminds her of the ones she'd been given as a child at school, the tackiness on her skin sticking for weeks.

He'd been right Wednesday night, before he whipped the fruit bowl across the kitchen. She hadn't liked him sometimes. Sometimes she's wished he was a different kind of child. It's hard to say exactly how, or what about him she wanted to change, or when she began to feel this way. But he had known.

There is a coat on the chair across from her that was not there before. She realizes it's her husband's coat. He's here.

She puts her head between her legs. Someone places a plastic kidney tray below her face and she spits stomach acid for a few minutes until she finally heaves. Nothing comes out. She is brought a wet cloth for her chin that smells like antiseptic.

She feels Jacob come into the room and she closes her eyes as he touches the back of her neck. She has failed him, she thinks. She always knew she would.

"You're awake."

But she's so tired. She lifts her head, and suspended in the familiarity of his voice, it feels for the first time as though she might survive this. But the feeling is gone just as soon as it comes. She waits for him to berate her. To smash something into her head, like she deserves. To kick her skull. So that it splits, blood dripping down her forehead, between her eyes, a river along the bridge of her nose. She wants him to be violent with her, just once. She wants to feel what it's like.

She begs him silently.

But of course, he would never hurt her. He adores her. He needs her. He is careful when he wraps his arms around her, like she is the delicate one on the brink of death, and not their son. And yes, maybe she is. His breath is warm on her neck and smells of coffee, and then her neck is wet with his mucus and tears, and she can feel the shake of his chest on her back. She lifts one hand to feel his hair and she thinks she can smell the stagnant air of the plane in his shirt.

When Jacob stops crying, he walks slowly to the other chair and takes a seat across from her. His wedding band clinks on the rail of the bed as he reaches for Xavier's other hand, and the noise rattles her— she looks at her own finger, bare where the diamonds he gave her thirteen years ago should catch the lights of the machines against the boy's pale skin.

She always sleeps with her rings on. But she had taken them off on Wednesday evening.

There had not been a second to think of something so obvious before she left for the hospital to see if her son was alive.

She is wondering if her husband will notice.

She is wondering if he's thinking about the bedroom window. If there has been even a fraction of a moment when he believed it was something as innocent as an unlocked pane of glass, a restless and sleepless boy, the complete misfortune of a freak accident.

He has asked her to stop yelling so much. He has said to her before, *Whitney, do you ever hear yourself? Do you know what that's like for the kids?* But he is more precious with her than he should be, like he's the only one who can see how delicate she really is. How close she comes to being pushed just a little too far.

She is wondering what her husband will ask her, what he might accuse her of, but he speaks at that very moment: "I'm sorry." His head hangs, his chin tucked into his chest like he wants to disappear inside himself too. "I keep thinking that if I'd been there . . ."

If he'd been there, nothing would have happened. Xavier would have been safe. He doesn't mean this exactly. But it is a fact that she was there, and he was not. And it is a fact that their son is fading away in a hospital bed. That the end is hours away, not months, not decades.

She thinks of what Xavier wrote on the wall.

She thinks of what happened right before her son fell from the window.

This is when she starts heaving again.

31

Rebecca

She isn't herself with the last few patients she sees. Her energy is low. Everything feels off.

"I'm sorry, can you tell me again what medications she takes?"

"Can you walk me through his past medical history once more?"

It is Xavier, it is Whitney, it is Blair who had left so upset, but mostly it's the conversation she will have with Ben when she gets home. She could wait, put it off another few days yet again. But there is, she knows, something about tragedy that can change a person's perspective on things. Maybe in the midst of a crisis, he'll find it within himself to forgive what she's done. She's more than eighteen weeks along. Only six weeks away from the baby being viable enough that a doctor would fight to save it. There is finally a reason to feel hope. And even gratitude. Their neighbors, she will remind him, are praying for their child to live.

She buys a pair of slippers from the gift shop before it closes for the night. Dr. Menlo, who is overseeing Xavier's case, is leaving his room as she arrives to give them to Whitney. The doctor tells Rebecca she's concerned about the depth of the coma. That the damage to his brain might be worse than they'd originally thought. The chances of recovery lessen by the hour, without some kind of positive indication. They'll wait overnight to see if things improve, and then they'll likely need to move forward with the surgery.

Rebecca knocks on the door to his room. She and Jacob hug.

"I'm so sorry. I'm so, so, sorry," she says.

Jacob says his head is spinning. He's thought of another question for Dr. Menlo. He asks Rebecca to sit with Whitney while he leaves to find her.

Whitney hasn't moved from where she first sat that morning. Rebecca puts the slippers on the floor near her feet and lowers herself into the chair on the other side of Xavier. She thinks of that gap the doctor had spoken of when she was a resident, the space between expectations and reality. That gap becomes tighter and tighter when all a parent can do is wait. Soon, there will be no room for hope at all.

The IV machine begins to beep, the antibiotic is finished. Rebecca silences the machine and feels fluttering in her abdomen again. "I'm pregnant."

She doesn't want to say this to a mother who is losing her child, but the words come out before she can stop them. The admission is an exchange of vulnerabilities. She's been privy to so much intimacy in that room.

"I went for bloodwork the other day, and the nurse who was filling out my form asked how many times I've been pregnant. I held up a hand. Five fingers. Five." Rebecca pauses. She leans forward, her eyes on Xavier. "And then she asked how many children I had. I watched her write the zero in the box and I thought, Wow. There it is right there, like a final score. Five-nothing."

She watches Whitney knead her son's knuckles like clay.

"People love to say there are so many ways to be a mother. Like it's some kind of consolation for women like me." Rebecca stands. She touches Xavier's foot under the blanket. "You asked me that question earlier, about why I haven't had a baby. I just wanted you to know."

She hears Whitney inhale, long and steady, and then: "Rebecca?" Whitney pauses and finally lifts her face. "I'm sorry."

It's the only time in three years that someone has said this, and only this—I'm sorry. Without advice, without platitudes, and she doesn't expect the simplicity of this validation to move her like it does. She clears her throat and gestures to Xavier. "I hope things go okay overnight. I'll call to check in tomorrow."

Jacob comes back to the room and motions for Rebecca to step outside. He asks if she'll walk to the cafeteria with him to get Whitney something she might finally eat.

On the way downstairs, Rebecca reiterates what she knows Dr. Menlo has already told him, and nothing more. Jacob seems to understand but wants to hear it all again from her. He asks her to repeat herself, like nothing is sticking. He touches the frame of his glasses, he is thinking, he is asking her questions about outcome probabilities that she doesn't feel comfortable answering for him. He orders a bagel for Whitney and a coffee for himself, and they sit on a bench in the atrium.

"He's not a heavy sleeper. He wakes up sometimes. We found him sleepwalking once when he was five or six."

He is trying to reason through the unreasonable. Rebecca watches the atrium begin to clear, staff going home to their families. Parents in slippers, with no appetites, wandering to the cafeteria where they'll stare at the options and go back upstairs empty-handed.

"They asked me a couple of questions as soon as I got here," he says, dazed. "About Xavier. And how the window opens." He gestures with his hand, like he's unlatching, trying to remind himself. "There was a woman from social work there too. She said it was just protocol. That she needs to make sure there's no reason to feel concern for Xavier's safety in our home." His finger pecks at the plastic lid of coffee. "Even the suggestion of that, about my wife. It makes me feel sick. Of course he was safe with her. With us."

"Of course," Rebecca repeats. Maybe he's only thinking about the window, how high it is from the ground, about the lock they never put on.

"So what now, we're going to be flagged in some system forever? Is that how it works? I mean, the injuries should show that he just lost balance and fell, maybe things were slippery from the rain yesterday. They can see the impact to his skull and measure the height and all of that, right? Doctors should be able to tell that kind of thing, it's a matter of physics. They have no reason to question anything. And I told them that. We're a good family, good people."

Rebecca nods. She wonders if he's thought through the scenarios of Xavier waking up and remembering what happened. There can be short-term memory issues with a head injury and loss of oxygen—but it can come back. Jacob is staring at the floor. His mouth opens. He wants to say something else, but he's hesitating. She should coax him: *Jacob, if you have anything you need to share about what might have happened, I'm here for you.* She swallows, clears her throat. But he lifts the brown bag apathetically.

"I should get back to the room, I guess. Try to get her to eat this. She still won't leave his side, she refuses. I don't even know if she's used the washroom yet."

They move into the flow of foot traffic and Jacob is quiet. She presses the button for him at the elevator. "How are the twins?"

"I told them we were taking Xavier on a trip for a few days. I asked Louisa to take them to her apartment until the weekend. I wondered if the police might show up at the house, I had this vision of yellow caution tape—" Jacob stops himself. He turns away from Rebecca, looks in the other direction. "I keep torturing myself, rehearsing what I'll say if we have to tell them Zags is gone, if things . . ."

"Focus on one hour at a time," she says, touching his arm. "If there's anything Ben and I can do to help you, just say."

She's uneasy, watching him go up the glass elevator. His assumption of a crime scene. But he's in shock, he's not thinking straight. And neither is she. She wants to go home. To Ben. He'd texted her while she was sitting with Whitney. He wanted to know if there were any updates. She calls him as she walks back to the ER to get her things.

"There's a lot of swelling. But there's not much they'll do tonight. It's a waiting game right now, but I don't know . . ."

"God."

She swipes her badge. "Jacob's here now. He got on a flight out of Heathrow earlier today."

"And Whitney?"

"She won't talk or eat. Won't leave Xavier for a second. I mean, she found him unconscious in the backyard. She's traumatized."

She'll see him soon, she says. She thinks about what Blair said earlier that day, about Ben playing catch with Xavier. He avoids any reference to children around her, not wanting to remind her about how much he'd like a son of his own to spend time with. Of everything he's giving up, being married to her.

She has to tell him tonight.

As she's pushing through the double doors, saying good-bye to the nurse at admissions, unclipping her pager to clear the messages, she thinks again of Whitney's despondency. It's pulling at her. And then, like a smack, she understands it, she can see it: a pane of freshly shattered glass, the millions of tiny shards not yet fallen to the floor, and it's so familiar to her, this place where Whitney is, of desperately holding on before the inevitable.

32

Rebecca

She lifts her head from the steering wheel and Ben is there, in the yellow light of the streetlamp, looking into the car window, always dusty from the underground parking lot at the hospital. He smiles. She is home, and she has the next forty-eight hours off, and he doesn't know what she is about to tell him. He opens the door and lifts her into him.

"You okay?"

She nods. In the kitchen, she sees he's made her a late dinner, but she doesn't feel like eating. She takes a shower instead and lets the water run as hot as it can get before she steps in. She is barely wet when she hears his knock, feels the steam in the air move toward the opening door. His blurred shape moves on the other side of the foggy glass.

"Can I join you in there?"

"I'll only be a minute." She turns her back to the glass.

"You must be beat."

The adrenaline races through her. She can't have him see the change in her nipples, the obviousness of her shape.

"I told Mara about what happened. She'd been out there on her porch all day."

"Did you ask if she heard anything last night?"

"She seemed shocked. She didn't know a thing," he says. She watches his shape come closer to the shower. She turns.

"What do you think the chances are that he'll be okay?"

"Well, they've got to see some progress soon, or the odds are he won't fully recover." She doesn't soften the truth with platitudes like someone else might. But anything can happen. But children are resilient. But the miracles we see in pediatrics. "The authorities interviewed them, apparently."

"The police?"

"Routine stuff. They mostly just need to know if the child dies. Because if so, they've got to treat it differently . . ." She rinses her hair, her back still turned. She looks down at her body, wondering what he'd say if he saw her right now. If she stepped out, brought his hand to her warm, wet belly and held it there. If he could hide the longing she knows is still in him. Hidden, because of her. "Blair said something today about you and Xavier playing catch."

"Once or twice, yeah."

She turns off the water. Blair had made it sound like a regular thing, but most people are like that, they speak in ideas instead of facts. She needs a towel to wrap herself in. But he'll expect her to come out like she usually does, dry off while they talk, lotion her body. Towel-dry her hair.

She holds out a hand. The other grips the shower door, holds it tight. She wonders if he'll tease . . . *Why so shy today?* She keeps speaking. The games of catch. "Did you think it would hurt my feelings, you spending time like that with a little boy?"

He is quiet. And then:

"He wanted to try out for the softball team, so I was giving him some pointers. He never came to tryouts in the end, I think he knew he wasn't ready. I felt bad, but it would have been even worse to cut him. Anyway." He sighs. "It was nothing."

She keeps the tiny baseball glove at the back of her closet. She had gone to the store where Blair works, minutes before it closed one day, to get a baby gift for a nurse. Her arms had been full of practical things, sleepers and swaddle blankets, when she saw a basket of little gloves, each with a soft baseball stitched in the center. She had taken the pregnancy test the day before. She hadn't thought of a way to tell Ben until then. Blair wrapped it carefully in tissue with the rest of the gift, but then Rebecca pulled it out of the bag when she got home and placed it on Ben's pillow. Later that night, she let him go up to bed first. He had picked up the glove and looked at her.

For real? He'd pulled her down and they'd laughed in a way they have not since. It was only three years ago, but in her mind, they were teenagers. Ripe and high and horny.

He's gone from the bathroom when she comes out of the shower.

33

Rebecca

S he tosses for an hour before she quietly gets out of bed, careful not to wake Ben. It's 3:00 a.m. The house is too warm. Downstairs she turns the dial on the thermostat and pours a glass of water in the dark. Xavier is on her mind. She lifts Ben's jacket from the hook at the front door and slips her feet into his running shoes.

Jacob's car is in the driveway now. She wraps herself in the coat and walks briskly across the street to the side of the Loverlys' property, Ben's shoelaces dragging. She lifts the latch on the gate and cringes at the click of the metal. The gate is heavier than she expects, and she reaches to catch it before it bangs against the fence.

She moves slowly along the side of the house into the backyard.

She isn't sure what she has come for, why she is trespassing like this. It feels more intrusive than she expected. The moon is covered by clouds tonight, and her eyes cross over the dark lawn. She turns on her phone's flashlight to scan the grass, as though she might find an imprint of

Xavier's body in the blades. There are faint lines that run like tracks where she is standing, wheels, maybe, from the ambulance stretcher. There's a soccer ball against the fence. A mini orange pylon. A wet paper airplane on the lawn. And on the concrete patio, just outside the back door, a stemless glass tipped on its side.

She picks it up and lifts it to her nose, certain of what she'll smell.

She takes a few steps back and looks up to the third story, to the bedroom window. She keeps her sightline there and shifts slightly to the right, to be where she thinks Xavier would have landed. The height is staggering from where she stands.

Does a ten-year-old have any concept of what his body can survive? Does he have the capacity to understand what his physical self is and isn't capable of? Does any of them? How can the human physical form create another life, regenerate tens of millions of its own cells in seconds, and yet be so precariously fragile? How has she spent decades going about her day, her work, not letting this discrepancy consume her, like it does now?

She lowers her chin, stares into the glass doors to the dark kitchen. She can see her own muted reflection, her hands clutched now at her chest, the jacket billowing gently. Her eyes lower to where life is growing inside her. She feels some kind of connection to Whitney. Maybe it's something maternal. Why has she been drawn there?

She hears voices on the street and then the close of a car door before it pulls away. She leaves the backyard with the jacket hood pulled up and her head held low. She sees the front door to Blair's house shut and a light come on. In the space between the curtains, she watches Aiden move through the family room. He's looking at his phone, his thumbs typing. He takes his shirt off and falls onto the couch.

Upstairs in her own home, she senses Ben is awake when she walks into the bedroom. She slips into the sheets, pulls herself close to him.

"I heard the front door," he says.

"I went across the street, to their backyard. To see where he fell."

She waits for him to ask why, but he is quiet.

"I think he might have been trying to hurt himself. Maybe to prove a point. Or maybe he didn't want to live anymore. I don't think it was a freak accident." She sits with the realization as she's saying it. An intuition. She slips her hand over her belly under the blanket. "I have no evidence, nothing to go on, and you know that's not like me. But there's this feeling I get in the room with her and Xavier. This . . . profound sadness about her, like there's something she can't bring herself to say. More than a sense of guilt, or regret." She rubs her forehead and feels exhausted now. "I don't know if I'm making any sense."

He turns onto his back, and so does she. She finds his hand and kisses his knuckles. He moves himself on top of her and puts his mouth to her neck, he tastes her, sucks on her cold skin. He's hard against her already. They haven't wanted each other like this in a long time, not through the years of calendars, and tests, and blood.

Tonight, something has changed. She lets him take her, her body hidden in the dark. She starts to get out of her cycling mind, but then she is thinking again of the grass where Xavier would have lain. The tremble of Whitney's hand in hers. Her broken uterus. Her lies. The one hundred and thirty days that tomorrow will mark. The feeling of blood between her legs. He is inside her now, he is filling her. She thinks of the wands they probe her with at the clinic, of how far they jam them inside her. The pain that makes her arch her back on the exam table, the whimpers she must stifle. She feels wetness then, real wetness, and the panic is back. But his hands have pinned her shoulders down and she can hear air hiss through his clenched teeth. She catches her breath every time he shoves himself into her, so much harder than he ever has before. Like he's angry. She can think only of his penis smeared in her blood, of the sheets soaked in red beneath them. Of what the sight of this will do to her.

She puts her hands on his chest and shoves him away. He slips out of her.

"You okay?" He is trying to slow his breath.

She flinches as his sweat drops on her face.

Her hand feels the stickiness on the inside of her thighs, and she lifts her fingers to her nose in the dark, searching for the familiar metallic scent. She feels him lie down beside her.

She is all right. She is fine. There's no blood. She rolls toward him, and they find each other's hands and hold tightly. Her mind had been elsewhere, but so was his.

She must believe they will be okay.

He turns on his side, she moves her body close. She wants to feel the warmth of his back against her growing middle, to believe in what they are becoming.

34

Whitney

Whitney sits at her desk and reads Xavier's October progress report from school. Louisa found it in his backpack and texted her a photo.

Below average. Below average. Below average. Nearly every line of the report. Needs significant help to complete. Needs daily reminders. Not meeting expectations. And perhaps the worst: Lacks motivation. Does not take pride in his work.

None of it is a surprise. They have hired a tutor. They have agreed to let him join the senior chess club with the older students, an opportunity to improve his confidence. He excels in math, in abstract reasoning, in pattern recognition. He struggles in everything else.

She knows this, but she feels nauseated seeing these failures on paper. She needs to be harder on him, despite what Jacob thinks. He defends him. He worries she puts Xavier down too much, that she speaks of him too critically to other people. And maybe he is right, and maybe she overstates his deficiencies because it helps her manage her own expectations of who he is. But look. Look at this report. This proof. She can feel the window closing on the time she has to mold Xavier into the child she wants him to be, instead of the child he is.

She is about to leave when Grace slips in and asks if she's seen the email. She has not, but she can tell by Grace's lowered voice, by the way she's clutching the side of the door, that the email is not something she will be happy to see.

And she's not. She is bcc'd and it is short and formal. The client has been fired from the telecom company. And if the client is fired, Whitney's firm will be let go next. There's a proposal for a half-million-dollar employee-engagement strategy on the client's desk that she had told Whitney she'd sign by the end of the calendar year, and Whitney had known then that the unusual delay was indicative of something. They have been the most impressive name on her client list for four years, they justify the salary of an entire account team of very good people, and she needs them.

She stares at the email and wonders who else she can call at the company, who she has a good enough rapport with. Who will likely be taking over. Maybe there's still a chance, if she can get ahead of it. She could ask for a meeting and reinforce everything they've done for them, present an amended project scope, and reduce their fees. She is looking through her emails to find the last correspondence with a director she once met at a charity dinner, a wet-mouthed, off-putting man whose name she cannot remember, when the client herself sends another email, just to her this time.

She's so sorry. She wishes it would end differently for Whitney's firm, but she has been told they'll terminate all consultancy contracts. Procurement would be in touch. Let's go for lunch after the holidays, she suggests.

Fuck. You. It is all Whitney thinks, and she says it to the screen, and she knows she should have more grace than this, she should write back to express her sympathies, tell her she'll move on to bigger and better things, thank her for the hundreds of thousands of dollars in fees. But right now, she lets the anger win.

These frustrations—the child doing terribly in school, the loss of her most lucrative client—are the excuses she will summon later, for the brief moment she feels the need.

She sends the photo of the progress report to Jacob, who is in Manhattan for the night, a gallery opening. She doesn't add any comments.

When she pulls into the driveway, she can see the children through the tall windows at the front of her home. The twins are chasing Xavier around the living room, scampering over her expensive glass table, and there is something dark, maybe a chocolate brownie, in Thea's hand. She wonders if Louisa has given up. She should go inside, let her go home early. But there is something uncomfortable growing up her spine and into her neck, and it is the anticipation of this: *Mommy, come downstairs! I'm hungry! Sebastian hit me! I need a wipe! Zags won't share!*

She cannot do it. She will sit in the driveway instead and stare at her phone. She puts the car in park, and that is when she sees a figure in her rearview mirror—it is Blair. Blair, who can make work disappear. Blair, who thinks her challenging and underperforming son is special. Blair, who will surely be up for a glass or two of wine. She turns herself on like a switch. She is out of the car, saying she'd just been thinking of her. Chloe is behind her; she is looking for Xavier.

"Go on in and find him, Chloe, they're running around with Louisa." Whitney never goes to Blair's house. But today she looks across the street and she thinks of the chaos on the other side of her own door and she says, "Do you mind if we go to your place this time?"

They open a bottle from a local winery Whitney hasn't heard of before, and it isn't chilled, but it is the only alcohol Blair has in the house. Whitney looks around the family room and can't remember when she was there last. There is something quaint and comforting about Blair's house. The slipcover sofa and matching chair. The television on an old pine bench that Blair whitewashed herself. The light cotton of the curtains, almost like children's bedsheets, so thin you can see through them.

She wanders to the shelves Blair has styled with horizontal book spines organized by color, a careful arrangement of photographs in rose-gold frames, tiny potted succulents. She picks up a photo of Chloe and Aiden and Blair, probably from last summer. Blair and Chloe have the same freckles, the same cuteness. Their heads are touching, and their hair falls so that she cannot tell where Blair's ends and where Chloe's begins. Aiden is behind them in the photograph, tanned, smiling. He looks ten, fifteen years younger than he is. There is something about him. She cannot help but think that he doesn't look like he belongs. To them, to the moment in the photo.

"I put some ice in." Blair is beside her now, handing her a glass, looking at the same photograph longer than for just a glance. She doesn't say anything. She turns back to the room, apologizes for the mess, although there isn't any. Whitney is assuring her the place looks good, the place looks great. She picks up another photograph, this one of Blair's mother and father, and tries to find her features in their noses, the contour of their faces, the way they stand, each with a hand on the neck of a horse that stares right at the camera.

"You don't talk much about your mom," Whitney says. "What's she like?"

"My mom? Let's see." She looks up to the crease where the wall meets the ceiling, as though she's never had to think about this before. "She's very simple. Likes to sew. She watches a lot of soaps."

Whitney can't help but laugh. "That's it? Oh my God, I hope my kids can come up with something better than that about me one day. What kind of woman is she? What makes her tick?"

Blair's hand is over her face now, laughing too. "Oh, she's just sort of . . . I don't know. Empty." The laughter is over. She takes a drink.

"How so?"

"Something changed in her at some point, when I was eight or nine years old, I'd say. Before then, she was lighter. Happier. We'd all have tickle parties and that sort of thing. But then eventually she and my dad stopped talking to each other and things were just . . . tense." She glances away from Whitney. "I think maybe my dad had someone—" She stops herself, shakes her head. "I don't know. Maybe not." She clears her throat and sits up. Whitney waits, but Blair looks stiff. She won't say more.

"I think my mom thought about leaving us when we were young. Leaving my dad, definitely, but also leaving us kids," Whitney says, running her finger around the rim of the wineglass. She hasn't shared this with anyone before.

"I'm so sorry."

"No, it's—sometimes I wish she *had* left, to be honest."

"But, Whit, that would have been traumatic. That would have changed your whole life."

"And it would have changed hers. Instead she barely functions now at seventy. She seems twenty years older than she is. Do you know she still lives in the same sad apartment we grew up in? She won't leave. Probably waiting for my dad to die."

"Yeah, but look who you've become. And the life you have now compared to how you grew up. I know she didn't have much, but she gave you something by staying, right? That kind of stability shapes a person for the better."

Whitney shakes her head. She doesn't want to tell Blair about how her dad used to speak to her mom. She sometimes wondered if her mom preferred him in pain and out of work, because he couldn't follow her around anymore, his mouth hissing in her ear. He could barely stand.

"No, she felt trapped, going through the motions," Whitney said. "I always knew it. She kept this bus ticket hidden in her pocket for years, like on any given day she might just go out for the groceries and keep walking straight to the terminal."

"I'll never understand wanting to leave a family like that."

"But the sacrifice of motherhood isn't for everyone, right? It changes who you are in the world. It's this irreversible decision that alters so much of you. She loved us, I know. I could feel it. But I think she daydreamed about who she could be without us weighing her down like a brick. It's not easy for everyone. Even if you think it's what you wanted."

Blair's eyebrows raise and she glances around the room. "I get that. But we go into motherhood knowing it's a selfless thing, right? We put them first, even when it's hard. We try to make the right decisions, no matter what. And then they turn out to be thriving, happy people who do good in the world. At the end of the day, that's the most important thing. That's all I want."

Are you kidding me? Whitney thinks. *Are we really going down this road?* As if wanting anything more for oneself would be excessive. As if they must satisfy the quota for selflessness, and only then, after the accommodating and the pleasing, can they be anything else.

"Of course, every mother wants their kids to be happy. I just mean, it's nearly impossible for a woman not to lose herself in the process. It's a kind of . . . voluntary death, in a way."

But Blair doesn't say anything. And then the silence feels too heavy.

"Well, in any event. Fuck. It's not for the faint of heart, is it?" Whitney takes a swig, exaggerated, wanting the tension to go away. Blair's attempt to laugh with her is throaty and insincere; she reaches for the bottle to top them up. Whitney knows she'll change the conversation now. She'll talk through their plans together for Christmas Eve, the fondue they'll have with the kids, the matching slippers she's ordered for them all.

But instead Blair is quiet. She tucks her legs under her.

"How was Chloe's report card?" Whitney knows she'll want to be asked.

"All fine," Blair says, but she's tempering. Chloe does nothing but excel. "And Xavi?"

"Not so fine. I mean, we got the tutor this year, but . . . I don't know."

"The tutoring will take some time, but it will help. He'll get there with the right support. And some patience. He's so capable. He's such a good kid."

Like she's the expert. Like Whitney needs to be convinced of her own son's potential. Like Blair could do for him what she cannot.

Whitney wants to go. She's feeling the wine now, and she's hungry, and wants to check the phone she made a point of leaving in her bag. "Well, speaking of, I should go relieve Louisa. I'll send Chloe home now."

"Yeah, Aiden should be here any minute."

They hug, and when Whitney pulls away, she keeps Blair's hand in hers.

"Everything okay?"

"Of course," Blair says after a pause.

But Whitney wonders if she should stay after all. She could tell her she understands more about Blair than she might think. That she wishes Blair had her own version of her mother's bus ticket hidden away in a pocket somewhere. An option. But Blair would never have bought the bus ticket. She would never have even considered it.

There is freedom in the truth, she thinks from the front door, watching Blair rinse their glasses over and over at the sink. And there is suffering in the lie.

Whitney leaves the house with her heels in her hand, and the pavement is cold through her nylons. She hears a car door close behind her.

"I've heard you tell your son not to be outside without shoes on."

She spins around. He is smiling.

Through the numbing of the alcohol, she can still recognize it. The moment that can go either way next. Teetering on something dishonorable, but not yet incriminating. Words, they are only an exchange of words. Seconds. Nothing to feel guilty about yet. Nothing a mother shouldn't do.

"We never had that drink, did we? We should, whenever, you know, it makes sense."

The glance at her home. At his.

That could have been it, a thing someone says and never follows through with. The proposition of it, the possibility, like the bus ticket in her mother's coat pocket.

35

Blair

It is 6:45 a.m. on the day after Xavier's accident, but he is not the first thing Blair thought of when she woke up. She slams the cupboard doors and rattles the dishes in the sink. This is a generous grace period. She's been seething for an hour. Chloe looks up from the word search she is doing at the kitchen table while she finishes her breakfast. Blair closes the next cupboard door gently.

Chloe calls to him in the family room, where he is still on the couch.

"Dad? Mom wants you to get up now."

He ambles into the kitchen and pours himself a glass of water.

"Good morning, darlings." He ruffles Chloe's hair and points to a word on the sheet. "Irate. I-R-A-T-E."

"Where?" Chloe looks closer and he grins teasingly at Blair, but she turns away from him. He comes behind her and puts a hand on her shoulder. He wants to soften her. She can smell the booze while he gets himself a coffee.

He still wasn't home when she fell asleep at two in the morning. She had texted him seven times. Where are you. It's late. Where are you. Jacob's car was at home by 11:00 p.m., so Whitney would have been alone at the hospital. She had tortured herself with speculation. She had held her head under the pillow and begged for her brain to stop spinning.

She can't do it anymore.

"Upstairs." It's all she can say to him.

She sits on the end of their bed and waits for him. He is expecting her to be the irrational wife, to spew the anger she reserves only for him. She thinks of how much to say. How far to go. She has nothing but a corner of foil packaging and a key. And hours and hours of assuming the worst. That is all she has.

There is no plan. No idea what to do next if he says, Yes. That's a key I gave her to my office, where we fuck. That's a wrapper from the condom I used. I can't keep lying to you anymore. Are we done here?

He lies on the bed next to her and puts his hand on her lower back.

"You want an apology, and I owe you one. I'm sorry I was so late."

"Where were you?"

"I should have called. We went back to Lin's house after the pub and he got the poker chips out. I didn't realize how late it got." He rubs her gently.

"You didn't answer any of my texts."

"I didn't have my phone out, I didn't see them until I left. I'm sorry."

She looks over at his hands, resting now on his chest like he might take a catnap. She thinks of who his hands have touched. Of how easy it is for some people to lie.

She walks downstairs to the living room to pick up the pants he left on the floor. She digs into each pocket. His credit cards, his car key, his phone. There is no receipt from the pub. She puts his password into his phone and scans his texts. There is nothing from the night before. Not even her own frantic messages to him. He has deleted them.

He has never deleted her messages before. Their text chain is like an appendage of their marriage. A record of their days. She is always there, at the top of his screen. The first thing he sees.

He looks asleep when she comes back into the bedroom.

"Why did you delete all my messages?"

"What are you doing?"

"Just answer me."

"I have no idea why. I just did."

"So someone else wouldn't see them?"

"They weren't exactly nice messages. The last one told me to fuck off. Do you think I wanted to keep them?"

She walks to the dresser and takes out the key. She places it in the palm of her hand and puts it close to his face.

"That's my key. Where'd you find that?"

He reaches to pick it up, but she closes her fist. There is something in his voice, a distinct patience she doesn't expect, an effort to remain calm. She warns herself again. She will not be able to rewind. She thinks of Chloe downstairs doing her word search. She can walk her to school, and then separate the laundry into piles by color. She can take the ground beef from the freezer to defrost for dinner. The day can go on, everything intact.

"Whitney had it," she says instead.

"Whitney? Why?" He's propped on his elbow now. He rubs the stubble on his face. The whites of his eyes are pink.

"You tell me."

He laughs then. He lies back down. He has mocked her concern. She is meant, now, to feel foolish.

"Maybe she found it at the gym? I thought I might have lost it there. I don't know, you're the detective. Ask her."

Her heart pounds as he tries to defuse the room. "She doesn't go to that gym anymore. Why wouldn't she just give it to you if she found it?"

"I don't know what you're getting at, Blair. Because she forgot, maybe? That's a key to the back door of my office. But it's useless now anyway, they had to change the lock because I lost it."

He leaves the bedroom and starts the shower.

She follows. She wants to run out of the house and leave him there with Chloe, with the breakfast dishes, with the empty fridge, the piles of laundry, the boredom, the routine. With the knot in her stomach that has weighed her down for weeks, since she found the corner of the condom wrapper. She wants him to feel what it's like to drown in all of it. She wants to strip him of the ease with which he walks through his life, the calmness he can so easily find. She wants to rip the shower curtain from its flimsy plastic hooks, she wants to crank the temperature to scalding hot, she wants to put her fingers in his pubic hairs and pull them all out.

She yanks back the vinyl. "Are you having an affair?"

Her entire body beats, waiting. Waiting.

36

Rebecca

She is roused in the morning by the feel of the mattress moving beside her. She has the next two days off. She waits in bed until she can smell the coffee Ben is making. Downstairs she pulls her robe closed, stands at the counter, watches him pull groceries from the fridge to make breakfast. She wonders if he's thinking of last night, of how it felt for her to shove him away. Did he feel that she was protecting something? Did he wonder?

"Ben."

He lifts his head, smiles at her. Asks how she'd like her eggs.

"I'm pregnant."

His eyes drop to the carton he's just opened.

Each second that he is quiet feels like he's backing up further and further away from her. But he is motionless. She wishes he would smash an egg. The whole carton. Tell her she is insane. Anything but the silence.

"More than eighteen weeks. The furthest we've been by five days."

She wants to tell him that she's scared too. That sometimes she feels like a monster throwing fetuses at the wall to see which one sticks, but here they are—it's working this time. She wants to tell him she's sorry, but this is what she had to do.

"You said you knew your cycle, that we didn't need condoms every time." He places his fingertips on the edge of the counter. "This wasn't—"

"I need you to want this as much as I do."

"It's not a matter of what I want." His sharpness startles her. "It's a matter of what we can survive. And you're not accepting that! You're banking on some miracle. You're not . . . you're not yourself anymore."

"There is a chance. There's hope."

The crack in her voice when she says the word "hope" makes her feel more vulnerable than she has with him in a long time. More than the hours together in waiting rooms and the nights on the cold tile floor and the blood he has helped to clean from her. She is tired of feeling resilient. Of being rational like a physician is supposed to be. Fuck the statistics she's become a part of. Fuck the chances of the outcome. Yes, it is science, it is biology, it is a matter of cells. Her body is either physically capable of sustaining a life or not. But she is also a woman who wants to feel the weight of her own writhing newborn on her bare chest. She wants to know what it feels like to be fanatically consumed. To catch herself in the gestures of her child one day and be stunned that this exquisite creature belongs to her. She feels owed that chance no matter what is rational or sane or likely.

He exhales long and steadily, and she doesn't want to be in the room with him anymore, not if he can't lift his head and say what she needs to hear. She waits.

And then she turns away, walks slowly up the stairs, into the room he painted three years ago, attentively, lovingly, as he wondered about who their child would be. She misses her, the first baby she held, although she doesn't know who she is. She doesn't know her daughter's voice or what it feels like to be seen by her. Or loved by her. She is undefined. She is ethereal. The room is empty, it is waiting, and Rebecca lies down in the middle of the hardwood floor to watch how the morning light changes the color of the walls.

37

Blair

Aiden does not open his eyes. He tilts his face up into the weak stream of their old shower head. He has had enough of her this morning. He is dismissing her. He won't even give her the dignity of denying it with his words.

"Did you hear me—"

"Yes, I heard you! And of course the answer is no. For fuck's sake, it's offensive that you're even asking." He tugs the shower curtain closed. She stares at the speckles of mildew along the edge that she hasn't been able to get out. She waits for him to say it—*Don't project your daddy issues on me. I wouldn't do what he did*. But he doesn't.

She goes to Chloe's room. She smooths and tucks the blankets on her bed, picks up her nightgown from the floor. Her chest aches and her face burns. She is tired of everything, every feeling, every thought. Of who she has become. She listens to the pipes turn off, to his wet feet slap the clean tiles of the bathroom floor. She wants him to come find her. To put an arm out for her to slip under. To deny it again and do whatever he has to do to make her feel better.

She thinks of how his hands shook when they stood at the altar. Of picking blueberries at the end of his parents' lane when Chloe was three, the purple stains on all their fingers that lasted for days. Of the humidity that fills the second floor when he showers with the door open, of how it makes the ends of all their hair curl. Of the scent of his skin seeped in their pillows, even after she's changed the cases. Of how sweet he used to make her coffee every morning, the extra sugar, too much cream. These are the unremarkable currents of a reliable life together, the life that once felt like it was enough.

She can't decide what it means to have finally confronted him. To have freed a vicious rodent from a cage, and although the threat isn't rattling in her hands anymore, it's still alive somewhere. It will come back.

She needs everything explained. Irrefutably. But she cannot, right now, ask Whitney.

"Why are you crying?"

Blair hadn't heard her footsteps. She turns away from the door so Chloe can't see her face. "Go back downstairs," she snaps.

"I was just—"

"Chloe, I need a minute! Go, please."

But Chloe does not go. She wraps herself around Blair's waist and she squeezes her. Blair thinks of the first time she thought of her mother as small. As sad. As weak.

"But why are you crying, Mommy?"

"I'm not, I'm okay. I'm fine. Let's finish the word search before school." Blair wipes her face and smiles. She tosses a rainbow-shaped pillow on the bed and pats Chloe on the bum. She pulls her hair back, wraps an elastic, and says, in the highest pitch she can muster, "All good? Let's go."

But as she jogs down, she feels Chloe pause at the top of the stairs, watching her.

A iden comes into the kitchen as Blair helps their daughter find the word HANUKKAH. She avoids his eyes as she rinses the spoon he used earlier, closes the carton of cream he left open, wipes the drops on the counter from his sloppy pour.

At the table she pulls Chloe onto her lap. They have to tell her about Xavier before she goes to school and the rumor mill begins churning. She pushes her hand into Chloe's small chest to feel it thumping and sniffs yesterday's playground sweat from the nape of her neck. She remembers her silky head in the palm of her hand, the weight of a grapefruit, all the comfort and promise a newborn life still holds. And then Chloe pulls away.

Thank God it wasn't her.

"Can you guys tell me what's going on? With Xavi?"

Aiden sits down and strokes her cheek. "Xavi had an accident," he says. "A bad fall from his bedroom window on Wednesday night. He's going to be in the hospital for a bit while he gets better."

"Oh." Chloe is quiet. She looks at Blair. "But how did he fall?"

"We aren't sure. It was late at night, so nobody knows what happened."

"Oh," she says again. She tucks her chin and stares at her lap. Blair pulls her in tightly. She didn't want to tell her. She didn't want her to worry.

"Is he going to be okay, after the doctors fix him up?"

"Of course he will, honey. Everything will be just fine, all right?" Blair kisses her head as Aiden stares at her. Blair shoots him a look to say nothing more.

"Is this why you were crying upstairs?"

Blair doesn't look at Aiden. She nods.

"Can we get him a card? And give him that old airplane he left here? It's his favorite one, so he's gonna wanna play with it at the hospital."

"You're a good friend, Chloe." Blair kisses her. "Why don't you get dressed and we'll go pick out a card at the drugstore before school? We'll have time if we leave now."

Aiden sighs audibly when she leaves the room. Blair stands to pace the kitchen.

"Hear anything more yet this morning?" he asks, with an ease that feels strange to Blair after what she's just confronted him with.

"Nothing."

She hadn't told him about Whitney's reaction at the hospital yesterday. She'd said only that she was coping as well as expected. That she'd brought her something to eat. He flips through the newspaper but doesn't take out a section like he usually would. He pushes it across the table and sips his coffee. Blair leans on the counter and watches him. Wondering.

He comes over and kisses Blair's head, puts his arm around her neck. He holds his lips there for a moment. Let's move on from that nonsense earlier, he's telling her. He can always seem to do this, forgive.

But this morning it feels different. She watches him move around her, studies the quickened rise and fall of his chest. He pours her more coffee, and then some for himself, and the silence is thick. He scratches his jawline, the jawline she can trace in her sleep. He rubs his neck, the neck she has hung from so often. There are physical parts of him that feel almost like physical parts of her, and while she can't find the attraction for him that she used to have, while she doesn't even like him most days, she feels possessive of him. That is her jawline. Her neck. Her whistling husband.

Perhaps they're just in the sagging, ambivalent middle of a marriage.

He goes upstairs to get ready for work. She waits for Chloe and looks around the kitchen, the table nobody has cleared, the pillows that are smushed on the couch from where Aiden slept.

She thinks about a night when they were early in their relationship. They were out for dinner after work. They were still finding things to talk about, stories and favorites and places they wanted to go together. She remembers thinking, as he spoke, that she didn't know what being lonely felt like anymore. She had lost the envy toward her thirtysomething friends who one by one had cocooned into their own relationships, ones they knew had a future. She had finally found that future for herself. She didn't have to fear that she'd never have the things she so desperately wanted: A child. A nice home. A nice life. She'd already established her career, and she didn't have to give that up. She came of age in the nineties, girl power, a woman's right to have everything, to be everything. And she was determined she would, unlike her mother.

When the server took their plates, Aiden had reached for her knee under the table. She'd thought of the painful wax she'd gotten the day before. The sex they would have that night. She had chosen a light meal for dinner. She reached below and took his hand, and they touched each other's nails, each other's knuckles. He had asked what she wanted to do the next day.

"Oh, I don't know. Pick up some groceries. Maybe go to yoga and then catch up on work."

"How about we look at places," he'd said.

"Places?"

"A house. Together."

He had laughed then at her delight, her surprise. He'd raised his glass in her direction, and she had lifted hers to touch his. She had felt like she'd won something. Him? A life that looked the way happy lives did? The champagne he had ordered made sense to her then. She had felt exhilarated. And in love. And then relieved. And then she made tracks with her fork in the chocolate mousse on the table between them.

She had mused aloud about neighborhoods they could afford on their combined salaries. About the number of bedrooms. He nodded along as she spoke, and when she lifted her eyes, he looked pleasantly focused on something behind her. She licked the chocolate from the bottom of the fork and held it in front of her, staring at the tines, his face unfocused in the background. She did not want to turn around to see what he was looking at. But she had. The woman looked amused, she spoke to her friend behind the cover of her hand, and then glanced up to see him again. Her eyes met Blair's instead. Blair turned back to Aiden. He cleared his throat. He dug into the last of the dessert and said to her, "So tomorrow. I've got showings booked for us at ten."

She understood in that moment something about him that she had not wanted to be true. But there are risks people take when they want something badly enough. There are things they learn to ignore. It was just a look. She loved him. He was the one, or at least the one she had chosen. She had already decided on a life with him. She had already come so far.

38

Blair

Outside, she sees Mara standing on her porch in her nightgown. Chloe waves as she scoots past, but Blair wonders why she's not dressed yet, it's unusual. She calls for Chloe to wait, and she jogs across the street, lets herself through the rusty iron gate.

"Did you and Albert hear what happened at the Loverlys'? Wednesday night?" The morning sun is in her eyes and she shields her face to see Mara.

"I did," Mara says. Blair waits for her to say more, there is always more. She follows Mara's eyes to the Loverlys' driveway. Jacob's car is there, but the curtains are drawn, the house still lifeless. Her lips look tight.

"Okay, well . . ." Blair takes a few steps backward, and for once, Mara says nothing to keep the conversation going. "We'll let you know if there's any news."

She walks fast to keep up with Chloe on her scooter, west across

Harlow Street toward the drugstore. It's the kind of spring day that makes everyone feel light and optimistic, but she can't relieve herself of the cement in her stomach. It is Xavier. But it is also the key she can't ask Whitney about. It is something in how Aiden let things go a little too quickly that morning.

She's not convinced of anything.

They stop at the light. The question comes out of her mouth before she can stop herself:

"Chloe, I need to ask you something. Have you ever seen Whitney get angry with Xavi when I wasn't there? Like, really, really angry?"

The words feel like a betrayal. Her best friend. A decision she won't be able to undo. In the swell of guilt is a shard of wanting to hear something damning about her. Something she'd be obligated to pass along.

She stares at the sidewalk as Chloe thinks.

"I don't know."

"Do you mean you don't know, or you don't want to tell me?"

Chloe bangs the rubber toe of her sneaker on the sidewalk. She thinks some more. "I've never actually seen her get mad. It was just that one time, at the party in their backyard. And the time we dropped off the cookies."

They'd gone over the day before Christmas, a tin with cookies still warm from the oven. Chloe wanted to leave it on the table in the foyer as a surprise, she'd written a note from Santa's elves and taped it to the lid. She'd taken a quiet step inside and then turned back to Blair with wide eyes. Blair heard it too. A child's screaming from somewhere, the growl of Whitney's voice. And thumping. And then slamming. And then crying.

Blair had pulled Chloe back outside, closed the door quietly, and placed the cookies on the doormat. She'd felt the same unnerving fear she had at the barbecue, privy to something far too intimate. She wanted to unhear it. At home, she'd sat on the sofa and pulled Chloe in to sit with her. She'd reminded her that sometimes grown-ups lose their patience. *But you don't do that,* Chloe had said. *You're never scary.* Blair had said something about everyone having bad days. And then she'd convinced herself of the same thing.

Now, Chloe's eyes stay on the sidewalk. Blair knows she isn't being honest. She has an intimate understanding of her daughter, every expression, every mannerism, and she knows she's hiding something. That she's doing what she thinks a good girl should do.

In the drugstore, she leaves Chloe looking through the row of get-well cards. She stares at the shelf of condoms at the back near the pharmacy counter. There are more choices than she remembers. More serums and textures and tingling jellies, a world she has no use for anymore. She imagines someone rolling the rubber taut over Aiden's dick.

She digs out the corner of the foil packaging from her pocket. One by one she opens boxes from the brand Aiden used to buy. She looks for the same shade of green, the same rippled edge, but she can only find a similar jewel tone in plum. She pulls a row of condoms from the box and holds the purple next to the ripped foil. They have identical weight and texture. The corner in her hand is the same dimension.

She could check the brand's website for their product line. She could ask someone who works there if they have other varieties in the back room. And then what? She'll be here in this place where she's been for months. Looking for more proof and then looking for more excuses.

She finds Chloe, who is reluctant to decide among the three cards she holds. She wants to leave without buying any of them. The news about Xavier is sinking in. Blair crouches to her level and takes her cheeks in her hands.

"Hey, honey, you okay? Tell me how you're feeling."

Chloe's face crumbles and Blair knows the tears will come next. "I just want to go home. I don't want to go to school today."

"I'm so sorry you're feeling upset. I understand, I really do. It's completely normal to feel this way, he's your best friend. You just want him to get better, right?"

Chloe cries into her chest and tries to stifle the noise. Blair closes her eyes. They shouldn't have told her yet, not when there is still so much unknown.

"But that's the problem. He isn't my best friend anymore." She pulls away from Blair and tries to catch her breath between sobs. "I said some mean things to him on Wednesday, at morning recess. Really, really mean things that made him cry in front of everyone. And then Hayden Ross threw a granola bar at his face. I wish I helped him. But I didn't, I just laughed and then everyone else did, too, and then he hid in the bathroom. I was going to say sorry to him yesterday when we walked to school, but now I can't."

"Oh, Chloe. Come here."

She pulls Chloe's head against her chest and it registers. Wednesday. The night of the accident. Xavier adores Chloe. She's his only real friend, but he's one of many for Chloe. This would have devastated him.

But it's not the time for reprimanding her. She hushes her instead, and then puts her lips to Chloe's ears: "Don't worry about that right now, okay?" She kisses her. She wipes Chloe's tears and takes her hand. "Come on, let's go pay for this and get to school."

"Will you take him the card and his airplane? And tell him I'm sorry I said that nobody would care if he died, and he should just disappear?"

Nobody would care if he died. Disappear. The words fold in Blair's mind, and then fold again, and then fold again, until they are as small as she can make them. She stares ahead at the display of wrapping paper squares and the poms of spiral ribbons for gifts, and she can see only one thing. Xavier, alone, leaning over the bedroom window. Not caring, either, if he died.

39

Whitney

The Hospital

Her phone appears in front of her, in Jacob's hand. He's back in the room, he smells like toothpaste. He's wearing different clothes. It must be morning. He's saying something about texts from her assistant, she's sent Whitney three messages, but the screen is locked, so he can't read them to her. Does she want to check? Does she want him to call the office for her? The meeting, there was that big meeting this morning. He can let them know what's happened to Xavier, that she won't be available for a few days. Whitney doesn't answer, she doesn't want to think about work. Jacob waits. He's unsure of what she wants. And then he makes the decision for her. He says he'll slip out of the room to call Grace, he'll be just a minute.

But then she snatches the phone from him. She sucks in the stale hospital room air, but her lungs don't fill like they need to. She grips the phone as tightly as she can, and she needs Jacob to back away, to leave the room. Because Grace doesn't ever text, she only emails.

Someone else in her phone is listed as Grace.

She asks Jacob to go downstairs to get her a sandwich. Says she thinks she might finally be hungry. Her voice is too tight; he's quiet for a moment. And then he looks around for his wallet, says he's glad her appetite is back, but she knows he doesn't believe her.

When he is gone, she unlocks the screen and reads the three texts.

I'm sorry. For everything.

I need to see you again.

I think she's close to finding out.

40

Rebecca

She is still alone on the floor in the empty nursery. She has an ache for something she can't recognize at first, and then the obviousness is overwhelming. She wants to see her mother.

Her mother's voice is full and hopeful on the other end of the line when Rebecca asks if she can stop by later that morning. She's avoided seeing her mother as often as she should. Being around her reminds Rebecca of the relationship she herself might never have. They usually talk about other things instead, politics, her work, the condo board her mother has joined, but she knows her fertility is on both of their minds.

Before she leaves, she digs out one of the pocket diaries from her bedside drawer. It's thin and worn, almost as old as she is, a freebie from the bank where her mother opened her first savings account. In tight, cursive handwriting, in the calendar squares, her mother had written the things they did together every single day. *Explored the free section of the museum. Worked on sounds "A" to "M." Practiced addition on our new* *abacus ($2 at the Goodwill!). Preschool tour.* As the years went on, the squares in each additional diary began to look like a storyboard for another family—not the poor, single mother and her scrappy daughter. *Third piano exam, passed! National debate championships. College loan application submitted. Freshman move-in day at Columbia. SHE DID IT!*

Thousands of squares in eighteen little diaries, the compulsion to keep a record of everything Rebecca ever did. Her mother gave them to her in a banker's box when she graduated from med school, and she keeps a few in her nightstand. Rebecca treasured them for what they were: acts of love, markers of her mother's pursuit to achieve for Rebecca a life she never had. But the squares were also a quantification—of everything she'd ever been given in her life.

And now she might finally give her mother a grandchild.

She'd had the idea in the shower. She'll hand her the last of the diaries and point to the new square she's drawn—her due date.

Her mother will make everything better for the hours she sits in her kitchen.

She stops for peonies at the market and then drives through the city to the highway. Her phone is on the passenger seat beside the diary, and she checks it every few minutes to see if Ben has texted her. She imagines him home when she returns this afternoon, sitting at the kitchen table, ready to talk. Ready to forgive her. He'll find hope again as the baby grows bigger inside her. This will become a slice of time they hardly remember. Everything will have changed.

She turns on the radio and finally feels herself relax.

Forty minutes later she pulls off the exit to where her mother lives. She shifts in the seat as she slows for the first lights. She feels hot in her jeans, and thinks she should have worn a dress, she is sweating even with the air-conditioning on. She puts down the car window and leans into the fresh spring air. She thinks about stopping to get them coffees. She shifts in her seat again at the next light, and feels it more distinctly this time, a warm dampness in her underwear. She reaches to pull the tight jeans away from her crotch. The obvious thought makes her anxious. But she is always on the brink of panic, always waiting to be flattened again. She pulls her mind back to the road, to the green light. She touches the smooth petals of the peonies in the seat beside her.

She parks at Starbucks and finds her wallet in her bag. The simmer of panic comes again and makes her angry with herself. She lifts her bottom from the seat, puts her fingers into her underwear, and then looks for the clear discharge that will settle her.

Her head becomes light.

Her fingers are crimson and sticky.

41

Whitney

The Hospital

Wednesday night replays in her mind on a loop. Over and over. Shame slithers like a worm up her throat and makes her want to gag. The very thought of what she's done.

After Louisa had left for the night, Whitney made a coffee to keep herself awake. She planned to send a text to cancel her plans. She would prepare for the next day's meeting instead. But then she'd gone into Xavier's bedroom to check on him.

She saw him twitch, and then his eyelids fluttered too much for him to be asleep. So she'd said his name. She'd said it again in a firmer tone. She'd wanted him to apologize for getting so angry in the kitchen. She'd wanted to end things on a better note. She wanted to give him a hug.

He'd turned onto his back, propped himself on his elbows, and adjusted his eyes to the light from the hallway. And then he looked toward the wall at the end of his bed, under the posters of the vintage racing cars. He looked like he was tracing something with his eyes.

She'd turned to see what he was looking at.

His printing on the wall was large, careful, and neat, the ink thick like tar.

The black marker was on the floor.

N ow, she lifts herself from his chest to look at him in the glow from the monitors, his open mouth, his gray and lifeless skin. Not a twitch. Not a flutter. *What would it be like if I wasn't here?* he'd asked her a few months ago in the car.

And now, he isn't here. Her own chest is tightening again, she must press her hands into herself to alleviate the tension. She is so empty. Every thought feels stuck in mud.

She wonders what his first thought will be if he opens his eyes and she is there, standing over him, moving her lips. What he will remember. *I'm here*, she'll be saying, *I've been here the whole time, I never, ever left you.*

She imagines him turning his face away from her. Wanting his father instead, his eyes searching for him.

There is not enough air. She is heaving for it. Jacob will be back with the sandwich any moment. Jacob, who she has lied to, who will leave her. Who might never let her see her children again. She will lose them all. She imagines what Xavier will say to him, if he lives, if he can talk, if he can get the words out that he is thinking. If he even has the capacity to think at all.

They have all been talking about this around her—his function, his mental capacity if he wakes up—they have been saying things she re- fuses to acknowledge about the pressure that is pulverizing his brain. He might not be the same Xavier anymore, he might not have an easy life, and it's because of her. She has never been a good enough mother to him, and she won't be good enough now, not when he'll need her the most. She is not capable. She will fail him again.

She puts her hand on his mouth, over the cross section of tubes. Her fingers shake running down the main line, to the soft accordion piece that attaches to the ventilator that keeps him alive. She glances at the door. Nobody is there.

Something takes over, a thought that finally promises her relief, and she wants to chase that feeling, she cannot let it get away from her, she is desperate. She coaches herself. Do it. Nobody will know. It's for the best. She has ruined him. She'd ruined him long before Wednesday night.

She closes her eyes and she pinches the tube.

She cuts off his air.

42

Rebecca

She is desperate enough that she lets her mind do what it needs to do. The blood could be from something else. Her placenta. A tear in her lining. It could be just this one bit of spotting, and then the bleeding will stop. She holds her hand out while she drives, she doesn't want to touch anything. She keeps looking from the road to her fingers.

She'd already searched this over and over in the pregnancy forums. Other women have bled and been fine. She clings to this as she speeds on the highway back home. If the cops pull her over, she'll tell them to fuck off. Show them her bloody fingers. She has never felt this reckless. She drives faster.

She doesn't feel the panic until she peels onto Harlow Street, and the delusion wears off. She throws the car into park and bangs the steering wheel. She puts her fingers back into her underwear and feels more fresh blood.

The contractions haven't started yet, but she knows soon she'll feel the first slow pull.

She can think only of the purply, translucent baby that must come out of her. The head and body will be in proportion now. There will be a cord. The beginnings of eyebrows and eyelashes. She doesn't want to hold it in her hand again, to be on her bathroom floor.

But the choices are bathroom floor or emergency room. Where they don't make situations like hers a priority. They will let her shift and ache and bleed in a waiting room chair until a space becomes available, and then a resident with no experience in the loss of a pregnancy will ask her questions too slowly about her history of family illness and if she's had this shot or that. And then after, if she's lucky, if there's room, she'll be shuffled to the labor and delivery unit, where she will see the massive bellies draped in gowns the color of robins' eggs, pacing the halls, steadying themselves with long, loud breathing. There, she might be given a bed, and next door she'll hear a woman laugh with wild awe as she meets her new screaming baby, as Rebecca lies in her empty room and listens.

"Are you okay?"

Mara's voice is distant through the car window. Rebecca tries to get out of the driver's seat but she can't stand. Mara puts her hand on her back, guides her head between her legs.

"Take deep breaths. It's all right."

Rebecca can smell herself, the mix of sweat and blood. There is a patch of darkness now coming through her denim.

"Your baby?" Mara asks. She pinches her lips, waiting for Rebecca to confirm. It is the way Mara says it—*your baby*. The validation of what is inside her.

Rebecca squeezes her eyes closed as she nods. Mara helps her to stand, walks her up the steps to her front door. She realizes that the woman is in her nightgown still.

"Your husband isn't home," Mara says. The word "husband" sounds bitter in her mouth. She looks past Rebecca through the entryway to the kitchen at the back of her home. There's an apprehension about Mara that makes Rebecca uneasy.

"I'll be okay, Mara, you can go. I've been through this before."

"I know you have, you poor thing."

Mara holds Rebecca's chin between her thumb and her other fingers, and this tenderness makes Rebecca want to crumble. Her eyes close and the tears spill. She leaves Mara outside and slowly walks upstairs to her bathroom. And then she sits on the toilet and stares between her legs and watches the thin stream of crimson curl through the water like smoke.

43

Whitney

The Hospital

She holds her breath and whimpers, she thinks *no, no, no,* but she is doing it, she is waiting for the beeping to start and for someone to come in and take her hand off his air tube. To save him from his mother.

She starts to count. The numbers are slow. They morph together in her mind.

This is the only option. She can feel the relief just ahead of her, she is running to keep up with it, she is almost there.

"Is everything okay?"

Whitney gasps and lets go of the tube. She stares at her hand.

The nurse pulls the chain on the overhead light and moves quickly to the other side of the bed, and Whitney is shaking her head and trying to find the words. "I think there was something wrong, I was trying to fix it."

"It's all right," the nurse says, but she is checking the tubes, the attachments, she is looking at the monitor and adjusting the clamp on his finger. Whitney's head is dizzy, and she wonders if they are going to take her away, if they will arrest her. She should be arrested. She is not safe for him, she never was.

She shakes so violently that she is sure the nurse will know.

"Is he okay?" Whitney asks.

"Hmm?"

"Is he all right?"

The nurse nods, she is holding her finger against the screen of the IV machine, she is saying something under her breath, repeating a number, checking the chart, checking the number again. She checks his arm where the intravenous is. And then she leaves.

It's then that Jacob clears his throat. *Oh my god*, she thinks.

He's in the chair at the back of the room.

She hadn't heard him come in. When had he come in? What had he seen?

She holds herself still on the rail of Xavier's bed and stares at the floor. Her face burns. He would have stopped her, she thinks. He wouldn't have let her do what she was about to do.

But sometimes she feels like he's testing her. To see how far she'd really go, before he's there, watching, saving, reminding her again of who she needs to be.

"You should leave here for a bit," he says. "You need to sleep. And see the twins, they miss you and Zags. I'll stay."

Whitney shakes her head and keeps her eyes on their son. She won't leave him. He can't make her go. She grips the bedrail. She won't let anybody move her.

A few minutes later, she hears the rustle of Jacob's jeans as he uncrosses his legs and stands. He doesn't say anything when he walks out of the room. He hadn't brought her back anything to eat.

Had she really just done that? She looks at her hand. Maybe she hadn't. Maybe she's so tired that she's hallucinated. She doesn't know who that woman was.

She thinks about the texts, about the repeated questions from the authorities, about how close she is to losing everything.

She reaches to find the lever and lowers the side rail of his bed. She shifts his body over just an inch. First his hips, and then slowly his torso, and then she gently lifts his head. And then she kneels on the bed and lowers herself down beside him. She faces him, and slides her arm across his chest, under the highway of tubes and cords, and puts her trembling cheek against him. She doesn't care if this isn't allowed. She doesn't care if it's breaching a safety protocol. She will lie here with her son on this bed until somebody carries one of them away.

She imagines them sitting together on the floor of his bedroom, while he talks her through everything he knows about chess. She has her legs crossed, like his, and she asks him questions. She takes notes, so that he feels important. She draws a sign on a piece of printer paper that says DO NOT DISTURB! EXPERT LESSON IN PROGRESS! and tapes it to his door. They spend an hour like this, together on the floor, and for the first time, she pays attention to every tiny thing. The wideness of his eyes when he's thinking. The gestures he's adopted from his teacher, the way he nods, praises her like an adult does. The new words he uses. The way he carefully draws his bangs away from his eyes like a curtain.

And then she remembers a particular feeling, a moment in an otherwise unremarkable day. Xavier was five months old. She was tired. She lay on the floor of his nursery, on a thick wool rug, staring at the glowing sphere of cloudy glass in the center of the ceiling, the pump sucking her milk into a flimsy plastic bag that would be sealed and dated and filed in the freezer. She couldn't get the smell of petroleum jelly out of her nose. She was lulled by the tempo of the motor whomping in her hand. The light above suddenly looked to her like the moon. The room felt like her whole world, and it wasn't enough. None of it was enough, not even the baby she loved, in the bedroom beside her, being soothed to sleep by his father. She had thought it then—I will always want for more.

She can hear the machines. He's still alive. She has not killed him. She never would have. In that cloudy state of waking, she has the relief of feeling nothing for a split second before the memory of what she's done crests again. She wants back into the obliviousness of sleep, but Jacob's voice is pulling her away. She hears other people then too. She smells strong coffee and opens one eye to see if there's sunlight behind the window blind, if she's slept all day or for fifteen minutes, but there is no sense of a daily rhythm in this room.

"It's positive, yes, but this usually moves slowly."

"We'll hold off on surgery for now."

"It's a critical time."

Jacob is promising them he'll wake her up now, he is thanking them for letting the rules slide this once. She feels the nurse behind her tinkering with the vial changes, the click of the tube clips opening and closing. She smells the tacky medical tape, the waft of sanitized hands above her head.

Jacob's breath is in her ear now. There was movement. He's saying Xavier was trying to open his eyes while she was asleep with him in the bed. That he must have felt her there with him. She puts her lips on Xavier's face, she kisses and kisses, until her husband pulls her shoulders back, away from her son.

44

Whitney

NINE YEARS AGO

I f you want her to pinpoint the moment she's hungry for, it's when they enter her. The submission of it. *I have you, you're in me, you've surrendered.* It's animalistic, she knows. Teeth of a predator in a neck.

In the hotel elevator, on the way up, she thinks about how to get to that point as quickly as possible, if she might ask him to sit at the foot of the bed, watching, while she eliminates the need for his rough finger pads on her skin, the performative removal of her underwear. No part of that exchange interests her, although they'll think it does, they'll think they are earning the part that comes next. But her arousal is in the very possibility—in giving herself the permission.

She's on a business trip in Paris. It's her last night here.

She keeps her wedding rings in the hotel safe.

She places her phone facedown on the bedside table, ringer off.

There are underclothes she saves for these occasions, so as not to mix the pleasures.

The smell of bar olives on their breath, the cocktail napkins in the pockets of their suit jackets. The socks, the collar stays that have occasionally been left behind, dropped in the wastebasket after they're gone, before she washes her face, settles the flush in her cheeks, brushes her teeth and then brushes again, and then rinses with spearmint mouthwash. Gone, it's all gone, she can let herself believe it's that easy.

Except this time there is a knock on her door at seven in the morning, as she's putting the pump's flange on her nipple. Her tits are about to explode.

She has had only four hours of sleep.

Her husband. Her unexpected husband. He has taken the red-eye to Paris, a surprise, the kind that takes weeks of planning and covert arrangements for childcare. He has takeaway espressos in his hands.

She is swollen and damp between her legs still, when he cups her in his palm on the bed. He'll think this is because of him. This, and the heat in her face, the pound of her heart when he puts his head to her chest.

They order breakfast to the room after and talk about their only child. The child she had not missed until she saw her husband standing in the hallway outside her hotel room door. They watch videos of this child while they are naked, feet rubbing. The first splash in the shallow end of their condo-building pool, the sour face of applesauce on the tongue for the first time. Things that matter more than any parent thinks they will.

Her eyes follow him across the room, and now that they aren't touching, she gives herself a handful of seconds to feel the terror. If the flight hadn't been a red-eye. If he'd landed last night instead. He calls for someone to collect the dining cart. He flips through the tray of hotel magazines on the desk where the phone sits.

"What is this?"

There is a note. On those pads of paper hotels always have.

Nobody has ever left a note. She hadn't thought to check. "Show me?"

She does her best to sound surprised. Amused, even. She sits up, steadies herself as the structure of her body disintegrates. She seems to float above them both. To watch from another place.

He doesn't look at her. He rips the paper from the small rectangular pad and sails it in her direction. The paper lands at the lump of her feet under the covers.

Her name isn't written. It could be a note left for anyone.

You were fucking amazing.
Can we stay in touch?

His phone number, his name.

"Looks like the last guest had some fun," she snickers. "Fuck, though. That could get a person in trouble. I mean, honestly! You'd almost think the maid left it there on purpose for a laugh."

"Maybe." He picks up a magazine about the hotel chain, but then puts it right down.

He must be thinking about the possibility. He shakes out his jeans from the floor, pulls the belt from the loops. He is quiet. He doesn't unpack. He usually likes to unpack.

She can feel how close they are to implosion. She must speak.

"I have the afternoon free, only an eleven a.m. and then a lunch meeting."

"Good."

"We could walk, get a drink on a patio somewhere and Parisian people watch."

"Sure."

He checks his phone. The doorbell rings to collect the dining cart. She runs herself a shower, where she bends over, puts her elbows on her knees.

The note is on the bedside table next to her phone when she comes out of the bathroom wrapped in a towel.

It occurs to her only then that her husband could call the number.

She needs to get rid of it, fast.

But then she understands something. Jacob has put the note there for a reason. Convince me that I'm wrong, the piece of paper says to her.

She sits on the bed beside him. He is reading something on his phone, one arm behind his head.

"Why did you put this note here?" she asks. "It's creeping me out. Makes me think some prostitute was in here before we checked in."

She makes a face, pops up, feigns lightness. She crumples it, throws it into the trash can under the desk. There is only one way forward, and there has only ever been. She opens the door of the wardrobe and sighs.

"Short sleeves? What's the weather supposed to be today, do you know?"

He looks up, but he does not answer her.

45

Whitney

The Hospital

The nurse is asking her if she'd like to help.

She feels a wet towelette against her fingertips, and then her hand is placed in a basin of warm water. There is a bar of Ivory soap. She should know what to do next. She is his mother.

But she is elsewhere.

His fingers, inside her. She can feel them, the way he strokes her, and she can't pull her mind away from this, not even as she's watching the nurse carefully peel the hospital gown down her son's body.

His hot breath in her ear. She tells him exactly what to say, and he says it. She is trying not to feel now the way she does when this happens. The nurse is telling her to make suds on the cloth with the soap.

She has bought Jacob plane tickets to art fairs, to exhibitions, to places where he'd need to be for several days at a time. She has made it seem like a favor she'd done for him. He has wrapped himself around her and told her she's the best wife in the world. That he appreciates her. He holds her longer than usual before he leaves for the airport.

The nurse is lifting her son's arm and gesturing for her to come closer. She squeezes the water from the cloth.

She always cleans up when they are done with a box of tissues she keeps in the shed, tissues they use to wipe the children's noses. She doesn't always get it all, and she knows there is sometimes still cum on the shed floor, on the edge of the shelf, and in the mornings, Louisa and the children go in to get their trucks, their skipping ropes, the attachment for the sprinkler.

The nurse is holding her hand now, she is showing her what to do, how to wipe away the smell from under his arm, three gentle motions.

She thinks of him while Jacob makes her orgasm in their bed, while Jacob is saying her name, telling her how beautiful she is. That he loves her. And she loves him, too, she loves him so much that what she's done to them all might kill her.

Her hand is in the warm water again, and the nurse is lifting the gown up from his waist now, she is telling her to make more suds.

The sting is back in her throat. She could throw up in the basin. She can't turn around to see her son's face again, and so she hands the nurse the soaking wet cloth and hears the water drip on the floor. The nurse is telling her it's okay, but it isn't.

There were others, long before this one, shortly after Xavier was born. Other fingers inside her, other whispers in her ear. Singular events that she can expertly forget, like the features on their faces, and the color schemes of their luxury hotel rooms. Blank, all of it. She'd never given her last name, not because she feared they'd look her up again, but because her last name was Jacob's last name, and she could never have brought herself to say it.

It has never been about Jacob, not even then.

It's about the way she needs to feel outside of him, apart from them all. From the responsibilities, the expectations she's mounted on her own shoulders for decades. From the three children she is no good at raising. The ones she will always fail, no matter how much money there is or how hard she tries.

All of this feels survivable, even palatable, when she exercises this one little freedom.

Of course, it is not a freedom at all.

The nurse is talking to her, she is speaking about the miraculous resilience of children, of their defiant young bodies. Of the hope she must hold on to as a mother. His eyes fluttered as she'd lain with him, they might flutter again if he senses her presence, calm and loving. They might even open, she says. Whitney wants to stuff the cloth in her mouth, she wants to be alone with her son without the sound of another voice. But the nurse's hand is on her shoulder now.

Nothing about it has been reckless, like an affair is said to be. She's never reckless. What she's done these past nine months has been calculated. There is risk and there is benefit, and there are good people she lies to, and good families she is threatening, and there is shame in this. So much shame. And yet it has always, every time, felt worth it.

But then she began to feel hungrier and hungrier. And the desire to be aroused by him crept into her mind when it shouldn't have. And then she felt anxious if a day went by without a glimpse of him, a reminder that she could have that feeling again, if she needed it. And was it about him, specifically? Or was it as simple as this: he is not the husband who is better than her, he is not her relentless obligation, and she does not fail him over and over. He is not melded to her like a heavy metal.

The pleasure became a habit. There was no control anymore, none at all.

She is banging her fist against her heart now. And she is replaying Wednesday night.

The nurse is saying she will get her a cup of water, that she needs to take care of herself. To be strong. That her family needs her. She is guiding her back to the chair at Xavier's other side. But she doesn't want the Styrofoam cup on her lips. She doesn't want to feel strong. She felt strong before. She felt invincible, she has felt the reins in her hands for decades. And now she is done. She surrenders.

46

The Loverlys' Backyard

Aiden and Blair are the only ones left at the party. The caterers are gone. The twins are in their beds. Blair helps Whitney clear the kitchen island, wrap the leftover food they've been picking at. They are unusually quiet with each other.

Chloe and Xavier come into the kitchen, and he unwraps the dessert platter, puts his fingers in the carefully arranged fruit, digs for a slice of pineapple. Chloe finds a place under Blair's arm, puts her face into her mother's chest.

"Please don't touch the food, Xavier," Whitney says.

"Do you want to play chess with us?" Xavier speaks only to Blair. Whitney pulls his hand from the fruit. He grumbles, she shushes. She wipes his fingers with the dish towel. She removes a perilous wineglass from the edge of the kitchen island. He is always doing what she doesn't want him to do, and she wishes she couldn't see these things, that she were blind to these irritations.

"I'd love to play with you, Xavi, but it's getting late." Blair touches his hair as his face deflates. She rubs the top of his arm and chases his eyes with hers until she catches him. She smiles playfully—he brightens again. Whitney stares at them, wondering if she ever falters. Yells. Screams.

"Say good-bye now, Xavier. Up to the shower," Whitney says, but he ignores her.

"Do you know that the longest ever game of chess was 269 moves? Or maybe it was 629." He tells this to Blair, but he looks at Whitney before he speaks again. She is rearranging the fruit onto a smaller plate, avoiding his eyes. "Once I played a game with, like, 120 moves. The chess club teacher said it was the longest game he ever watched."

"Wow, good for you. Can you come over next week to give me another lesson?"

He nods, puts his fingers into the icing on the mini cupcakes and licks them. He's not usually this chatty. Whitney watches in silence. Whitney wants Blair gone.

"And did you know the longest flight of a paper airplane is 29.2 seconds? From a fold called the Star Fighter. I've made one before. You've gotta pinch the tip, like this." He squeezes Chloe's nose between his thumb and index finger and she giggles before she swats him away.

"Xavier, I said go upstairs."

"Chloe, can you please tell Daddy it's time to go?" Blair kisses her, pats her bottom, and then a pleasant sigh. As if there's no tension. Tonight, this pretending makes Whitney feel foolish, like Blair is doing her the favor of pity.

"Are we going to pretend it never happened?" Whitney asks.

Blair is stunned by Whitney's words. She can't find a reply. Isn't that what we do for each other? she thinks. We turn a blind eye? We protect each other's dignity? How dare you do this to me, Blair thinks, how dare you humiliate me? She is stunned Whitney would bring up Aiden's gaping at her like this. They've never had a confrontational moment before, and the discomfort is engulfing. She turns to look out the back of the house to the yard, to see if Aiden is coming. To make sure Chloe can't hear them.

But then Whitney says, "The way I screamed at him up there. I lost my shit. It was bad, wasn't it."

Blair exhales. The yelling, that's what she means. Whitney's arms are crossed high over her chest now, like she's conceded that it was a questionable choice of dress for a neighborhood barbecue, and Blair can see the boldness has finally left her. Blair turns off the water in the sink and wrings the dishcloth. She knows they aren't talking about the fact that Whitney treated him so cruelly. She knows they are talking about the fact that everyone heard.

"Look, you can't let this consume you. People will forget it ever happened."

"No, they won't."

"Xavi already has—he was in a great mood just now." She knows it will sting to point out how cheerful her son is in Blair's presence. Whitney presses her hand into her forehead.

Blair can insist the screaming from his room wasn't as bad as it was, she can talk until Whitney is convinced. Lies that might make Whitney feel better. But she thinks of Whitney's perfect breasts on flagrant display, and of the catering bill paid without a glance at the total, of Whitney pulling her up to dance when she knows she hates to dance, and Blair decides she doesn't want to make this any easier for her.

"That thing you said about Xavi, though, to the moms from school. Afterward. About him having serious problems right now, and seeing the behavioral specialist. Is he?"

Whitney puts down the tray of picked-over desserts. Her lower jaw slides and Blair regrets bringing it up. There was the embarrassing display of rage. And then there was the lie about her son.

"I had to say something to those women, Blair. They already think I'm a shitty mom."

"They don't think that. They know you have a lot on your plate." A pause. Blair could keep reassuring. But instead: "I just wanted to make sure everything's really all right with him. That there's nothing concerning you about him. Is he struggling with anything, is he—"

"It was just a white lie. He's fine, and you know that."

Blair thinks to herself, for the first time: *Do* I know that? Do I know that Xavier is okay? Does Whitney really believe he's fine? She thinks of how it must have felt to be the target of that explosive anger. Of how often that might happen. Of how pleasant and easy the boy is when he comes over to her house, without Whitney.

Whitney is about to say something when Aiden and Jacob come in from the backyard.

"Great party, Whit, thanks." Aiden touches her shoulder, kisses her good-bye on the cheek. "I've got a three-hundred-dollar bottle of tequila with your name on it, a gift from a client. You've got to try it. I'll bring it over."

"Anytime, yeah." But Whitney is busying herself, she is fiddling with plastic wrap. She doesn't look at him. Chloe is pulling Aiden away from her side, leading him to the door.

Whitney gives Blair a final stare in the kitchen that says, I thought you were on my side. I thought I could count on you to make this better. What Blair would never admit is that it's not the rage that concerns her the most, or even the lie she told about Xavier. What she can't shake is how effortless the lie was. How easily those words seemed to roll off Whitney's tongue.

Blair is following her family out of the kitchen when she hears Whitney's voice, low.

"Blair, there's something else."

Whitney looks back over her shoulder toward her front door, where Aiden is speaking with Jacob and Chloe is tying her shoes. They are out of earshot. Whitney's hands slide to the back of her hips, and she bites on her lower lip, and this makes Blair more nervous. Whitney opens her mouth, there is something she needs to say, something that has tempered her eyes in a way that tells Blair it is Whitney who holds the pity now. That Blair has a reason to be worried too. In that one beat of silence, Blair knows she cannot let herself hear whatever comes out of Whitney's mouth next. She has a terrible feeling it will be something about Aiden. She cuts her off before her first word.

"I should get going, Whit, I'm sorry."

Whitney's jaw closes. Blair expects her to be annoyed, but instead she looks relieved. It's this relief that makes her worry more than everything else she will replay about the party in the days that follow. Before Whitney turns back to the plastic wrap, Blair feels her stare at the olive-green shorts Blair is wearing, at the bulky pockets, at the cuffed, wrinkled hem, and when she gets home, she throws them in the garbage can at the side of the house.

47

Blair

Blair sits at the bench near the front door with Chloe's card and Xavier's die-cast airplane in her hands. She'd thought Whitney might have been involved with what happened to Xavier, but it's her very own child who might be responsible. She isn't sure if she can go to the hospital, knowing what Chloe has done. She's been Googling phrases on her phone that feel impossible: *Can a ten-year-old commit suicide? Rates of suicide in children under 12.* Pressure creeps around her skull, from the back of her head to her temples. He's so young. But she can see it now—there was a darkness in him. There was always a sadness. It was part of what Whitney couldn't deal with, his long face, his unsettledness. His anxiousness.

"Was she okay at drop-off?"

Aiden stands over her, his suit jacket hanging from his index finger; he's late for work.

"Seemed to be. I'll email her teacher, I'm not sure what the school knows." She folds her shaking fingers into her lap. She can't bring herself to repeat what Chloe told her at the drugstore. She needs to keep control of this and make it go away. What if Xavier dies? She can't have them bear the burden of that blame for years to come, with the kids at school, the teachers. The parents. She won't. She needs to get ahead of this before everyone makes up their minds about why this has happened. "I think I'll go to the hospital to see Whitney again."

She watches Aiden bend for his dress shoes, wincing. She waits for his reaction to the mention of Whitney's name, but he says nothing. She'd gone the whole last hour without thinking about the possibility of them fucking each other. She can't decide if she regrets showing him the key or not.

"Can I ask you something?" she says slowly. She wants to give herself time to back out. But this is her family. Her daughter. "Do you think it's strange nobody's talking about how Xavier fell? Why he was up so late at night at the window like that? If he was really alone?"

He sighs, ties the laces. "I don't know, haven't really thought about it. They probably asked some questions at the hospital and were satisfied it was an innocent accident. It doesn't do us any good to be speculating, does it?"

Blair opens the card and reads Chloe's message. *I love you Xavi. I want to be friends forever.* "But if you had to speculate. If you had to guess."

He rests his forearms on his knees and keeps his face down. A subtle nod as he thinks. "You're suggesting that Whitney lost her temper with him."

Blair is quiet. If Aiden was having an affair with Whitney, he'd want to disassociate right about now, when her world is on the brink of chaos. She can't be trusted to remain discreet, not in her state of crisis. The affair would need to end. Maybe he was rattled by seeing the key. Maybe he's decided to start protecting himself. And maybe that could work in their family's favor.

Blair wants him to keep talking, to start a narrative they can build and build until it begins to feel like the truth. They need a different theory than the one involving Chloe. Something for Blair to plant, inconspicuously, delicately, with everyone who will ask. The flood of messages will surely start soon, she's waiting. She pushes him: "I mean, accidents happen. But it doesn't really add up. And Jacob wasn't there, and Louisa would have gone home already. So if he woke up and wouldn't go back to sleep . . . if he was being difficult with her. Pushing her buttons. Making her angry. She might have just . . . snapped."

She could mention the smashed cup of coffee in Xavier's room, but then she'd have to tell him she was over there. She waits to read his reaction, but he keeps his eyes on the floor.

"It's a pretty serious assumption to make."

She keeps silent. He looks thoughtful, like he's trying on an idea. And then:

"I guess you know her better than almost anyone," he says. He thinks some more. "It's certainly possible. But if something along those lines did happen that night, Whitney isn't going to admit it to anyone, that much we know. She'll lie her way through it."

Blair's head pulses as he speaks, the tension growing in her temples. She closes her eyes. He has his own motivation for her to run with this, she can feel it. The implication makes her sick, but this is what she needs. Something they can mention to Rebecca, with concern. And the women at school who want to know more. Inquiring neighbors. "Why do you say that?"

"Look, I don't want to speak badly about her, especially not right now. But she always puts herself first, doesn't she? Why would this be any different?" He shrugs. "And if Xavier doesn't make it, then . . . she's got nobody to challenge her."

"Aiden." It's unlike him, this cold pointedness. He used to think Whitney could do no wrong. Something has changed. And although she needs this, their disloyalty feels disturbing. She thinks of how lifeless Xavier looked in the hospital bed. The disability he might face if he lives.

"I'm sorry, I know it's harsh. But you asked. I'd take her version of most things with a grain of salt. That's all I'm saying." He bends again and ties the other shoe. He picks up his briefcase. He's about to walk out the door, when he turns. "Do you really think you should be going to the hospital today? Seems like yesterday was tough on you. Stay home and try to get your mind off this for a bit."

She can see it in his face. Yesterday he'd urged her to go to Whitney's side right away, but now he doesn't want her anywhere near her. He wants her to think Whitney is a liar. A bad person. His cheeks are unusually red. His forehead is damp. She looks down at the vent blowing cool air into the foyer, at the hair raising on her chilled arms. She knows she has to see her again.

48

Mara

The way Blair's tires peeled away makes Mara wonder if there's bad news. If she's going to the hospital, she might be surprised to see who else is there. Although like most things worth knowing about these days, that's supposed to be none of her business. And those women certainly don't make it their business to know hers.

She crosses her ankles and folds her arms. She's chilly on the porch this morning, but she can't bring herself to get dressed, to brush her teeth, to eat. She hasn't focused on a thing since yesterday. She wonders how long it will take for them to notice her husband is gone. They didn't know Albert any better than they know her, but if they did, they'd have thought him as nice a man as everyone else. Hardworking. Asked all the right questions in a conversation. Sixty-two years of marriage, they'd say in disbelief. They'd say that number over and over, trying to grasp how long it would feel; Mara would be surprised if any of them ever finds out for themselves.

Everyone will want to think she was left with her own broken heart the minute his gave out on her kitchen floor.

His cruelty was covert.

People are rarely who they seem.

But sometimes it's the good ones who do the very worst things.

Yesterday, as she'd sat on the basement sofa about to fold the last pile of laundry, she'd heard Albert call for her from the kitchen.

"For heaven's sakes, can he not wait a few minutes?" she'd muttered to herself.

She'd told him twice she was going to do the laundry. She could not walk all the way up the stairs to see what he wanted, and then all the way back down to finish the folding, and then all the way back up again with the basket. He'd have to wait for whatever he needed.

He'd called for her again. Twice. Three times. She'd stopped folding, held his yellowing undershirt in her hands. And then she'd heard something slam into the kitchen table, and then clang off the chair's metal leg, and then a thud on the floor.

Her heart jumped. She'd sat still and stared at the pile of his clothes. There was another noise, a groan, a moan, and then maybe her name. And then definitely her name. And maybe a mumble of prayer. In her periphery, she'd thought she saw the shape of Marcus, near his old kitchen chair in the corner; Albert had insisted they didn't need it at the table anymore. Ethereal, like smoke. She'd whipped her head toward the bottom of the basement staircase and listened.

She'd picked up the undershirt from her lap and folded it in half. And then into quarters. She'd heard something stomp against the floor, his foot maybe. She'd placed the shirt in the teetering pile with shaking arms. And then reached for Albert's navy sweatpants. She'd smoothed them. She'd swallowed. She'd folded them. An ambulance. She would need to call an ambulance. She would fold just one more thing. She would not look for the shape of Marcus again, she wouldn't let her mind tease her like that.

She'd held up another one of Albert's undershirts, stained at the armpits, stained at the collar. Her mouth went dry, she couldn't swallow anymore as she stared at the dingy ribbed cotton. She'd thought about the possibility of this over the years, of what it would feel like. She'd even fantasized. She'd folded the undershirt. Reached for the next. And then the next. And then the next. And then the next.

"I'll go upstairs now. I will," she'd whispered eventually, when she was sure the noises had ceased from above. When she was certain it would be too late. Her legs were weak when she stood. She'd put the basket on her hip, and she walked slowly across the basement to the bottom of the stairs. She could have sworn she'd felt Marcus in the room.

I don't know what happened, I came up and was shocked to see him there on the floor," is the lie she told the paramedics. "He has a heart condition."

When they'd given her a minute alone in the kitchen to say good-bye to him on the stretcher, she'd put her lips right up to his ear, the way Marcus used to do to her before Albert took his whispers away. She'd said the only thing she had wanted to say to him for decades:

"I hate you for how you treated him. I always wished you were the one who was dead."

49

Blair

She shows her visitor's pass as she walks by the ward's reception and down the hall to Xavier's room. The nurse from yesterday tells her Jacob has just left—he's gone to spend time with the twins for a couple of hours. She's more nervous than she'd been on the drive over, when she'd felt determined to figure out what was really going on. All the whispers she so masterfully ignores, they are screaming at her now, and she'd felt a moment of confidence in the car. She did know something. She could trust herself. The key, how Whitney had treated her yesterday, the way Aiden had wanted her convinced that Whitney is a liar.

But now Blair stares at the hospital room door, that conviction waning. She can't get Chloe's words out of her head. The cloak of guilt loads her down. She walks in slowly, wondering if Whitney will tell her to leave again. She's in the same chair, wrapped in the sweater Blair brought yesterday, still stroking Xavier's hand with her thumb. She doesn't look up.

There are more machines than last time, more bags of liquid draining into him. There's gauze taped over his heart with two thin white tubes hanging from it, the other end entering a hole through his neck. A patch of his head is shaved now. He looks barely there. Blair had forgotten about the swelling of his eyelids, the plastic brace around his neck. She holds her fingers under her eyes to dam the tears. From the chair on the other side of his bed, she reaches for his limp, warm hand.

Nobody would care if you died.

He already looks dead.

She feels light-headed.

He's only ten. But he was wiser than those ten years. And he hadn't been himself, not this school year. He was shrinking, as her own daughter was flourishing. Retreating, while Chloe was melding with the other girls. Blair feels the shame grow. She was raising her to be kind and good. But somewhere along the line, Blair has failed.

She puts her mouth close to Xavier's ear.

"Chloe didn't mean it," she whispers. "She's so sorry."

The nurse knocks to say the surgeon is coming by in a minute. Blair stands and wipes her face. She can't plot against Whitney—she can't try to make her the villain in this, when her own daughter might be to blame for what's happened. It's not right. She's not that kind of person.

But she needs Whitney to give her a reason to stop thinking the worst about her and Aiden, to stop obsessing over the key. Anything.

"Have I done something wrong?" Blair asks. Her voice shakes. "Or is this about Chloe?"

Whitney finally lifts her eyes from Xavier. She stares past Blair, at the wall. "I can't talk about this right now, Blair, I asked you not to—"

"About what Chloe did at recess?"

Whitney is eerily still.

"Come on, Whit, we're closer than this." Blair reaches for her arm. She wants to shake her awake, pinch her until she speaks, end this ridiculous tension between them, but Whitney yanks her arm away.

"Blair, please." Whitney looks irritated with her. She shakes her head. Closes her eyes for just a moment, the way she's seen her do when her children frustrate her. She looks back at her son.

Blair feels humiliated. She was wrong—they are not closer than this. She doesn't mean much to Whitney at all.

Betraying her must have been so easy.

The key she found in Whitney's drawer is in her coat pocket. A grenade with the pin pulled. She slips it out and holds it inches away from Whitney's face.

"Why do you have this?" Blair asks.

Whitney looks slowly to Aiden's key chain. The initials. She is unblinking again. And then her face tilts, as though something has just occurred to her. Something has finally pulled her mind from the clench of a vice. Only then does Blair realize what she herself will have to answer for.

Whitney looks up. "I could ask you the same thing."

50

Rebecca

It's been three hours since the blood started and the cramping hasn't begun yet, but she's taken three naproxen. She wants to evaporate into a place where she can feel nothing. She is on the cusp of sleep, thinking of lying on an operating-room table, slicing herself open with a scalpel, splaying her insides, throwing every one of her reproductive parts on a metal cart and kicking it across the sterile room, the crash of the instruments, the steel kidney basins clanging on the floor, her womb splattering like a water balloon. The sound of the splash wakes her.

She opens her eyes, sees the lamp on her nightside table, the empty glass of water, the pocket diary. Three seconds, four, and she remembers. She doesn't want to live through what's coming for her.

There are no more chances after this. She is done. There is finally no hope at all, and the unfairness is unbearable. She rolls to put her face into the pillow.

Downstairs she paces in the kitchen, she shoves things, the kitchen chairs, the garbage can. She throws her keys across the room. She waits for the pain to take hold of her lower back as the fog of the painkillers begins to lift. Her brain recognizes what's coming and her body is tense, it is already exhausted. The gully under her tongue fills with saliva and she spits, her head hanging over the sink.

Ben hasn't texted, he hasn't called. It's nearly noon. Her face crumples with the regret of telling him about the pregnancy. Four and a half hours too soon. She bangs a fist on the cupboard door.

He could come home any minute and say that he feels it—the hope. The best chance they've had. That he forgives her, that he is grateful she never gave up, that she was right about miracles after all. And she will fall to her knees.

She walks to the living-room window with her lower back in her hands to look for him. There is a ripple of something coral pink—Mara's cotton nightgown, in the breeze. She is on the stairs. She hasn't left. Rebecca opens the door, but Mara barely turns as she speaks.

"I wanted to make sure you're okay," she says.

"Thank you. You can go, though, really. You've left your door open." She thinks she can hear Mara's phone ringing. "Is Albert there? Is that your phone?" But Mara doesn't seem to hear her. "Ben will be home soon, it's really okay."

"Ben's gone to the hospital. I heard him tell the cabbie when he left." She gestures to the street.

"The hospital?" Rebecca thinks of the emergency room they'd gone to the first time. She cannot make sense of how he knows she's losing the baby again. And why he'd go to the hospital without her. She can't make sense of anything.

"The hospital where you work," she says. "Where the boy next door is. And his mother."

Rebecca moves through the explanations. Ben must have thought she was called back in for a consult. He must be looking for her.

But it's the way Mara said *his mother*. The way her eyebrows lifted. The way she's now kneading her thumb into the palm of her other hand.

Mara looks back at her again. Rebecca watches the woman's chest rise and then fall, one long, weighty breath.

She leaves the front door open and turns to find his laptop on the kitchen table. She has never done this before, invaded his privacy. She has never had a reason to. But she opens the screen and clicks on the email icon. She types Whitney's name into the search bar and presses enter.

Whitney Loverly (No Subject) November 2, 2018

One email. Only one email. She imagines what it will say: Could you put the garbage out for us while we're away? Collect our mail?

> **Hey! Thanks again for the new glove, he loves it. I wish you'd let me pay you back. If Rebecca is working tonight and you're looking for some company, pop by for a drink again. Btw, meant to ask you—maybe text is better? W.**

51

Blair

It isn't until she's in the parking lot of the hospital, furiously searching her bag for her car keys, that she realizes she forgot to give Xavier the card from Chloe and the die-cast airplane. Chloe will ask the second she walks in the door. And the optics of a gift would look good. She runs her thumb over the fading American Airlines decal on the side of the yellowed airplane. It must have been Jacob's when he was a boy. She'll leave it outside the door.

She peeks into the room from the hallway to see if the surgeon is there yet. Instead, she sees Jacob, his back toward the door. She must have just missed him in the hallway.

He reaches out to touch Whitney's cheek with the back of his hand. Whitney pulls slightly away from him. He tries again, and this time she doesn't move. Her hair curtains her face, and her shoulders begin to shake. She is crying—Blair's visit must have upset her. Jacob slides his hand to the nape of her neck and strokes her with his thumb, as her head slowly moves closer into his chest, like she's finally succumbing to some sense of relief. His hand slides into the neck of her shirt. And then he looks back to the door.

Blair moves away from the glass, but before she can avert her eyes, she's caught staring—at Ben. His gaze darts to the floor as his lips move quickly and his hand pulls away. He is saying something brief to Whitney. Something panicked. Whitney turns her back to him and the door. He walks to the far corner of the room, where he knows Blair can't see him.

Blair places the airplane and the card on the floor. She can't process exactly what she's witnessed, but something has just implicated them all, and each second is more loaded than the next as what's happening becomes clearer.

She bangs the elevator button and replays the way Ben touched Whitney's face, her neck. The intimacy more shocking than the visions of flesh she's tortured herself with for weeks. She bangs on the button again and the elevator doors open. The repercussions spin so fast she can barely process them. This is happening to Jacob and Rebecca. Not her. The key doesn't mean anything.

Aiden. Aiden, who was right about the kind of person Whitney is. Aiden, who isn't perfect, but forgives the way she treats him over and over, because he loves her. Aiden, who hasn't ever not been there for their family. He wouldn't do this kind of thing to her. He might look, he might fantasize, but he wouldn't stroke another woman's face with the kind of tenderness she just saw. He isn't anything like those two. Standing in the wake of what she's just witnessed, she's never felt surer. She wants to fold to the floor of the elevator and weep in relief.

The elevator dings. Parking level 4.

She wants to be far away from what is happening in that hospital room. That disgrace. That putrid taste they've left in her mouth. They'll all have to pretend she was never there.

In the car, though, she cannot bring herself to start the ignition. The adrenaline has worn off and her chest is tightening. She is shaking. She tucks her chin and presses her temples as hard as she can, and when she lifts her head, the noise that comes from within her is monstrous. She has only known herself capable of it once, when she pushed Chloe out into the world. She lets the sound fill the car for as long as her lungs allow, she feels out of herself, spliced open, she is everything she is never allowed to be. She feels the reverberation of her voice long after she can no longer hear it.

She looks around her at the dark empty cars. She is exhausted.

Everyone seems to think only of themselves. When has she ever made a choice with only her needs in mind, just because she wanted to? Put herself before her own family? Put *their* happiness at risk for her own? She never has, no matter the cost to herself. She's never been so selfish, so reckless, so cruel. She is a mother. She is a wife. She is a good person.

She bangs her hand on the car window. Her throat is raw.

She still has it, the real estate listing for the apartment, although it's long leased by now. It's curled into a scroll at the back of the junk drawer in the kitchen. She'd had a meeting at the bank a few days after, then a call with a family lawyer, one of those big franchise places that give twenty minutes free. She'd needed to know how it all felt. And she lets herself relive that feeling every day. Just to see.

But who is she without this life she has, if she's not this mother, this wife? Who is she?

She blows her nose and then she looks at the time. She needs to get groceries for dinner. And they need paper bags for the yard waste because the collection is tomorrow. These mundane responsibilities do not end. Some days these mundane responsibilities are all she has. She takes a deep breath, and she presses the puffiness out of her cheeks. She straightens her back. She puts on her seat belt. And then she finally starts the engine.

52

Blair

W hat date are you looking to move in? First of March?"

She is quick to shake her head. She doesn't like the question, it feels too certain. "No timeline. I'm flexible."

She runs her finger along the laminate counter and then opens an empty cupboard with shelves lined in floral wallpaper. An older woman lived here alone. Maybe died here. She thinks of stocking it with things that only she likes to eat. How it would feel to shed herself of the dozen expired cans and unused spices and untouched cereals and the stale bag of marshmallows.

She puts her hand against the glass of the window in the apartment's main room, because it's something people do. Something about temperature escaping, she isn't sure. There is a lever on the window frame that turns, that lets air in through a six-inch gap, and she could let the cool breeze in all night long if she lived without Aiden. He insists the room be warm.

The shower is combined with a shallow tub. A pane of bubbled glass runs along the side, on a track that is black and mucky. But she can clean mold. She can clean the mirror. She can replace the vanity light that belongs in a motel.

There's a closet with hangers that have been left behind. She thinks of the grown children who might have cleaned out the dead lady's things. She pulls one down and smells it, expecting the smell of death. Loneliness. Floral perfume. But nothing.

There would be a new order for her clothes in this closet, there would be only one laundry basket waiting underneath to be filled. Sometimes she would wear an outfit all day that not one other person would see before she took it off again.

She turns to the place where a bed would go, and it barely looks like enough space for a double. Something about the possibility of this being self-fulfilling is comforting to her. Well, the bed isn't big enough anyway. Well, there was never any room for someone new. She is lonely, desperately and achingly lonely, the way a mother with a family is not supposed to be. And yet here, the loneliness would feel different. Self-imposed, and reasonable.

The second room has the better view, and this is how she'll sell it to the innocent daughter whose life she would be upending. They can almost see the waterfront from here. They'll almost see the sailboats when the weather warms. This is almost like our family was before, almost the life I wanted for you, she thinks. And the thought of Chloe in this room makes her mawkish.

"Would your sofa fit? Do you have a sectional?" The Realtor keeps her hands clasped at the tail of her dark green blazer as she circles, the heels of her ankle boots driving like stakes into the parquet flooring.

"I don't know what I have," Blair says. And it's true that she does not.

There's a hint of pity on the Realtor's face, like she's had this situation before. Like she knows exactly why she's there, and that there will be no commission, and that this woman in front of her, rolling the brochure into a scroll, is only testing herself. It's the way Blair stands in the middle of the apartment and turns herself around like she's a frightened child in a crowd, looking for the grown-up who brought her here. That, and she doesn't ask enough about the rent. She doesn't try to negotiate.

In the elevator on the way down they are both quiet.

"I'll be in touch," Blair says, in the unremarkable lobby.

"Sure."

Blair warms up the car and waits for her pulse to come down. She is exhilarated and liberated, and there's a buzz in her head that she can't remember having before. She could drive to the bank and open her own account. She's used a free calculator on a divorce lawyer's website to estimate how much support he'd have to pay her each month, and it could work. Just barely. She tries to imagine herself living there. Being separated, selling the house. Worried about money. Working every day, a single mother. Is it freedom? Is it insanity? She thinks of what Whitney said a few months before when she came over for a glass of wine. About her mother. The bus ticket she kept for years. The way out. She hasn't been able to stop thinking about it. She wanted to know how the possibility felt. She stares at the brochure in her hand.

But then all she can feel is foolish. And a walloping ache for the expired cans of soup in her cupboard, and the mess of her husband's shaving bits in the sink, and the way her toes feel in the stair carpet that she hates. The sound of him coming home. Chloe in between them in their bed. The routine they know. And this is what happens when she fantasizes about a separation; she always flips back. To the security of living diminished.

She takes her phone from her bag and calls her mother.

She tries again. And again. Her mother so rarely answers her cell phone anymore. At least not for Blair's calls, fizzing with updates about Chloe and Aiden and the latest ongoings. She never tries the landline at their house, in case her dad answers.

She's about to give up, when she hears her mom clear her throat.

"It's me," Blair says. Her voice catches. She swallows. "It's been awhile. Just wondering what you're up to."

Her mother asks her to hold on, and Blair can picture her moving through the house to the backyard, where her father won't hear her. She puts the phone back to her ear and sighs.

"Thanksgiving, I think it was," her mom says, but she doesn't think, she knows. Blair looks up to the roof of the car and wants to tell her the phone works both ways.

"Well yeah, things have been busy. And I've been feeling . . . not quite myself." She's regretful as soon as she says it. They're both only comfortable at a distance. But she wonders sometimes if her mother resents her for the seemingly happy life she has. Maybe they could salvage something between them if she understood Blair could relate to her more than she thinks.

"Mmm-hmm," her mom says. "Well, you've always been quick to feel stressed out. Everything good with Chloe?"

Blair pauses before telling her she's working on her first science project. That she and Aiden go swimming twice a week now, she's learning all the strokes.

"Well, I'm glad things are fine, then."

Blair waits for her mother to ask why she's feeling off. But she's moved on, to the deal she got on a train ticket to stay with Blair's aunt at her new town house where the property manager cleans the exterior windows and does everyone's seasonal planters.

And then her mother says she has to go. Blair knows she can't think of anything else innocuous to fill the conversation with. Neither of them mentions her father.

She drops the phone on the seat beside her and stares at the tired entrance of the condo building.

When she gets home, Aiden asks where the bags are, and there's a split second when she thinks he knows where she was. That he's ready to pack her things in those bags, and there'll be papers drawn up by a lawyer in a big manila envelope on the kitchen table. And this house can't be hers anymore, and he can't either, and the family she has made is really gone.

"The bags of groceries?" Aiden clarifies in her silence. "Weren't you just at the grocery store?" He pops something in his mouth. Cashews, maybe. The last of them. Waiting for her to refill the jar, to replenish everything they ever need.

Although she will fall asleep that night hoping for the courage to change who she is, to be a stronger woman than her mother, she puts her arms around his shoulders and convinces herself that everything will be fine. That these phases come and go, and soon, once again, it will be gone. This life will be enough. He stiffens; he pats her back. They don't kiss anymore. She can't remember how kissing him feels.

"I forgot my wallet" is all that she says.

53

SEPTEMBER

The Loverlys' Backyard

Whitney's lace underwear is at her ankles, and she is breathing into her palms that smell like strangers, like the hands she's been shaking all afternoon. She's replaying her reentrance into the party fifteen minutes ago. The averting eyes. The disparaging look on Jacob's face, how she's failed him again. She fights the humiliation, but it's there, it's hot on her skin, her anger still pulsing in her ears. Xavier's recoil from her. She's finished peeing, but she can't move, she can't leave this powder room. She leans her elbows on her knees and grabs fistfuls of her hair. Her eyes are welling but there is makeup to preserve, and there are hours left to go, and—

"Oh shit, I'm so sorry," someone says.

She scrambles to cover herself. She isn't in the habit of locking the bathroom door at her own home. She wipes, quickly tries to rub out the smudge around her eyes, and hopes the person who walked in on her is gone when she opens the door. But he's not. Ben.

"I am so sorry about that, Whitney. I would have saved myself the embarrassment and gone back outside, but you looked . . . are you good?"

Whitney smooths her dress over her hips, *tsk*s his concern. Of course she is good, of course she is great, is he having a nice time? Does he want another drink? Has he tried the mini burgers yet? She straightens her bracelets and tries to smile. Finally, he leans in, repressing a grin.

"What happened earlier isn't a big deal, really," he says. "The magician's rabbit got a little wild right at the same time, so. You weren't the only show in town."

Whitney shields her eyes. She mumbles, "Oh God," and then an apology, but they're both smiling. They step to the side, let someone else through to the powder room. She remembers then that she had felt Ben's eyes on her earlier that afternoon. Before she screamed at Xavier. When his hand was in Rebecca's back pocket, cupping her ass.

"I heard you're coaching the junior school softball team? Xavier wants to try out in the spring, but he's not the most athletically inclined." She raises her eyebrows, wants to seem softer now than she is. He seems a bit nervous around her. She likes this. She likes that she does something to him.

"I'm happy to spend some time with him before it gets too cold, throwing the ball around. We can work on his skills so he's ready for tryouts."

"That would be nice of you. Sports are not Jacob's thing, but don't tell him I said that." And then because she feels she needs to: "He's a good kid. That incident upstairs, it was just . . . that was on me."

It feels easier to be honest with Ben than with those women outside. He shakes his head, he mumbles quick words about understanding, about forgetting it ever happened. They look at each other, directly at each other, and she waits for it to feel uncomfortable.

She thinks of what Mara had said to her about Xavier the spring

before. She'd left an armful of beautiful lilac boughs from her bush at
their front door. A reminder, maybe, that she was still there. Whitney
stopped by Mara's porch the next day to thank her.

*And by the way, if Xavi ever gets to be too much, poking around the
fence, just say so.*

Mara had clucked, waved the concern away. And then as Whitney
turned to leave:

*Your son reminds me of a quiet little boy I once knew. Something in his
eyes—*

She had cut herself off, like she'd said too much. She didn't look up
from her marigolds, turning the terra-cotta pot so it sat in more sunlight.

Whitney thinks of this now, speaking about Xavier with Ben. Ben's
eyes feel familiar to her. They feel like her son's. Was it sadness that
Mara had meant? Is that what Mara had seen in Xavier's eyes?

"You sure you're okay?" Ben's hand moves to her shoulder.

"I feel better now, knowing about the rabbit."

They smile again, he at the floor, she at the boyish curl of his hair
around his neck. Neither of them begins to walk away. Neither of them
says, Well, better get back out there. Thanks for coming. Thanks for having me.

"I'm going to take you up on that offer to help Xavi with his throw."
She looks to the backyard where Rebecca is asking the bartender for a
water, where Jacob is tipping the magician.

"Happy to. If it comes with a cold beer after."

"Maybe something a bit stronger. But yeah. Let's do that."

The slow pace of their nods. The restraint of their smiles. And then
the pink in his cheeks, the parting of his lips. Like there's more he
wants to say to her.

Much later, the conversation with Ben outside the powder room will
not leave her. Not that night as she lies awake on her bed, Jacob's screen

glowing on his lap beside her. Not when she showers the next morning, eight hours of back-to-back meetings before her. Not that next evening as she stands in her kitchen after work, still in her suit, listening to Xavier kick the leg of the table over and over and over as he slurps a bowl of melted ice cream, and she feels the grip of this life tighten inch by inch up her spine, until she slams her hand on the table and the rage takes over again.

54

Rebecca

She slams Ben's laptop closed.

Her brain finally cycles faster. *Again*, Whitney had written in the email. Ben's never mentioned going over to the Loverlys' for a drink. In the evening. He's never mentioned the Loverlys at all. They were just the family across the street. She stares at the initial she signed off with. *W.* Something about it feels too intimate. Far too casual for a woman he barely knows.

She looks down at the feet moving across the white-oak floorboards as though they are not hers. She goes back to the open door and says Mara's name. She knew about the pregnancy. And the other ones too. And she had waited outside to tell her this.

Mara is still sitting at the top of Rebecca's stairs. She doesn't turn around.

"I told you I had a son, and that he died." Mara pauses. "Well, what

I didn't say is that I could've prevented it. I was responsible. And I think about that every day."

Rebecca leans down and touches her shoulder.

"Oh, there's no need for that, it's okay. It was a long time ago." But Mara puts her hand over Rebecca's anyway and rubs it. "You don't need to hear my problems at a time like this. I only wanted to tell you that no matter how bad things get right now, you'll find the resolve to keep going, in ways you won't expect. Something'll land right there for you to find, just when you need it," she says, gesturing to her worn slip-on shoes on the bottom step of the porch. "But, you have to wait. Be patient."

She pats Rebecca's hand and then struggles to stand. Rebecca steadies her. She wants to thank her, to say something kind, but Mara won't want to hear it. She's already down the steps and on her way back across the street. Rebecca moves slowly inside to the living room and stares at the laptop.

The heaviness growing from her pubic bone up her back starts to make her nauseated. She twists to get away, but it's here. She goes to the powder room toilet, covering her mouth to keep the vomit in as the contractions begin to engulf her. She kneels on the tile and hangs her head over the cold lip of the toilet seat. She tries to find one last breath in the space between doubt and certainty, but the sourness fills her mouth, and she gives in.

55

Blair

After she comes home, with the dinner groceries and yard waste bags, she kneels in the front garden and pulls on the stubborn roots of prickly weeds while berating herself for not seeing it all before. Whitney's affair with Rebecca's husband, the extent of her selfishness. It's hard to admit how much she loved her. How much she'd envied her life. It's unsettling how a friendship as close as theirs can so quickly be diminished. How hurtful the end feels, and yet how uneventful. How little her life will change without Whitney, not in the way the loss of her marriage would turn herself and everything else inside out.

And yet losing Whitney feels more tender. More personal. Like a death. Their friendship was the only space where they both were better versions of themselves, and now Whitney has stolen this space and all that it held. But it wasn't hers, alone, to destroy. Blair rips up forget-me-nots by the fistful. Why has Whitney done this to them? Missing Whitney will consume her. But Whitney has other problems to contend with,

Blair thinks, stuffing weeds in the yard bag and swallowing the lump in her throat. Blair will be an afterthought, their relationship forgotten in the wreckage.

And maybe it's for the best, given what Blair knows. She remembers, then, about the key that's still in her pocket. About the explanation she never got.

She checks her watch. It's almost time to get Chloe from school. She looks behind her across the street and sees that Jacob has opened the curtains at the front of their house. She shields her eyes from the sun and sees him moving around in the kitchen, maybe putting something together for Whitney to eat at the hospital. She'll have sent Ben away by now, although it doesn't look like he's home.

She knows she should stay where she is, right there with her knees in the dirt. She shouldn't go anywhere near the Loverlys' house again.

But she feels the escalation of an audacity she's never had before.

She thinks of the way Jacob places his fingers on his wife's waist when she walks past him. The emphasis he puts on Whitney's name when he speaks of her, like he's saying the name of royalty. Whitney deserves none of it. And Blair can take it all away from her, in one conversation. The scale of their friendship had never tipped in her favor like this. She's never felt this kind of power.

She stands in her garden, the opportunity becoming clear. She peels off her gloves and finds herself walking up Jacob's driveway on legs that might wilt underneath her.

He opens the door and embraces her. She smells sandalwood in his neck. She lets her fingers run all the way down his arm as he pulls away.

Her own voice echoes in her ears as she speaks. She says she is so sorry, that she cannot believe this has happened. She asks how Xavier is doing that morning, what the status at the hospital is, as though she hasn't been there that day at all. Jacob tells her about the flutters, about the small, subtle movements they've seen. That it could be a good sign, or it could be false hope. That surgery has been scheduled. He's just come from a visit with Thea and Sebastian, but he's about to go back to the hospital again now. He hasn't slept since he got the call. Whitney won't eat.

But Blair can only think of what she'll say next:

I have something to tell you, and I know this isn't the right time, but . . .

I'm only doing this because I respect you, and I think you should know . . .

I hope you'll forgive me for this, Jacob, but it's not right to keep this from you . . .

That simple. Like jumping into a cold lake. Just do it without thinking, is what she would tell Chloe. Just count to three and jump. Be more than they expect you to be.

She opens her mouth, she interrupts him, she says his name in a voice that doesn't sound like hers.

"Jacob, I have to—there's something . . ."

He puts his hand back on her shoulder. His tight grip. She thinks of how intimately she's explored his things, how she's held his underwear to her nose.

"I know. We should talk," he says. His face grows red. "I didn't want to have this conversation with you. I'm sorry. I think the authorities are satisfied now, but people might ask you some questions. And there'll be rumors. And we need to be able to count on you to, you know . . . set things straight."

Blair starts to nod because he wants her to understand what he means without having to say the words. But she doesn't know what he means, not exactly. He seems uncomfortable. Are the police still sniffing around? Did Whitney admit to something? Did they see the broken mug, the coffee all over Xavier's room? Or worse, did they speak to the school, have they found out about the incident with Chloe? They will—it's only a matter of time unless a more damning rumor takes over.

He's still gripping her shoulder.

She mumbles—of course, there's no need to mention it. She's there for them. She tries to smile. He leans in to hug her again and she feels his hand rub her back slowly, over the clasp of her bra. She thinks of touching herself on his bed upstairs. She replays Ben's hand stroking Whitney's neck in the hospital room.

"How did Chloe take the news?"

She pulls away to read his face. Did he emphasize Chloe's name? Is she imaging that?

"Chloe, she's fine . . . I mean, she's devastated, of course. I dropped off a card she made at the hospital. Earlier today."

"Oh," he says. He looks confused, and she remembers she'd implied earlier that she hadn't been to the hospital today. "I must have just missed you?"

"I guess so," she says, and then shrugs, although it feels a beat too late.

"She's a good girl. His best friend." He nods as he says it, but he looks serious. Too serious. His face is still flush.

She feels like he can read her mind and she wants out from under him. She can't find the bravado she came over with; instead, she feels threatened somehow. Is that what this is, a threat? Does he know how Chloe treated his son?

She's flooded with the relief of having kept her mouth shut just now. What she knows about Whitney and Ben might have more value if she keeps quiet for the time being. Should she have her own family to protect from rumors.

She walks slowly across the street back to her house, trying to process what Jacob has just done. Or what else he might know about what's going on. The devastating mistakes his wife has made. Maybe, in his own way, he's just as weak as she herself is. She feels Mara's eyes follow her all the way to her front door, even as Jacob is calling Mara's name, jogging across his property toward hers.

She slips her phone from her pocket, opens the group chat with the moms from school, and starts typing.

> I'm not sure if you've heard yet. There's been an
> accident at the Loverlys.

She stares at the text. And then deletes the last sentence. She writes again.

> There's been an incident with Whitney and her son. I'll
> let you know when I find out more. We're all devastated,
> especially Chloe.

She presses send, and goes back to the weeds.

56

Whitney

The Hospital

S he feels shaky until Jacob is back. He comes behind her and puts his cheek against hers, where Ben had touched her. She wonders if he can smell Ben in the room, like she still can. She squeezes her eyes closed and waits for him to notice something is different, to make an innocent comment that grows and grows in his mind until everything she has done to him becomes clear. She wonders when he's going to pull her hands away from her face and finally say, *Look at me. You need to be honest with me.*

But instead, he talks to Xavier as though he can hear him. And maybe he can. His voice is tender, the voice of a dream. He puts his little toy airplane in his hand. He's telling him about how much Thea and Sebastian miss him. About how they want to run through the sprinkler with him when he gets home. But the words hurt. The hope hurts, and she knows they can both feel it.

He turns toward her now. Who does he believe her to be? What does he think her capable of? She wants to tell him she never would have gone through with cutting off the oxygen. That she only wanted to see how it would feel. How it would *almost* feel. Like someone standing at the ledge, high up. Toes over. Looking down.

But he tells her he's met with the surgeon again. They've decided to go ahead with the procedure tomorrow. That is the word he uses: "procedure." Like something's just clipped or tightened or tuned. But no, they'll remove the plates from his skull. Whole pieces of him, gone. The OR is booked for first thing in the morning. There are pages of risks they need to sign off on.

She doesn't want him to tell her anything more. She cannot think of his brain exposed to the air. The sharp blade of a medical instrument. Everything about him is in there, his thoughts, his feelings, his personality. That brain is who he is, who she so desperately wanted to change. But now she wants to fight them all off, rip their hands from his body, she wants them all to leave her son alone. If he's going to die, she doesn't want him to die at their hands, prodded and undone.

Or maybe they'll make an error. The smallest slip of a hand. One that impairs Xavier's memory. And then she'll get away with everything. What she's done. Who she's been.

It's a microflash of thought, but it's vile.

Jacob pulls her up, tells her she can't keep going on such little sleep. He wants to stand with her, sway with her, feel something for each other. She thinks of everything he doesn't know. They didn't feel like lies before. They felt like private decisions, choices that were her right to make because they fed a need inside her, one that Jacob does not have. This life was enough for him; he was good at this life. But she was not, and she wanted more. She wanted to feel different eyes on her body. The arousal affirming for her: you aren't like other mothers. Other mothers can't do this.

She took responsibility to ensure he never knew. All those careful measures, all those rules she had made for herself, had felt like the set of precautions someone ran through before setting out on a sailboat; yes, the boat could capsize, it was always possible with an unexpected change of wind, but it probably wouldn't if you knew what you were doing.

After, every time, she had been a better mother. Had they felt it, sometimes? That she had days when she enjoyed them more? And so, if that is what she needed, that one little thing, then could she be forgiven?

But now.

Standing in their son's hospital room, their foreheads pressed together, his fingers in her hair, all that hungry wanting feels atrocious.

"We're going to get through this, Whit. But we need each other. We need each other."

He keeps saying this to her. Again and again. Almost like he knows everything, and he's trying to convince them both. He grips her head. And then his hand slides down to her neck. She swallows.

It crosses her mind. That he could choke her. That he might know this is what she deserves. He keeps his hand there, his fingers slowly digging into her. She tries not to cough. She can feel him begin to cry.

57

Mara

The phone won't stop ringing, the shrill bleat blaring through the house, each time more jarring than the last. She's moved between the porch and the kitchen all day, wondering how long she can avoid the things she has to do next. The body. The calls to Lisbon. It's nearly 3:00 p.m. Nearly a full day since Albert died.

She can't trust herself to do anything rational. Maybe she should have kept her nose out of these people's business, especially right now, given Xavier.

She knows what it feels like.

As she'd reassured Rebecca that she'd find hope in the most unexpected ways, she remembered she still needed to check the backyard. Sweep the bushes to see what she can find. Jacob had come over a bit earlier. He'd had sweat on his brow. He'd looked wrecked.

"Did you hear anything?" he'd asked her. "Wednesday night?"

"Hear anything? Like what?"

"I don't know," he'd said. He'd looked at her kitchen window, he'd tilted his head like he was trying to see inside her house, looking for Albert. "What about your husband? Might he have been awake around midnight? Can you ask him?"

"We were both asleep," she said. And that was all.

She was responsible for too much already.

She'd watched Blair fill two whole yard bags with weeds about an hour ago. She'd ripped each one from the ground like the cord of an old engine that wouldn't start. Every once in a while she stopped and stared at the dirt, her elbows on her knees.

Mara could have gone over to have an eye-opening chat with Blair too. Brought her a fist of parrot tulips from her back garden and asked nicely if she had a few minutes.

But she'd interfered enough for today.

Rebecca, though, she had a soft spot for. It didn't feel right to let everyone else off the hook at the expense of Rebecca's dignity. She deserved to know the truth. She's the only person who looks at Mara and sees the woman behind the age on her face, someone not so unlike the rest of them. Because of Rebecca, she hasn't yet disappeared from Harlow Street, not completely. She imagines she'll be the first one to notice Albert's gone. She'll stop by the porch one day to chat, she'll gesture to the house and say, *By the way, how's he doing? Has he gone out of town for a little bit?* Maybe next week. Or next month.

Maybe it would have been better if she'd sat on that porch for however many months it would have taken to watch everything implode. Without her meddling in the lives of all these women. Either way, the Realtor signs would pepper the street again soon.

She goes inside the house and leans her back against the front door. She couldn't have prepared herself for how it feels to be the only one left. The only one with any memory of who they were together, the three of them. The only one who can think about Marcus every day. Who knows the weight of him on her lap. Heavy and real. When she goes, he'll be gone, too, and it's only for this reason that she's relieved when her eyes open each morning to see the popcorn plaster ceiling of her bedroom.

He was sixteen, in the mid-1970s, when she finally bought two airplane tickets. She would try again. For years she'd been putting away a bit each month from the allowance Albert gave her, skimping on the groceries and lying about things they'd needed repaired so she could pocket the service fee. She told Albert her great-aunt had paid the airfare. He didn't question it, whether he believed it or not. They didn't need to discuss whether he would come with them on the trip—she knew he'd stay home.

Marcus had a whole shelf of books about airplanes by that point. A pilot's handbook they found at a secondhand shop, an aeronautical information manual, and *Stick and Rudder: An Explanation of the Art of Flying*. She wanted him to finally feel what being on a plane was like. She wanted them to leave Harlow Street, for once. And the deadening weight of Albert.

She daydreamed again about watching Marcus absorb the details of the airport, the planes rolling slowly into the terminal, the smartly dressed flight crew rushing to their gate, a glimpse of the cockpit controls over the heads of the pilots before takeoff. She wanted to see his face light up, and revel in the joy that would rumble through him. There wasn't much that seemed to excite him in his teenage years, but that's how boys his age were. The trip would be different.

She kept it a secret until the night before the flight, when she showed him the tickets. He studied the cardstock in his hands. She jiggled his shoulders.

"We're doing it! We're finally doing it. A whole seven hours in the air. We'll stay for two weeks with my family." She pointed at the seat designations. "22A and 22B. I got you a window."

He chomped on the inside of his cheeks and put the tickets on his bedside table.

"Marcus. These cost a lot of money. You love airplanes. You'll love going on a trip, I promise you. This is what families like ours do. They fly back to where they came from, they meet cousins and grandparents. We have to go, it's so long overdue. Do not make this difficult, please."

She regretted the tightness in her voice. She had to temper herself. They were both thinking about what happened the last time they'd planned this trip. How everything had changed after that. But she didn't ask much of her son. And a part of her felt owed the thrill of doing something *she* wanted to do, for once. She hadn't been home to see anyone in nearly seventeen years. She wanted her family to meet her son. And Albert's family, too, although he'd wanted nothing to do with their plans. He warned her that the trip was a bad idea, that Marcus wouldn't do well somewhere new, meeting houses full of strangers, the chaos of the airport. As though he knew anything about what was good for their son.

She kissed Marcus good night and finished packing upstairs.

In the morning, he dressed in the nice clothes she'd laid out for him and sat for breakfast while she double-checked she had the passports and read through their itinerary again. Albert had left for work earlier than usual.

"Are you excited for the airplane, Marcus?" He wouldn't look at her. But he nodded. "Good! I can't wait. Let's get going. You're going to love it."

She had kissed him on the head, and let her lips stay there in the part of his chestnut brown hair. In that moment she let herself believe they could both feel like new people.

. . .

At the airport, Marcus took everything in a few paces behind her. They sat right beside the gate and waited for the boarding call. Mara held his knees to stop his legs from bouncing. His anxiousness was inevitable. He would be calm once they took their seats. When their row was called, she nudged him along down the boarding bridge. She could always find patience with him; it was a necessity of their life together. But she was finding that hard now, with the tension of travel getting the better of her, the heavy tote on her shoulder, the line of people they were holding up, the mess of documents in her hands that she didn't want to drop. She wanted him to enjoy this. She wanted to enjoy this herself.

"Come on, Marcus, hurry up." A young couple pulling carry-on suitcases brushed by, knocking her elbow, and the tickets and passports and her wallet scattered on the floor. Marcus watched her scramble to pick everything up while the line grew behind them. "Marcus, help me, for Christ's sake! Don't just stand there!"

She was flushed with embarrassment as he stood over her. She heard a *tsk* from a passenger stepping around them and wanted to tell the woman to go to hell. She stuffed everything in her shoulder bag and fixed her bangs, which were matting to her forehead.

"Listen to me," she hissed to Marcus, his chin pinched between her thumb and her index finger. "Smarten up. Walk faster and act your age for once. I've had enough."

She flicked his head away from her before she let go. She'd never said it before—I've had enough. But she had. Her eyes brimmed quickly as she marched to the plane door, not looking back at him. She composed herself in time for the cheery attendant to welcome them on board.

It was just before takeoff when she heard the change in his breathing as he looked out the window at the tarmac. He twisted uncomfortably.

She had taken his hand in hers, stroked his knuckles. She felt bad for losing her patience earlier, she wanted them both to start again.

"Close your eyes and count," she reminded him. "It'll be okay."

The plane rumbled down the runway. She heard the metal clink against his armrest but realized too late that he'd unbuckled his seat belt. She smelled the odor of his armpit as he reached over her to grab the headrest of the man beside her in the aisle seat. He was trying to climb over her, to leave the plane. She pushed him back into his seat and wrapped herself around him as tightly as she could. He was as big as she was now, and strong. His shirt felt damp against her face. She could feel his heart pound against her. He panted in her ear. She whispered to him.

"It's okay, Marcus, just sit still, just breathe. You're okay. Lots of people feel anxious on a flight. It's completely normal." The man beside her shifted away from them. He lit a cigarette before he shook the page of his newspaper. Mara's face burned.

Marcus touched his chest where the anxiety often gave him pain.

"I know," she reassured him. "You'll feel better in a minute. Look." She pointed out Marcus's window to the layer of pulled, white cotton sinking lower beneath them. She was overcome with the sensation of something she had already seen. And then she placed it: the dream she'd had when she was pregnant with him. Of her womb padded with clouds like the ones they could see now. Of how peaceful he had floated inside her. Of the quiet.

She let go of him and leaned back in her seat then. She rested her eyes. The white noise on the plane was soothing for them both. He'd be all right. The most stressful part was behind them. They'd be able to see the deep green shores of Lisbon as they descended, and he'd like that. She wondered when the coffee might come by. If Marcus might want a glass of tomato juice.

And then she felt Marcus's fist hit her stomach. The wind was knocked from her.

She gasped for air as she watched him go rigid in his seat, trying to grab her. Trying to tell her something. His other hand yanked at the collar of his shirt and his face was distorted in pain. He was in agony. His heart. She gulped desperately and finally found a breath.

"My son! Someone help us! Something's wrong!"

He was pulled into the aisle on the floor and disappeared from her view. She climbed over the seats, screaming for him, shoving bodies out of her way. Someone grabbed her by the armpits and dragged her to the back of the plane, thrashing. Her head smashed on the corner of a serving cart. They held her against the emergency door with her hands behind her back and her face pressed into the cold metal. She tried to shake the din of the overhead speakers from her ears, to scream loud enough for Marcus to hear her, but someone's hand pushed harder into her skull.

When they landed the plane in Houston, she was brought to a hospital for stitches and sedation. They kept her overnight. She didn't see Marcus's body for two more days. They told her it was his heart, that he went quickly. Likely a preexisting condition, triggered by stress. She refused the autopsy—she didn't need anything confirmed, it didn't matter. She knew she had killed him by making him get on the plane. If she'd listened to Albert, he'd be alive.

She called home to tell him the morning after Marcus died. He'd sobbed. His heartbreak felt cruel and undeserved, but she'd always known there'd been love, somewhere deep underneath the cruelty. She'd hung up the phone as he'd cried.

After the morgue, back at the motel, she sat in an empty bathtub with a steak knife she stole from the diner where she'd stared at a plate of food for two hours. She thought long and hard about what she believed to be true. There was heaven, and there was hell. And there was the promise she had right then, the guarantee that if she stayed alive, she could see him when she closed her eyes. She could bury her nose into the smell left on his pillowcase at home. She could hold his die-cast airplanes while she slept. And she could eat her breakfast, looking at his empty chair, knowing that he had mattered.

The afternoon sun has another hour until it dips below the roofline of the Loverlys' third story. Mara makes her way across the street to the Loverlys' front door and bends down to place the paper airplane at their doorstep.

58

Rebecca

Whitney jumps when Rebecca's cold hand touches her forearm. She puts her mouth close to Whitney's ear. "Was my husband here?"

Whitney doesn't answer.

Rebecca tells her to follow her out of the hospital room. That she obeys her is the only confirmation Rebecca needs that, yes, he was there. Yes, there is something between them. The adrenaline dulls the ache in her lower back. The pad between her legs is heavy.

She opens the door to a small empty room down the hall. Whitney hesitates.

"Sit down. I need you to sit down."

Whitney does. Rebecca paces in small steps. She's got her here in this room, but she has no plan. She wanted Ben to be here, she wanted to feel what it was like to see them together.

"How could you have let me comfort you? Hold your hand?"

"Rebecca, I can't do this right now, I need—"

"Don't," she snaps. She looks away as Whitney starts shaking. She is losing her son, but Rebecca has nothing. She is wrung. She cannot formulate the questions she should be asking.

She tries to put together a story of what's happened, but nothing fits. There is no space for misunderstanding or a different explanation. *You're not yourself anymore*, Ben said to her that morning. Her, it is her. The losses have changed her, yes. The obsession has consumed her, yes. But what he'd meant was, you are not who I want you to be. You are no longer enough for me. They were broken, but they had not shattered together.

There's a knock on the door and then Jacob slips his head in. He tells Whitney he's back, he's brought her a change of clothes. And then he sees that she looks panicked. He takes a step into the room. "What's going on, you okay?"

Whitney moves so close to Rebecca that she can smell Whitney's sourness, the odor of her armpits. This is the woman Ben touches. He holds this woman's flesh against his own. She wants to reach out to touch Whitney, too, to imagine what this feels like for Ben. Her sweatshirt. The maintained tips of her hair. She wants to twirl the diamond stud in her earlobe. There are feelings, there must be feelings, but she can't make sense of his having the capacity to love someone else. This person. She is nauseated. She turns her face away from Whitney's breath—she's whispering in Rebecca's ear:

"Please don't do this. Don't say anything to him."

Whitney, with her three children. Breasts that have fed. A cervix that has delivered.

"Whit," says Jacob, impatient. "Are you going to tell me what this is about?"

"Everything's okay, honey. Let's go. I need to be with Xavi."

Whitney takes a step back from Rebecca, but she does not look at her husband. Her eyes beg Rebecca instead. Jacob puts his hands on Whitney's shoulders, and then she finally turns and leans into him. He rubs her arms briskly, like he's trying to warm the life back into her.

Rebecca steadies herself on the back of a chair, the pain taking over again. She feels her phone vibrate in her pocket and knows it's Ben.

"Whit," Jacob says. "You go ahead. I want to ask Rebecca about the surgery, and I know you don't want to hear this stuff."

Whitney and Rebecca look at each other. The fear grows in Whitney's eyes, but she must tread carefully. So she nods and walks slowly out of the room. Jacob watches to make sure she's out of earshot.

"I know you're in a compromised position and you've got ethical duties as a doctor. I'm just asking that you let us know if anything else comes up around what happened. Okay? Just a heads-up, that's all I'm asking for. Like I said before, she wouldn't have done anything wrong that night, I can assure you." He pauses. He swallows. He seems more desperate for her to believe him than he did yesterday.

"So what do you think happened then, Jacob? It was late. He should have been asleep." He looks stunned that she's questioning him. She sees his jaws clench. "I see your light on at three in the morning all the time. She's an insomniac, isn't she? Does she take anything for that? Pop a few pills while she's drinking every night? That combination can really fuck with someone's state of mind. And their judgment. Do the police know she was into a bottle of wine Wednesday night? She left her empty glass right in your backyard. It's still there." She can barely recognize herself. But she keeps going, her voice sharpening. "You know how lucky you are to be white and have a bit of money, right? That even these trained social workers are going easy on you? Negligence doesn't even hit their subconscious when they look at you two."

Jacob stares straight at her. "Why are you doing this?"

But then Whitney is back in the doorway. Rebecca stays silent.

"Jacob, what's taking so long? You should come," Whitney says, her voice cracking. "Please."

Rebecca watches them leave. And then she crouches to the ground to collect herself. She has to think. Her phone vibrates again. And then again.

Her uterus tightens as she walks the opposite way from Jacob and Whitney, down the hall to the nursing station. The pain wraps around to her back and she tries not to grimace. She begs for the blood not to soak through her pants. For nobody to notice the dampness of her hairline.

She could find the social worker right now, admit she has concerns about Xavier's mother, previous behaviors she's aware of. She could have things escalated very quickly.

But they'll ask why Rebecca didn't speak up sooner.

She sees Leo rolling a blood pressure machine a few feet ahead of her.

And then she thinks of what Dr. Menlo told her outside the elevators when she arrived. Xavier's sedation is wearing off, and they've decided not to give him more. They want to see how he does without it. Dr. Menlo hasn't told the parents yet. She doesn't want to get anyone's hopes up—things could go either way. But she has reason to believe there's a chance.

That he might wake up, Rebecca had clarified, gripping the hallway railing. She knows Dr. Menlo can't share anything specific.

Well, let's keep fingers crossed, Dr. Menlo had said. *I have some cases to get to upstairs, but I'll be back in an hour. We'll see what happens.*

The moment Whitney has been waiting at his side for. A moment that would kill her to miss.

She checks the time now on her watch.

She pulls Leo aside. She asks him if he'll do her a favor.

"I need you to give a message to Xavier's parents. Right now. They're back in his room."

He looks at the floor while Rebecca speaks, ready to focus on her instructions.

In a voice that echoes in her ears, she tells him Dr. Menlo insists they take a break while they bring Xavier down for another scan. They should go home, they should shower and regroup before the surgery tomorrow, see the twins for a bit. Dr. Menlo will call with anything urgent. And then she tells Leo to escort them to the elevators. To make sure they really leave. That it's very important he does this.

"But . . ." Leo looks confused. "I think anesthesiology is holding back the sedation, and wouldn't they want to be here for that?"

Rebecca's heart races. She tries to keep her expression neutral through the pain as she shakes her head. "It's fine." It's all she says. She waits for Leo to question her. But he only nods.

And then she asks, like it's an afterthought, that Leo not mention she was the messenger. She doesn't want them to be offended that she hasn't come to see them; she's only at the hospital for a quick meeting, and she's already late. She puts her hand on her watch.

She's never given him a reason to question her integrity. But just in case he does, she walks away before he has a chance to speak. She steadies herself with the railing along the way. Her eyebrows furrow, her forehead wrinkles. She can't keep it together anymore.

Ben is calling her again.

She finds a bathroom and rips off the pad that is now the weight of a football. She is hot and clammy and starting to shake. She sits on the toilet and opens a photograph on her phone. It is of Whitney. She had taken it when she first brought Whitney to see Xavier, when she had sat across from her on the other side of his bed and felt, somehow, that there was a connection being drawn between them. It's why she told her about her pregnancies. Why she'd gone to the backyard last night. A part of her had known there was something more.

She wipes the smear of blood from her inner thighs and replaces the pad in her underwear. She will take herself to the hospital across the street. She will answer their questions. Five pregnancies. No children. She will write her mother's number as her emergency contact. She will stare at the clock on the wall until they call her name, she will lie down on a gurney behind a thin blue curtain, she will pull her knees into her chest and rock through the pain, and she will not hope, and she will not pray, she will do the only thing she can. She will wait.

59

Blair

Aiden and Chloe are playing hangman again at the kitchen table. The spaghetti sauce is simmering on the stove. Blair is sitting across from them with her laptop open, searching again. Causes of suicide in children. Suicides misreported as accidents. News stories of elementary kids bullied to death.

She has another swell of fear.

Chloe squeals, victorious. Aiden rubs his knuckles on her head. He came home early from work to be with them. One more game, she begs, and he agrees. She draws the gallows.

Aiden and Blair look at each other, and he holds her there in his gaze. She can feel herself softening toward him in the wake of everything that's happened. She has to. He's starting to feel, for once, like the only safe thing in her life. She doesn't want to treat him like the problem anymore. She needs to heal from the animosity she's become addicted to.

Later tonight, she will roll toward him, and she will say that she is sorry. That she shouldn't have believed he would have an affair, and she will mean this. That she wants them to be in a better place. She'll hold him under the covers, wait for him to grow hard in her hand.

He will tease her, he will let it go like he can so easily let go of everything else, and then he will pull her into him, and he will nip at her bottom lip that will still have the taste of toothpaste on it, and he will kiss her shoulder, and then the breasts she will want to cover, and they will have sex for the first time in a long time. She will tell him to put his mouth on her. She will feel the relief of never having to let another man touch her in the places that he does.

Blair hears car doors. She closes the laptop and walks to the front window. Jacob is holding Whitney, taking her slowly to the front door. Blair feels a pang of missing her already; her heart hasn't caught up to her conscious brain, and maybe it never will. But nothing will ever be the same between them. She steels herself with a sharp breath. She'd texted Rebecca that afternoon for an update on Xavier, but hasn't heard anything yet, which is unusual. She watches Whitney stand back to let Jacob unlock the door before he puts his hand out for her again. They stand like this, still, before he leads her in.

Blair thinks of the betrayal that smolders below this tenderness. The admirable marriage that Whitney threatened so stupidly. And for what? Yet more attention? Someone to fuck her better? She should have known Whitney was dangerous. This makes Blair, too, feel the betrayal again. For being lied to so effortlessly. For envying that love so deeply.

She closes the curtain.

The group chats were filling up. The questions, bookended with vague sympathies, wondering what more Blair knows. How Whitney is coping. If there'd be a routine investigation of any kind, given the nature of the "incident," the involvement of a child. There's a tone of assumption in their language, like she'd hoped for. About Whitney. The careful treading, texts expertly constructed by vultures. So far nobody has mentioned what happened with Chloe, not to her. But she can feel the momentum of their curiosity, and it makes her nervous. Blair had turned her phone off and put it away for the night. She isn't sure yet how she'll respond next.

Back at the kitchen table, she leans to kiss Aiden on the cheek. She runs Chloe's long ponytail through her hand. A waft of Whitney's perfume—she lifts her wrist to her nose. At the kitchen sink, she runs the hot water, squirts lemon dish soap on her skin, and winces at the sharpness of the bristles on the scrub brush. She had gone to the Loverlys' house this afternoon after Jacob left. Just one last time.

Everything had felt different when Blair walked through it. Cold and lifeless. She had stood at the bathroom counter and sprayed Whitney's perfume once and then twice. She noticed the wedding rings were gone from the jewelry dish.

She'd walked carefully up the stairs to Xavier's room. Nothing had been touched since she'd been there the day before—the spilled coffee had dried on the floor and the window was still wide open, the room cool. She'd rubbed the top of her arms and looked outside to the backyard, but everything seemed as it always did. She saw Mara in her garden next door. She was sweeping her hand through her hydrangea bushes, like there was something specific she was looking for.

The messy, black scribble of ink on Xavier's wall. She'd run her fingers over it, and then she could see there'd been something written underneath that he must have been trying to cover up. She'd squinted, putting the letters together, and then stepped back, until she could see what Xavier had written.

The words had taken her breath away:

I DON'T WANT TO BE YOUR SON ANYMORE

Chloe and Aiden start a tie-breaker game of hangman. Blair says she'll be right back to put the noodles on, and she walks upstairs to her bedroom. She'd gone to the Loverlys' house that afternoon looking for the conviction she needed. Be thankful for the life you have. For the little girl who still holds your hand. For the husband who helped you build this life, who you made this precious daughter with, who still wants to slip into bed with you at night, to wrap his leg around you under the covers. Because it can all go in an instant, if you're not careful. If you let down your guard.

Marriage isn't about love; it's about choices. And she has chosen this person, and this life. Her longing now for something that she cannot place, something she'll never find, feels like nothing but ingratitude. A selfish hunger. She can't live like that anymore.

She pulls the keychain from her pocket and drops it into Aiden's gym bag. Nothing but a lost and found key. And then she opens her dresser drawer and takes the emerald foil corner into the bathroom. It feels pathetic to her now, nothing but a piece of garbage in her hand. She drops it in the toilet and watches it float. And then slowly, the triangle begins to submerge, like the sail of a capsized boat. She puts her finger on the handle. She has a good life, a blessed life. She will stop convincing herself otherwise.

60

Mara

She stares across the street at the paper airplane she left on the Loverlys' porch and wonders again how Xavier is doing. If he's still alive. She'd feel more responsible for the whole thing if she hadn't been up late herself on Wednesday night, unable to sleep through Albert's snoring, and heard the noise in the Loverlys' backyard. She'd slammed her window shut and slept downstairs in Marcus's old bed instead.

Little had she known it would be Albert's last night alive.

Xavier used to join her for gardening last summer. Early every Thursday morning, he'd poke his head over the fence to ask if he could help, although it turned out he didn't like getting his hands dirty. She'd bought him a pair of junior gardening gloves and told him her son hadn't liked the feel of dirt under his nails either. She'd never mentioned a son before.

One morning at the end of the summer, out of the blue, Xavier asked about him again. Mara had told him he'd been gone a long time.

"Gone where?"

"He died," Mara had said. "He died while he was flying."

Xavier had looked pensive, tracing the wings of the die-cast jet she'd given him a few months before, the one Marcus had loved. He reminded her so much of him. She sensed he wanted to know more. Flying, how? Flying, where? But he must have known not to ask too many questions about a dead boy.

She first found the paper airplanes the following Thursday morning, the first week of school, when he couldn't come over to watch her do the gardening anymore. It had been a particularly bad day, her mind stuck chasing the hardest question again . . . what if, what if, what if. And then there it had been, right at her feet when she looked down.

After that, she would circle the yard early every Thursday and collect the paper planes from wherever they'd happened to land. Sometimes lodged in the branches of the bushes, sometimes near the back fence or scattered on the grass, the noses bent or the paper soggy from the dew. She never told Albert, for fear he'd say something to the Loverlys about it.

She'd asked Xavier once if the planes were from him. He'd looked worried at first, knowing it'd be over if he got in trouble for being up late, with that window wide open, launching airplanes into the old couple's backyard.

He swore they weren't, that he had no idea what she was talking about. She'd mumbled, *Oh, well never mind then.* And then she saw him stifle a satisfied grin. Maybe he wanted her to think, for one wonderfully foolish moment, that they might have come from heaven.

She smiles now, thinking about this.

It's been a long time since she's had a proper drink. She pulls a glass from the cupboard and then the bottle of rum from the hutch in the living room, and she heads to the basement.

She's going to miss those paper planes.

61

Whitney

Jacob turns off the engine in their driveway and they sit.

He made her leave the hospital, he insisted. He was relieved, she knows, that Dr. Menlo ordered her out of the room for the first time in two days. They want her to shower. To sleep and eat. To see the last bit of daylight in the sky. She has nothing left in her.

Maybe they don't think she's helping anymore.

Maybe the doctor knows something.

She didn't want to leave, but it was safer to acquiesce, to get away from the hospital, where Rebecca could change her mind at any minute. Where Ben could come back to find her. She'd barely breathed while Rebecca was in the room alone with Jacob. She'd slid down the wall in the hallway and sat on the cold resin floor, watching feet pass her. Anticipating the end.

She doesn't know why Rebecca spared them.

Blair might not.

Unsullied, virtuous Blair. She'd been someone Whitney aspired to be—the kind of mother she could learn to emulate. She should have known that attempt was futile. Despite Blair's best intentions, there's nobody who makes her feel like a more shameful mother. Nobody who would judge her more harshly if she knew the truth about Wednesday night. She could barely stand to breathe when Blair was in the hospital room next to her. Her very presence buried Whitney under a mound of guilt.

I will fucking handle this, Whitney had hissed to Ben when they saw Blair watching them together. *Calm down and leave before Jacob gets back.* But she didn't know how she'd handle this at all. The shame was paralyzing. She'd never get Blair back, she'd known that instantly. She was losing everyone. One by one. She'd needed to think.

She can't figure out how Blair got the key. And what else she might know.

A month ago, Whitney had pulled into her driveway at the same time as the red Honda had pulled up outside of Blair's house. She had noticed in her rearview mirror how quickly the car had stopped, like the driver had thrown it into park before she'd taken her foot off the gas. A blond woman in skinny jeans and a cropped T-shirt—she was maybe thirty, Whitney wasn't sure—got out and slammed the door. The woman had stood facing Blair's house. Whitney had watched her in the mirror and didn't feel right about her. She just didn't. She did not look like a woman Blair would know.

Whitney had moved quickly out of her car toward the woman as she approached Blair's house. She called out to her in the lowest voice she could so Blair wouldn't hear from inside.

"Hey. Hey! Can I help you?" The woman turned around and Whitney saw she looked nervous. Like she was about to do something that scared her. Whitney came closer to her. She could see the whites of her eyes were too pink, her cheeks too flush. "I said, can I help you?"

"I'm here to return something to the asshole who lives here."

Whitney knew it right then. "You mean Aiden?"

The woman's jaw jutted to the side. She was thinking. She was thinking about how much to say, and the muscles in her arms looked tense. She was taut and shiny. She reached into her bag and took out a pair of sunglasses, rooting for something else, and Whitney recognized the frames right away. Their square shape, the fleck of peach in the tortoise-shell. She'd been at the neighborhood barbecue in September. She was the girlfriend of Jacob's college buddy.

She remembers, then, how she had overheard this woman and Aiden talking at the party when Blair was inside tidying up. The brazenness with which Aiden had flirted, the way this woman had held on to his arm for a moment too long. She heard him tell her which office building he worked at downtown. That he often grabbed a drink after work at the pub at the bottom of the tower. Whitney hadn't liked it. She'd almost said something to Blair at the end of the night, in the kitchen, as she was leaving with Aiden and Chloe. Hey, I don't want to upset you, I don't want to cause trouble. But if I were you, I'd want to know.

But then she hadn't. Because it was Blair. And Blair wouldn't have wanted to know. Whitney was reminded, that afternoon, how essential Blair's friendship was to her life. She couldn't have risked what they had, not to place a bomb in Blair's hands that she'd never have wanted.

The woman pulled a small, pink satin pouch from her bag, and slipped out a key with Aiden's initials on the tag. Whitney glanced toward Blair's front window to make sure she wasn't looking out between the curtains. She didn't see Aiden's car anywhere. She needed this woman gone before Blair noticed them and opened her door.

"Give me that. I'll return it for you," Whitney had said. The woman stared at the palm of Whitney's hand. "The key. Give it to me now. And then leave."

The woman looked stunned. And then she glared at the house again. She slipped the key back in the pouch. Whitney could see it in her face, the playing out of what was supposed to have happened, the revenge fantasy she'd convinced herself of for weeks. The dowdy wife opening the door, her sweetness dissolving to fear.

"You don't want to do this. Trust me. I'll make sure you regret it." The woman looked at her hand for what felt to Whitney like a whole minute. And then she dropped the pouch and key into Whitney's palm. Her lips pursed. She might have thought about snatching the key right back, but it was already in the pocket of Whitney's jacket. "Go. And don't ever fucking come back here."

As she drove away, Whitney saw Mara on her porch, her eyes following the car down the street. They looked at each other, and then Whitney went inside, her heart pounding. She'd smelled Louisa's lentil curry, heard the squeals of the three kids playing hide-and-seek with her upstairs. She'd walked straight to the stove and lifted the lid to see what was left in the pot; they'd all eaten already. She moved her spoon through the leftovers, convincing herself she'd done the right thing. Did Blair suspect anything? Has this been quietly destroying her? She wanted to go over right now and hug her. Whitney didn't want this knowledge, but now she had it, and her friend would be humiliated to know that she did. Blair would want to deal with this privately if she ever did find out. So Whitney would not say a thing. Like at the barbecue in September, she would give her the dignity of pretending it had never happened at all.

And then there was the other complicating matter. The hypocrisy of how it felt to be so concerned for her best friend, so disgusted with Aiden.

She kept stirring. Thinking.

She heard Jacob's feet descend the stairs. And then felt his lips.

"Hey, can I ask you something?" she said. "That girlfriend of Jamie's, the one who came to the barbecue. Is he still seeing her?"

"They broke up awhile ago. She wasn't relationship material, apparently." He pulled away from her. He opened the fridge, took out a sparkling water. "Why do you ask?"

"No reason. Just thought I saw her the other day in the elevator at work."

He nodded. But he was quiet.

"I think she's got a red Honda," Whitney pressed. "You ever see it around here?"

His brows lifted. He shrugged. He shook his head. He could have said, how do you know what car she drives? Why would she be around here? But then he turned to leave the room, and she knew there was something he was not telling her. Maybe he knew about Aiden too. But she said nothing else; she'd already gone too far. She didn't want to have those words— "an affair"—floating in the air.

The shrapnel, she knew, was all around them, a threat underfoot in their homes, in between them while they slept. This damning debris— the hiss as it nears, the weight as it hits—was the most betraying. And discomforting. Life could explode at any moment.

No, she wouldn't mention this, not to Jacob, not to Blair.

So much was traded in what went unsaid. In what was protected.

This was the way she could think about it, then. She could carry it all inside her, divided, like the dinner served to her fussy little children, the foods on their plates never allowed to touch.

62

Rebecca

Ben is the first person she sees when she walks through the doors of the emergency room across the street from the children's hospital. He stands up from the chair in the waiting room. She can see the uncertainty, the lift in his eyebrows, the slack of his jaw that's meant to make him look innocent. Like he has nothing to apologize for, nothing but leaving her in the kitchen when he should have stayed. When he should have put his hands on the sphere of their baby and said something about wanting them both.

She walks past him to the registration desk and digs for identification in her bag. When they're done with her at the plexiglass window—*Miscarriage. Yes, I'm sure. No, I'm not twenty weeks yet. No allergies*—she lies down in the first empty row of seats. Her eyes can't be open anymore. She breathes through the next wave of pain and then hisses out through her teeth. There's relief, for a moment, but she knows it's going

to end, the pressure is starting between her legs, and there's a red OCCU-
PIED sign on the bathroom door ten feet away.

"Mara told me you'd be here," he says. She feels his weight on the
seat cushion next to her. She feels his hand on her ankle. "I shouldn't
have left like that. I'm so sorry."

The pain is back quickly. She hums, long, droning stretches.

"I left because I was scared, and I was shocked. But the second you
told me, I knew I wanted this baby too."

She can only chuckle. Delirium. She wiggles her legs, tries to find
relief in moving differently. Like jiggling a crying baby, this crying baby,
four months from now. She keeps her eyes closed. She listens, eager to
hear the click of the bathroom door. Below, she has the sensation of
opening. She knows she should walk to triage, tell the nurse she needs
a bed, but it doesn't matter to her right now where it happens, it doesn't
matter if she squats on the waiting room floor while the seven people
there turn away, hide their eyes from what comes out.

There was a question on the fertility clinic paperwork they each
had to fill out last year. Why is it important for you to have biological
children? He had turned to her. *How did you answer this one?* She'd
shrugged, she'd been staring blankly at the question, too, thinking it
wasn't fair they had to articulate this when millions of other parents
didn't. To see how their facial features morphed together? Because it's a
natural thing that humans of a reproductive age are supposed to want?
They'd never talked about *why* they wanted a baby, they had only talked
about *if* they wanted a baby. He'd put a line through the answer box, a
protest. She'd looked at his paper and then did the same on hers.

She doesn't want him to explain why he's having an affair. She knows
he felt claustrophobic in her presence. That he'd quietly disassociated
from the future they had together, stitch by stitch, an undoing, while he
tried so very hard to convince her otherwise. That he lay awake at night
feeling sorry for himself, like a petulant child who couldn't have the one

thing he wanted. The one thing he felt owed. And while Whitney wouldn't give him that one thing, there's no doubt in Rebecca's mind that being with her made his childless fate easier to live with. Rebecca soured his life; Whitney was a neutralizer. She made being with Rebecca bearable.

Or maybe it was just animalistic. An attraction to a woman with reproductive organs that worked. The mother he can fuck.

Her moan escalates. The pain climbs ruthlessly, ravaging every inch of her back. There are hands on her now, hands that aren't Ben's. There's a blood pressure cuff around her arm. The heaviness between her legs feels threatening now, like a soggy paper bag about to rip, and she knows what happens next.

"I'm done," she whispers to Ben. "I won't do it anymore."

He kneels at her head and takes her hand, presses his forehead on hers.

"We don't have to give up on a baby," he says to her softly. "We don't have to lose hope. I was wrong. Let's get through this, let's go back to the fertility—"

"I mean I'm done doing this, *with you*. I won't do it anymore, *with you*."

He's confused. He looks at the nurse who is back with a heating bag. She tells Rebecca there's a bed coming free in a few minutes.

"You're upset and in pain, let's just get you—"

"You started fucking her in November," she says. "When you told me you didn't want us to try for a baby anymore. That's what changed, wasn't it?"

Ben sits back. His eyes move to her belly. "You can't possibly understand how much I love you, how much I want—"

"Go home and clear out your things. Leave me the car and your set of house keys."

She squeezes her eyes closed again. He's quiet. She rolls from the bench, stabilizing herself on all fours. The nurse rubs between her shoulders. She says she'll walk with her, that they'll get the IV going right away. Come. She helps to steady her as she stands and guides her toward the hall of beds.

And then Rebecca starts to feel what she was waiting for. A growl of strength. Like she could reach inside herself and carry the sleeping baby out in the safe, warm palm of her hand. Like she is a mother.

63

Whitney

Jacob takes her hand and walks her to the front door. He bends to pick something up.

A paper airplane made from a piece of yellow notepad paper. Something is written in tidy cursive between the fold in the center.

> *How'd I do? Not bad for an old lady.*
> *I'll be waiting for you.*
>
> *Yours, Mara*

Whitney turns to Mara's house, expecting her and Albert to be there as they always are in the evenings. But nobody. And the lights are all off.

She moves into the entryway and looks through the kitchen, into the backyard. The emptiness of the house is striking.

She makes her way closer to the back windows and sees the grass.

It happens all over again in her mind.

The thwack of his head.

She wants to run back to the car, to the driver's seat, peel down Harlow Street, across the city, back to him. Blow every red light. Take the stairs to his floor three at a time so that her thighs catch fire.

Jacob takes her to the bottom step of the staircase and helps her sit. He puts their things one by one on the kitchen counter, the duffel bag, his watch, his keys. The paper airplane. He seems measured, methodical. He empties his pockets.

"Oh. Right. I forgot I brought these for you. To the hospital." He opens his hand. Her wedding rings. She stares at them. "You weren't wearing them Wednesday night."

It isn't a question. He doesn't ask why. Her heart pounds. He pours them both a glass of water very slowly. He lifts one in her direction and they both watch her hand tremble as she reaches for it.

"Listen," Jacob says. "I've been thinking. That thing Louisa told me on the phone yesterday. About how upset Xavi was on Wednesday after Chloe treated him like shit at school. Do you remember I told you about it this afternoon?"

Whitney remembers, although she doesn't acknowledge it. *Is this about Chloe?* Blair had asked her at the hospital. And of course it had been, in a way; Chloe, the ideal daughter for the perfect mother. The measures none of them could live up to.

"I think we need to say something to the social workers," he continues. "And to whoever else asks. That he was having a tough go socially at school, and then his best friend in the world basically said he should kill himself. In front of everyone."

Whitney inhales sharply through her nose. Kill himself. Why is he saying those words aloud to her? She thinks of what Xavier wrote on his bedroom wall. Of the things she has said to him. Threatened him with.

"Jacob. Have you been upstairs yet, to his room? Since it happened?"

"I can't go in there."

She watches him refill his glass of water, the tap stream thin, nearly a drip, like every move they make right now must be careful. Everything they say.

"Why haven't you asked me, Jacob?"

"Asked you what?"

"ASKED ME WHAT THE FUCK HAPPENED?" Her glass spins across the floor and the puddle of water grows between them. She stands, shaking her head, her face crumpling as she cries. "You haven't asked because you don't trust that I have nothing to do with it. You don't believe I wouldn't hurt him, despite how desperately you want to. You're terrified of the truth, you always have been. So what does that leave us with? A freak accident in the middle of the night that nobody else will believe? A suicide we pin on a little girl, whose mother is a fucking martyr? Other women don't like me enough, Jacob, they don't think I'm worth protecting. I've been too selfish. I've missed too much. I've let them hear me scream at him!" She catches her breath, the shame of that September afternoon swamping her all over again. She wipes her nose with the back of her hand. "I'm not like them. Don't you understand that?"

Jacob's hands are on his hips. He doesn't look away from the water seeping closer to his feet.

"Were you watching me in his hospital room earlier today? Were you testing me?"

His eyebrows furrow. He shakes his head. "What are you talking about?"

They stare at each other. Daring each other. What are each of them willing to live with?

He looks away first.

She knows the conversation is done, because the alternative, the truth about what she's done, and what he really thinks of her, is too painful for them both.

"I'm going to run you a bath," he says.

She waits until he's at the top of the stairs before she lies across the bottom step.

She can get them out of this house, off this street, out of this city, and they can all start again. She'll take a leave from the company, step aside for a while. She'll find a way to live with herself after what she's done to them all. For what she's nearly destroyed.

But Jacob is right. She does need a plan. Because if Xavier wakes up, he might remember what happened Wednesday night. And she cannot lose them. She cannot let this life explode.

She sobs into her hands. She shouldn't have left Xavier. She should have fought to stay by his side. What if, at this very moment, he can sense she's gone? What if he finally opens his eyes and he's alone? She needs him to see her there. She imagines the ring of strange faces hanging over him, his small hands ripping the catheter from his penis, yanking at the tape on his skin and the intravenous in his arm. Nurses running to restrain him. It's visceral, the commotion of the room thumping in her now.

She hears Jacob turn off the faucet upstairs, and she wipes her nose on her sleeve. She'll have the bath quickly and change her clothes. And then she'll get back to Xavier. There is a tickle of nausea in her that comes from nowhere, and she thinks of how empty her stomach has been, of how she'd needed to feel deprived as she sat by his side. But the nausea rises again and it's stronger this time.

It reminds her of something: her pregnancies. She lifts her thumb up under her shirt to touch her left nipple beside her racing heart, and it's only then that she feels the unmistakable sensitivity. Time does not register for her anymore, and so there is no use in counting through the weeks, the months, that have passed since she has bled. The times she has let each of them come inside her. She knows. And the knowing stuns her.

She realizes then that Jacob's phone is vibrating on the kitchen counter while she is trying to process what she has let happen. The buzz stops. The hospital, it could have been the hospital. They said they'd call if anything was urgent. And then their home phone rings from the kitchen, and the noise confuses her, it is nearly unrecognizable. Nobody ever calls them at home. Her legs barely carry her to the handset, but she gets there, and she answers.

It is Dr. Menlo.

She hears Jacob running down the stairs. She turns her back to him, she hurries through the kitchen to the backyard, clutching the receiver so he can't take it away from her, so she can be the one to hear the words.

"Is he gone? He can't be gone, I need him! Tell me now!"

Jacob is telling her to stop. He is shushing her. He is wrestling the phone from her hand, but she shoves him away as hard as she can, she presses it to her ear.

She falls to the grass.

Xavier is awake. And he is crying for his mother.

WEDNESDAY

The Night of the Fall

S he slams her coffee onto his bedside table as she stares at the wall. There's just enough light coming in from the hallway to read it.

I DON'T WANT TO BE YOUR SON ANYMORE

The words hold her throat. Her eyes well with tears too quickly for her to swallow everything down. She feels Xavier watching her, she feels his fear. He is waiting for her to explode. They both are.

But the anger isn't there like it always is. She feels weak. And empty.

He has exhausted her for ten years with how much he has needed of her and wanted of her. And now he understands what she always has, it's written there on his wall: she will never be enough for him.

"Get me your wallet," she tells him.

He is still. She yanks open his top drawer where he keeps his small canvas wallet with the bit of money he's collected from birthdays and the tooth fairy. She finds it under his socks and throws it at him in his bed. "You're paying to have this wall repainted."

Xavier slowly pulls back the covers and sits up. He takes out the paper bills and coins. Whitney holds out her hand. But he looks her in the eyes; he is looking for the flame. Waiting for the match to catch. He throws the money at her feet. He lies back down.

"You don't want to be my son?" she says, pausing. Testing herself. "Then I'm leaving you. And I'm never coming back. You don't have a mother anymore."

She holds her breath, the words ringing in her ears. She doesn't expect his chin to quiver like it does. He rolls away to face the window. She scoops the money from the floor and leaves his room.

Her chest pounds. She leans her back against the closed door. I'm leaving. I'm leaving. It's the first time she's said anything like that. An acknowledgment of the possibility that she could. That she has the choice.

But the only difference between her and a mother who leaves, if there's much of a difference at all, is that Whitney already knows there's no relief in having left. Not if her son is in the world, existing without her. He will never not be wrapped around her conscience, infiltrating her dreams, an endless feed of shame. Instead, she's learned to be absent when she is near. She has the ability to stare through the children, see their lips move while she nods her head, she can be elsewhere and she can be there. She is an illusion. But she has never left.

She should tell him she didn't mean it, she thinks, she should go back in to comfort him before he falls asleep. She is tired of failing him. The cruelest part of motherhood is that she has made him the way he is, every frustrating part of him. She is the source of everything that troubles him, she is the reason he's lonely even when she's there. She presses her hands to her cheeks. She doesn't want to be crying.

But there's a heavy thump against the door and then a shatter on the hardwood floor. The scent of coffee hits her nose, and then her heels begin to feel wet. And just like that, the anger wallops her again.

An hour and a half later, she wakes up with the pages of her presentation on her chest—she hadn't meant to fall asleep. She has the sense of something strange, an electricity in her, as though her dream had carried a current. What had she been thinking of, in just a short nap? In fragments she can't place with any sense of time or space, she is dragging him by the hair across the grass. He is screaming, begging for her to stop, but she is so consumed by the rush of this, by the sexual pulse she is feeling (Had she reached down to touch herself in her sleep? Had it felt that real?), that she cannot let go of him.

She wipes her hand across her eyes and wants it all to go away. The fight with Xavier. The horrible dream. She stares at the time glowing on her phone. It's 10:45 p.m.

Still no response from Jacob in London. He's read her last six messages.

She's uneasy about his silence.

She should have canceled. To be safe. She still could.

But she runs the shower.

Afterward, she puts on a navy silk robe that falls just above her knees. She listens outside the kids' rooms to make sure they're all asleep.

She pours less than half a glass of wine.

Outside in the backyard it's still damp and humid, and she puts the dry cushions on the patio furniture. She scrolls through news headlines on her phone and is about to take a first sip of the wine, when she feels hands touch her shoulders.

His breath hits her neck. He reaches his hand lower, to her breast, and he strums her nipple with his thumb. She likes when he doesn't want to talk first, when he comes ready for her. She puts her head back against the chair and she doesn't want to pause, but they have to go to the shed. That's where they do this, every time, Whitney bent over with her elbows on the steel shelf after she's swept away the plastic pails and the miniature dump trucks. She says to him quietly, let's go to our spot, but he pushes her down again, he tells her he wants to fuck her outside tonight. In the expensive outdoor chair with the wide wicker arms.

"Someone might see us out here," she whispers to him. And as she says the words, she gets wetter, and feels his finger slip inside her.

She arches, she wants him deeper. She slips off the robe. She wants to be on top of him now. She pulls his sweatshirt over his head, wiggles his pants from his legs. She sits on his cock, facing away from him, and he reaches around to feel everything he wants to touch. The clouds move fast and the moonlight comes back, and she wants to be seen by him. She orders him to kneel in front of her. She likes to feel on display, exposed, ripe. She gets lost in what happens next, she disappears into herself.

She doesn't realize the sound she's making until his hand is over her mouth, the reverberation of her pleasure cut like a wire. She can taste herself on the roughness of his palm. He pulls her head back and the moon feels bright against her lids.

"Mom, stop!"

Her eyes open.

And she sees Xavier at his bedroom window above. He's watching them.

Ben shoves her off his erection and turns himself away from the house. Whitney scrambles on her hands and knees for her robe. The wine spills, the glass spins across the concrete.

"What do we do? Fuck." Ben fumbles with his belt.

"Shut up," Whitney hisses. She ties her robe. She cannot look up. She can feel Xavier there, unmoved from the open window. "You need to leave right now."

She moves out of Xavier's view, holds herself up against the glass door to the kitchen, and she tries to get more air into her lungs. He'll tell Jacob, he'll tell everyone. Their lives will fall apart over this. Why the hell was he awake?

"Mom!"

She wants to yell for him to shut up.

"BEN?" he calls. He is looking for them. She sees his shadow grow longer, he is leaning out the window.

She squeezes her eyes closed. She thinks of how she'd spread herself for Ben to see her in the moonlight. Of how ferociously she'd licked him, how she'd spread his cum over her like finger paint, the vulgar words she'd said. Of how long Xavier might have been watching.

"MOM!"

He sounds angry now, or panicked, she isn't sure. She should rush upstairs to comfort him, to hold him and say she is so sorry. Convince him that what he saw isn't what he thinks it is. But he'll know. This will smolder between them for the rest of their lives. She's been fighting against the mother she's supposed to be since the day Xavier was born, and now she can see she was never going to win.

"MOM! BEN!"

She slips through the back door to hide from him, leans over the marble island, and tries to find a way out of the panic, but she cannot. Her mouth fills with saliva and she might be sick. She needs to think of what to do next. What to say.

"MOM, are you still out there? Did you already leave?"

He thinks she's leaving him, like she said she would. He believed her. Why had she said that?

She turns around to face her reflection in the glass door.

And that's when she hears it.

The faint thwack of his body against the ground.

She steps slowly to the glass door and slides it open with a trembling hand.

He looks dead.

There isn't any space inside her for panic or fear or any sensation at all. She kneels at his head in the damp grass and feels underneath for blood on his scalp. But there is nothing. She cups his face in her hands, and she lifts the lids of his eyes with her shaking thumbs. *See that I'm right here*, she begs, *reach up for me!* But he doesn't move. She pulls him in. She wants him back inside her again, the only place he was ever safe from her.

The smell of semen on her hands. Her swollen vulva.

The operator tells her what to do, she puts the phone on speaker as she goes through the motions. She finds air to fill her own lungs, and then blows that air into his. The adrenaline helps her focus, to do exactly what she must do, but she knows this gift of senseless time is fleeting. It is a race, and it will end. She is listening intently to the woman on the other end of the phone, she wants to do everything exactly as she says. She tells her she's done well, that all she can do now is wait, that the paramedics are minutes away, they'll come straight to the backyard to find them.

She sees, then, the paper airplane near Xavier's side that must have been in his hand when he fell. She remembers seeing it earlier that night. In his room.

His room.

She takes the stairs two at a time, she feels wild, knocking into the walls. In his bedroom, she slips in the coffee and scrambles to reach the black marker on the floor. She scribbles as hard as she can over every word he wrote. He had meant it. She is frantic and she is whimpering, and her fingers are burning, and she wants to go back to hold him on the grass. The parcel of time she has been given to be weightless and fearless is over. She's almost done. She will keep answering the operator's questions, she'll tell Xavier she loves him over and over and over, she won't leave him ever again, but first she needs these words covered up.

The yip of sirens. She drops the marker. And she runs to him.

Epilogue

TWO WEEKS LATER

W hy are you here?"

His words stop her in the doorway of Xavier's hospital room. Jacob's tone feels accusatory, but she reminds herself this is just the paranoia. The suffering of a lie.

"I woke up early so thought I'd relieve you. Why don't you go home, see the twins for a bit?" She looks down to Xavier, his torso raised in the bed, playing a game on the iPad. He hasn't spoken yet. This can happen, Whitney and Jacob are reassured, getting back to baseline can take some time, even in the best-case scenario, like his, when the tests check out fine. They all move around him pretending this new normal is bearable, half watching movies on the bulky television mounted to the wall, talking around him, about him, about all the things they'll do together again as a family when he's soon discharged. It's for the good of Xavier's spirits, of course, but Whitney wants it too—this comfort. This guarantee.

Jacob puts his few things back in his overnight duffel bag, folds the sheet, and then uses the phone in the room to order Xavier's breakfast from the meal service. He slings the bag on his shoulder.

"You sure?" he asks.

Whitney has avoided being alone at the hospital with Xavier since he woke up. Jacob stays with him every night, sleeps on the bench in Xavier's room, while she lies awake in their bed at home, Thea and Sebastian on either side of her. He only leaves for a break when Louisa and the twins come.

Nobody talks anymore about what happened that night—they've all let it go. The repetitive questions, the quiet conversations she could hear just outside the door.

And she should let it go too.

But she can't live like she does, numb with the fear of what might surface once he begins to talk.

She needs to be alone with him.

Jacob looks hesitant to leave. She stands with her hands on her waist, she stares at him as he stares at their son. The paranoia again.

"Is there a problem?" She swallows.

He touches Xavier's foot under the blanket. And then he comes to her slowly, puts a tender hand between her shoulder blades, his lips lightly to her cheek. "Not at all," he says. She hopes he can't feel her beating heart. "Call me if you need me. Love you."

She steps into the hall and watches him get on the elevator. And then she goes back to Xavier's room, flips the sign on the door to PRIVACY.

He's put the iPad down and now he's staring straight ahead at the whiteboard on the wall, where they're meant to keep track of things, to note the time of any cognitive changes so the nurse can record them in his chart. Tremors. Stutters. Confusion.

She sits on the side of his bed and finds his hand. She shakes it a little, playfully, trying to jostle a smile from him. She does it again, puts her forehead to his. I'm different now, she wants to say to him, I am really here. I am really listening. I see you.

"You can tell me anything, you know."

She wonders if this is what it's meant to feel like, if this is what she's been missing all along. Is this the yearning she never knew, this desperation to be loved in the way only her son can love her? This urge to swallow him into her soul, to exist only and exactly in the way he needs her to? I'm yours, she wants to say. I can forget who I was before, can you?

She pulls away and strokes his cheeks, so swollen from the steroids that he'd barely be recognizable to anyone else. They call it moon face. The moon, the moonlight. Her nakedness, illuminated.

"Anything," she says quietly. "We'll keep it between us. Even if it's about that night. About what happened." She hopes he can't hear the tremor in her voice. She hopes she feels safe to him, for once. Will she ever feel safe to him again? She doesn't want to push him too far. But then, quietly, "Even if it's something you aren't sure is true . . . something that your brain might be mixing up. It can just be our secret. Do you understand? I don't even have to tell them you've spoken. Not until you're ready."

She strokes him again. He doesn't take his eyes off the whiteboard.

And then he nods.

"Can you tell me?" She looks to the closed door, and then to his hand squeezed in hers. She can feel his eyes tracing her face now. He has something to say. He's been waiting for them to be alone. She feels it.

"Tell me." She wants to reach inside him and pull it out, to have his words right there in her hands. To mold whatever he says into what she needs it to be. "Please."

He strokes her knuckles with his thumb. The gesture is so tender, so reciprocal, and the relief brings tears to her eyes.

"Okay," he says. She gasps softly at the sound of his voice. She was right, he'd needed to be alone with her, only her. They stare at each other, and then he inhales, looks down at their hands instead. She holds her breath. He bites his dry lips. The tears trickle along the ridge of his swollen cheeks. He wipes his nose on the back of his other hand.

"What will happen?" he asks, and runs his thumb over her knuckles again, just once.

She cups his big face and aches with how much she loves him. With how much she wants to make everything better. She shakes her head, she doesn't know what he means.

"To you," he says. "When I tell them everything."

Acknowledgments

Thank you to the marvelous Madeleine Milburn and the team at Madeleine Milburn Agency, who are second to none. I'm grateful to benefit from the support of Esmé Carter, Hannah Ladds, Liv Maidment, Giles Milburn, Valentina Paulmichl, Georgina Simmonds, Liane-Louise Smith, and Rachel Yeoh.

Thank you to Pamela Dorman, Maxine Hitchcock, and Nicole Winstanley, who were so patient, thoughtful, and encouraging as I wrote this novel. It's a joy and privilege to work with you, and I'm incredibly grateful for your commitment to my writing.

To the phenomenal publishing teams who have brought *The Push* and now *The Whispers* into the world with such care and enthusiasm, thank you for all that you do. In particular, to Brian Tart and the Pamela Dorman Books and Viking team: Diandra Alvarado, LeBria Casher, Tricia Conley, Andy Dudley, Tess Espinoza, Matt Giarratano, Rebecca Marsh, Randee Marullo, Nick Michal, Marie Michels, Lauren Monaco, Patrick Nolan, Jeramie Orton, Lindsay Prevette, Jason Ramirez, Andrea Schulz, Kate Stark, Mary Stone, and Claire Vaccaro. To Louise Moore and the Michael Joseph

ACKNOWLEDGMENTS

team: Clare Bowen, Jen Breslin, Riana Dixon, Helen Eka, Christina Ellicott, Laura Garrod, Sophie Marston, Kelly Mason, Sriya Varadharajan, Lauren Wakefield, and Madeleine Woodfield. And to Kristin Cochrane and the team at Penguin Canada: Beth Cockeram, Dan French, Charidy Johnston, Beth Lockley, Bonnie Maitland, Alanna McMullen, and Meredith Pal.

Thank you to Dr. Lennox Huang of SickKids, Dr. Kim Aikins of Starship Children's Hospital, and Dr. Sony Sierra of TRIO Fertility, who generously gave their time and expertise to inform parts of this novel related to medical care and fertility. (I must note I've taken small liberties for the purpose of story and character, therefore not everything is a reflection of their knowledge—forgive me!)

To early readers Beth Lockley, Ashley Thomson, Robin Kotisa, Karma Brown, and Dr. Kristine Laderoute for her psychologist's lens—thank you. And to Carley Fortune, Nita Pronovost, and Harriet Alida Lye, thank you for being such a lovely bunch of writer friends.

My writing partner, Ashley Bennion Tait, has read more terrible drafts of my work than any person should be subjected to. I have benefited enormously from her talents, and also from her friendship. She'll publish her debut novel, *Twenty-Seven Minutes*, by Ashley Tate, in January 2023, and I hope you'll buy a copy—it's as brilliant as she is.

My treasured girlfriends have supported me as a writer in such kind and thoughtful ways—please know how much I love you all. A special thanks to my dearest Jenny Leroux, for every reason.

Thank you to the readers, booksellers, librarians, and authors who championed *The Push* over the past few years, and to those of you who have reached out with a message, written a review, or shared a post on social media. It means so much.

The greatest privilege of my life is having the family I do. Thank you to my exceptional and loving parents, Mark and Cathy Audrain; to my sisters, Sara and Samantha; and to Alex, Brendan, and Brayden. Thank you to the Fizzells and to the Aikinses for all of your love and support. And thank you to our devoted nanny, Jackelyne Napilan.

Finally, to MJF, for everything, always. And to Oscar and Waverly, for indulging my writing life so patiently and being endlessly, wonderfully inspiring. I love you.